The
Mommy Fund

The
Mommy Fund

Madeleine K. Jacob

A PLUME BOOK

PLUME
Published by the Penguin Group
Penguin Group (USA) Inc., 375 Hudson Street, New York, New York 10014, U.S.A.
Penguin Group (Canada), 10 Alcorn Avenue, Toronto, Ontario, Canada M4V 3B2
(a division of Pearson Penguin Canada Inc.)
Penguin Books Ltd, 80 Strand, London WC2R 0RL, England
Penguin Ireland, 25 St Stephen's Green,
Dublin 2, Ireland (a division of Penguin Books Ltd)
Penguin Group (Australia), 250 Camberwell Road, Camberwell, Victoria 3124,
Australia (a division of Pearson Australia Group Pty Ltd)
Penguin Books India Pvt Ltd, 11 Community Centre,
Panchsheel Park, New Delhi – 110 017, India
Penguin Books (NZ), Cnr Airborne and Rosedale Roads,
Albany, Auckland, New Zealand (a division of Pearson New Zealand Ltd)
Penguin Books (South Africa) (Pty) Ltd, 24 Sturdee Avenue,
Rosebank, Johannesburg 2196, South Africa

Penguin Books Ltd, Registered Offices: 80 Strand, London WC2R 0RL, England

First published by Plume, a member of Penguin Group (USA) Inc.

First Printing, February 2005
10 9 8 7 6 5 4 3 2 1

Ⓡ REGISTERED TRADEMARK—MARCA REGISTRADA

CIP data is available.
ISBN 0-452-28576-3

Printed in the United States of America
Set in Caslon Book
Designed by Eve L. Kirch

PUBLISHER'S NOTE
This is a work of fiction. Names, characters, places, and incidents are either the product of
the author's imagination or are used fictitiously, and any resemblance to actual persons,
living or dead, business establishments, events, or locales is entirely coincidental.

For Dave, Maddy and Caleb
&
For Pete and Jack

ACKNOWLEDGMENTS

Special thanks to the incomparable Karen Gerwin at the William Morris Agency for her vision, enthusiasm and editorial insight; to our editor Julie Saltman, whose unwavering belief in the book and ongoing support are deeply appreciated; and to Brant Janeway, Trena Keating and everyone else at Plume.

Heartfelt thanks to the brilliant Laura Dickerman for her input; Mija Strong for West Coast promotion; Kristin "K." Kiser; Mary Frances Turnbull; Suzy Palitz; Kathy and Greg Karlik; Alan and Jennifer Gates; Esther Gates and in memory, Douglas Gates; Pat and Stan Parsons; Betsy and Larry Stern; Jeanne Birdsall; Melissa Nebelski; to Cathy, Annie and Lorraine at Cathy Cross for shopping and fashion inspiration; Lane Zachary; Todd Shuster and Esmond Harmsworth; Sara London and Dean Albarelli; Scott Gold; Elizabeth Hayes; Jen Marshall; Amy Greeman and Leanna James. We couldn't have done it without you.

Part I

~

*"Since everything is in our heads,
we had better not lose them."*

—Coco Chanel

Chapter One

It's 11 a.m. and Kate Thompson is still in her pajamas. Charlie, her three-year-old, is in the corner of the den playing with a stack of red cardboard bricks. He builds a tower until it teeters a couple of feet over his head and then, with a swift kick, sends the stack flying, scattering the dust bunnies that threaten to overrun the floor. His face lights up with glee.

Kate is sitting on an oversized couch with a book open on her lap, her coffee cold on the table beside her. She sticks her hand deep inside the pocket of her flannel pajamas and comes out with a handful of M&M's, slipping them into her mouth and trying to chew without crunching. She is thumbing through something called *Gratitude: The Simple Truth of Abundant Living.* She must admit, her life at the moment is not feeling particularly simple or abundant. Her thoughts drift to the refrigerator: *We're out of juice, eggs, almost out of milk.* She'll run to the store as soon as she gets dressed, she decides. Then she remembers that the car's in the shop until tomorrow night. Her husband, Andy, is bringing the loaner home after he teaches his late-morning physics lab.

"What are you eating, Mommy?" Charlie asks.

"Uh . . . why do you ask?" Kate replies guiltily, through a mouth of chocolate. Charlie looks as though he's about to say something, then turns his attention back to the blocks. Kate surreptitiously licks the colorful candy coating stains from her fingertips and reads on: *Make a list of all that you are grateful for.* She reaches over and grabs the new blank journal that she's just bought. The clean white pages stare back accusingly. *OK, I am grateful for* . . . Charlie is tugging on her pajama bottoms.

"I'm hungry, Mom. What's for lunch?"

"It's a little early for lunch, buddy . . . don't you think?" He stares up at her, tufts of thick brown hair sticking up at odd angles.

"What do you want?"

"PB&J."

She sighs. "OK, you got it, buster. Sit at the table and I'll bring it in."

Hauling herself out of the pillow pit she's sunken into, she shuffles from the den into the kitchen and slaps together a peanut butter sandwich with a thick slab of strawberry jam, just the way he likes it. She pours what's left of the milk into a sippy cup, licks the extra peanut butter off the edge of the knife and returns to the den, setting the sandwich and the milk in front of Charlie, who is waiting expectantly in his seat at the children's-size table. Their golden retriever, Chance, ambles over and wedges himself underneath, ready to clean up the inevitable crumbs. Kate flops back onto the couch and settles in. She grabs the journal and leans into the deep pillows.

She jumps when the phone rings. *I'll let the machine get it. Probably some telemarketer.* Then a voice is booming, "Hey, Kate, get your butt off that couch and pick up the phone." It's Dani, her closest friend. Dani's got a seven-year-old daughter and a "real job" as a lawyer in an office downtown. Kate can picture her sitting at her desk, in her sleek navy suit, tapping her pen impatiently. Dani's probably accomplished more already this morning than Martha Stewart could in a good week.

"Pick up the phone, Kate. I know you're there." Dani sounds tense.

Kate knows what a late-morning call means. She leaps to her feet and grabs the receiver from the phone resting on the table nearby.

"Hating Your Boss Hotline, may I help you?"

"Can you believe he did it again?!"

"Left the toilet seat up in the ladies' room?"

"Kate, I'm serious. He knows it's my weekend with Brianna and yet *who* does he ask to come in Saturday to prepare the Holskin brief with him for a Monday court date?!"

"Judge Judy? . . . OK, OK, I'm sorry." Clearly this has already passed the defuse-with-humor possibility. "That totally sucks. Tell Bryce you'll do the next one. You've been really clear with him about which weekends you can't work." She tries again, "Maybe his Rogaine treatments are beginning to affect his memory."

She is rewarded with a snort of laughter. "Seriously, can't that new guy Schlomo, or whatever his name is, cover it?"

"You mean Cuomo? He's in court for two weeks. I don't know. You know what Bryce had the nerve to say? When I told him that I couldn't come in because it was my weekend with Brianna, he just laughed and said, 'Well, that's why they invented babysitters.'"

Dani pauses, running out of steam. She sighs. "Maybe Brian will take her for two weekends in a row. If I have to keep doing this, Brianna's going to start thinking of Allison as her mother, instead of her stepmother.

"Don't be ridiculous," Kate says.

"But Saturday is her soccer game. How can I miss that? Be honest with me Kate, am I a bad mother?"

Dani's voice suddenly sounds tight and far away.

"You're not a bad mother," Kate says firmly. "But you do sound like you could use a break. When was the last vacation you took?"

"Hey, I was just in San Diego two months ago."

"For a conference on estate planning, if I recall correctly."

"Steak dinner at the Ground Round, all expenses paid. Balmy, late-night strolls back to the Days Inn. Complimentary continental breakfasts . . . Who needs all that lounging around a pool being waited on hand and foot, and sipping little umbrella drinks between seaweed wraps, anyway?"

Kate remains silent.

"Yeah, you're probably right. I just don't see when. Anyway, sorry to call and complain. What are you doing?"

Kate stares at the pile of pillows, the blank book. "Uh, not much really . . . I have that end-of-the-year presentation at the Honeywells' this afternoon."

Dani's intercom beeps loudly and she responds in a clipped voice.

"Yep, got it. Be right in. Hey, Kate, gotta run. Good luck this afternoon. You'll be brilliant. I'll see you at the soccer game tomorrow, right?"

"Yep, I'll be there. Talk to you later."

Kate hangs up the phone and catches a quick glimpse of herself in the hall mirror. *Yikes.* Dark circles ring her green eyes. Her skin is pale and blotchy. She peers closer. Is that a *pimple* on her chin? Her hair is pulled back in a messy ponytail. In the sunlight, she sees big streaks of gray sweeping through what's left of the dark blonde. *When did this happen?* Her two-piece flannel pajamas billow and bulge. Braless is no longer sexy and pert. She resembles someone out of *National Geographic,* modeling for Lanz.

She looks away quickly, her glance falling on the heap of laundry piled on the floor at the top of the basement stairs. She starts to move toward it, then hesitates. *It can wait.* She goes back to the couch, picks up her pen and the journal, and tries to get her mind back on the task at hand. *Grateful, so grateful.* She looks through the glass door of the den, out into their backyard. The leaves on the large maple are already tinged with orange. In a few weeks, they'll be fiery red.

She glances at the small boy eating quietly at the table, a spray of freckles across his nose. She examines his feet, flat with long slender toes, swinging as he chews. Undeniably, his father's feet, she thinks. While Henry, their seven-year-old, is the spitting image of her grandfather. Her heart swells. *Lucky. I am one lucky gal. No doubt about it.* She settles back into position on the couch and closes her eyes for a moment. She lifts her pen, pauses.

Smack. She is suddenly staring at a mutilated half of a peanut butter sandwich and a smear of red jam on the white page. Before she can even say anything, Charlie has hightailed it to the glass door where the McNairs' Yorkie is now yipping and jumping. She takes a deep breath. A glob of jam is wedged into the journal's slender crease. The vague cloud of discontent that's been hovering all morning takes form. She realizes that she would be grateful, so very grateful, for one weekend away. Perhaps a seaweed wrap would do her good, a sauna, a facial, a dinner where she doesn't have to cut anyone's meat. Then when she got back . . . this journal would be bursting with gratitude, *such* gratitude. Ms. "Simple Truth of Abundant Living" would be writing *her* letters for tips on how to be more grateful . . . A little R&R and that would be her, the queen of gratitude. The faint scrape of the sliding door breaks her reverie.

"CHARLES THOMPSON, IF I HAVE TO TELL YOU ONE MORE TIME TO KEEP THAT DOOR CLOSED!" Kate is on her feet. Charlie stands with one hand on the now open glass door, his back to her. He turns, stares at her defiantly and bolts into the backyard. "CHARLIE!" Kate is right behind him, the legs of her flannel pajamas flapping as she runs over the lawn, the dry grass prickling her bare feet. Charlie drops to his knees, bent over the small dog who is jumping and licking his face. Kate is skidding to a stop when she hears a voice to her left.

"Good morning, Kate . . . Or should I say, *afternoon?*" Kate becomes acutely aware of the bright sun overhead as she turns to finds herself face to face with Mrs. McNair. Her neighbor's puff of white hair is neatly coiffed above the starched collar of her printed shirtdress and there's a disapproving look on her deeply creased face. Kate quickly pulls the folds of her pajamas together, noticing that one of her breasts is partially exposed. "Come, Napoleon," the old woman says, averting her eyes as she calls to the small tan dog who promptly responds.

"Good morning to you, too, Mrs. McNair," Kate says weakly to her neighbor's back, one hand tightly clutching Charlie, the other gripping her pajama top.

———

Dani Strauss is sitting at her sleek metal desk staring absently at the sleek black phone in her minimalist office. Sunlight streams through the tall casement window. Dani looks past the stack of papers and the silver-framed photo of Brianna on the corner of her desk, wondering if her assistant Matt has already gone to lunch. There are no sounds outside her frosted glass door. *Of course he's gone to lunch,* she thinks. *Everyone is out enjoying this gorgeous Indian summer day. Everyone except me.* Dani picks up the phone, puts it down, picks it up again. She glances at her watch—a thin gold Rolex—a small, shiny reminder of the days when such things mattered. Almost noon. She punches a button for an outside line, listens to the dial tone, sighs and hangs up.

"*Hi, Allison, it's Dani.*" In her mind she hears her voice, breezy and light. "*I need to chat about Brianna's schedule.*"

OK, that's good. She takes a deep breath and dials.

"Hello?" Allison's soft, sweet voice fills her right ear.

"Hi, Allison, it's Dani." She tries for breezy but the stress in her voice is evident, even to her.

"Dani." Still soft, but not as sweet. "What can I do for you?"

"It's about Brianna's schedule," Dani rushes on. "I've got a conflict for this weekend and I'm wondering . . ."

"If we'll take her. I suppose you have to work through the weekend again."

Dani can't tell whether it's pity or judgment she hears in Allison's voice, but either way it's making her feel inadequate.

No, you blonde-tennis-playing-perfect-second-wife, I'm running off with my yoga teacher. But if I wasn't, I'd definitely be working because I love working for a moron who pawns all his work off on me while you and my ex-husband and your new baby make a cozy family unit for my daughter.

"Unfortunately," Dani says instead.

"Well, I really should clear it with Brian, but you know we love having Bree."

Dani closes her eyes and pictures Brian, Allison and baby Connor, their blond hair shining in the light of their spotless, spacious kitchen. She pictures Allison at the stove making blueberry waffles (with maple compote and homemade heart-shaped honey butter), Brian reading the paper, Brianna playing with the baby.

"Actually, Brian said to clear it with you," she says through gritted teeth.

"Well, if you've spoken with him already . . ." Allison says.

If you refer to leaving an obsequious message on his voice mail and having his secretary return the call saying "Check with his wife" speaking to him . . .

"Yep," Dani says.

"OK, then, we'll expect her after school on Friday."

"Actually, I'm taking her to soccer Saturday morning. I'll bring her by after that." *See, I can still work and spend quality time with my daughter.*

Dani places the receiver back in its cradle, takes off her tortoise-shell "serious lawyer" reading glasses and rests her head in her hands.

Her phone rings again.

"Dani Strauss," she says crisply.

"I'm not grateful." It's Kate. "Not grateful at all."

"You're not watching Oprah are you?"

"Why can't I feel grateful for what I have?"

"Is this some kind of Buddhist riddle?"

"Really, Dani. I know I have a nice house and a good husband and two adorable children, and my life is full of all the things life is supposed to be full of. So why can't I appreciate it just the way it is? Why can't I stop thinking about getting away from all the things I'm supposed to be grateful for?"

"Put down the self-help books and step away from the bookshelf, Kate."

"I'm not kidding."

"Be grateful you don't work for Bryce. Be grateful Andy doesn't have a perfect new wife. How's that for starters?"

"Don't be bitter, Dani." Kate's voice is serious. "Tell me: What are you truly grateful for?"

While Dani wracks her brain for a sincere answer, her office door swings open and Bryce stands in the doorway, one hand on his hip, his other hand waving a sheaf of papers. She can smell his cologne from across the room.

She clears her throat.

"Let me get back to you on that," Dani says.

"Tell Bryce he's an ass who makes your life miserable," Kate says as she hangs up.

"Bryce." *You're an ass and you make my life miserable.* "What can I do for you?"

Dani hates how cheerful she sounds.

"My notes for Monday's brief," he says, dropping the papers in a sloppy pile in the middle of her desk. "I'm leaving early today. I'm taking some potential clients golfing. I'll check in with you though, so keep your cell phone on."

"Please," Dani mutters at his retreating back. "Keep your cell phone on, *please.*"

He turns in the doorway.

"And don't forget. I need you here at 8:00 sharp Monday morning to review before court. I'll have my usual from Starbucks."

He doesn't even close the door behind him.

Dani's ears are hot with anger. *Who does he think he is? Who does he think I am? At my old New York firm, I ate twerps like him for breakfast. He would have peed his pants if he ever had to face me in court.* But she knows that was ages ago. Before Brianna, the move to Easton, before Brian met Allison, the divorce, before her expensive shrink pointed out the obvious: that her self-esteem had taken a beating and then some.

Get a grip, Dani tells herself. *You know Easton is a great place to raise a kid. And this is a good job for a single mom.* Or at least that's what they said when Dani interviewed. She can still hear Bryce's little speech: "The law firm of Detwiler, Turnbull & Bendickson is firmly committed to quality of life." She realizes now that he was only referring to the quality of *his* life.

It doesn't have to be this way. Why should Bryce be the only one to enjoy the benefits of a small laid-back firm? Just because I have a child doesn't mean I can't be a good lawyer. I mean, who says I can't be a good mother and a good lawyer?

Dani's little pep talk does her no good and, worse, she can feel the tears threatening as she realizes that she'll have to ask Allison to keep Brianna Sunday night and drop her at school Monday morning. She shakes her head hard, shuffles the papers into a neat pile and begins to read.

She's just finishing her notes on the last file when there is a soft tap on her door. Dani lifts her head as Matt comes into her office. "I'm back from lunch, boss lady," he says. Crossing over to Dani's desk, he drops an issue of *People* magazine in front of her. "Check out the profile on the new CEO for WorldWide Music Productions," he says. "Sounds like he's on the market. You two would be perfect together."

Dani flips through the article, taking in the photo of an elegant dark-haired man in a perfectly tailored pin-striped suit, standing near a window with a view of the New York skyline in the background.

She begins to read a portion of the article aloud. "Of course I would rather be with someone, but it is so difficult in this business to find a supportive partner. Not everyone understands the time commitment involved in supporting the artistic sensibility. If I had to name the ideal partnership in this business, it would be Elton John and David Furnish."

She waves the magazine at Matt. "Sounds like he's more your type than mine."

Matt runs his fingers through his short, streaked hair. He leans over to study the picture again. "Mmmmm, so he does. Sorry to get your hopes up." He grins at Dani.

"I'll step aside," she says dramatically.

"Frankly, my dear, you need a good man more than I do." The teasing tone is gone from Matt's voice. "When was the last time you went on a date, anyway?"

"I've dated."

"Since the divorce?" Matt asks innocently.

"My life is full enough," Dani says, more sharply than she intended.

Matt is silent.

"Shouldn't you be getting back to your desk?" Dani asks, pointedly changing the subject. She sits back down, leafing through the magazine.

Matt reaches the doorway and turns around, his gaze directed at the corner of the room. "Shouldn't *that lunchbox* have been dropped off with Brianna this morning? Or have you developed a thing for the Powerpuff Girls that I should know about?"

Oh, hell. Dani drops her head into her hands. She can picture Ms. Crandall, Brianna's teacher, huffing as she wrangles up an extra sandwich for the kid sitting hungry and empty-handed at the table. The kid with the working mom who will never be Parent of the Year.

Chapter Two

K ate hears a car in the driveway. *Must be Andy—finally. He should have been here a half hour ago.* She parts the curtains and sees Claire Howard maneuvering her Buick Skylark into the extra space. Claire gives Kate a wave when she sees her at the window.

"Thanks so much for coming over, Mrs. Howard." Kate says opening the door. Claire Howard is a heavyset woman in her early sixties with silver hair and a broad, pleasant face that could make Mrs. Claus look edgy. Charlie appears and throws his arms around her legs. "No trouble at all, dear." Mrs. Howard smiles. "I'll take any chance I can get to spend time with my favorite guy." She ruffles Charlie's hair and then scoops him up, his head resting on her shoulder. "We always have such fun together. Now, you run off to your meeting and we'll see you soon." Claire carries Charlie to his room and pulls a book from the over-stuffed shelves, showing it to Charlie for his approval. Then they settle on the edge of his bed together. She's Charlie's absolute favorite sitter—Kate's too.

Kate heads down the hall. *Where the heck is Andy?* She closes the bathroom door and faces the mirror over the sink. *Ugh. We have got to replace these fluorescent lights,* she thinks. She digs her makeup bag—a Ziploc baggie—out of the drawer under the sink and begins dabbing foundation over the dark circles under her eyes. Charlie's been having bad dreams lately and is convinced that there are monsters in his closet.

He crawls into their bed in the middle of the night, pushes Kate to the edge and falls back into the thrashing, twitching sleep of a three-year-old. Andy doesn't even notice. Which seems fair since Charlie doesn't seem to notice Andy's impressive snores. Between Charlie's sleep gymnastics and Andy's sonic serenade, Kate is allowed only a few fitful hours of non-REM sleep before it's time for the breakfast rush. *Maybe a little more blush?*

She adds lipstick and steps back to survey the result. She shuts off the light. *That's not so bad.* She pulls back the curtain and the morning sunlight bathes her face in a definitely flattering glow. Ignoring the flattering glow cast on the dirt ring around the inside of the bathtub and scooping up the pile of still slightly damp towels from the floor, she heads back down the hall.

Claire's high-pitched giggle and Charlie's manic laugh ring out from his room. Kate sticks her head in.

"You look very nice, dear," Claire says. "That's a lovely shade of lip color you're wearing."

"Yeah, Mama, you're fancy." Charlie runs over and hugs her pant leg. Kate fights her first instinct to pull away and spare her only good pantsuit the wrinkles, drops the towels on the floor and leans in close for a big hug.

"I'm off, then," Kate says, planting a kiss on Charlie's head.

She goes downstairs, dropping the towels on the laundry pile that has managed to spread throughout the kitchen. Athletic socks and underwear have crept under the table. The dog has made a bed out of a pile of dirty jeans. Kate pushes everything back into a heap. It's gigantic. It has multiplied overnight. She sighs, knowing it will be there for her when she gets home.

She looks at the clock: 2:05 p.m. *I can't believe he's not here. I'm supposed to be at the Honeywells' at 3 p.m. If he doesn't come in the next five minutes, I'm late.*

Kate dials Andy's office number and to her surprise he picks up on the first ring.

"Andy?"

"Hi honey, sorry—can't talk now, I'm with a student. Call you in a bit?"

"Andy. I don't *believe* this. You were supposed to bring the loaner home forty-five minutes ago."

"Wow, I'm really sorry baby. I completely forgot . . . the lab ran late. Listen, my office hours just started and I can't get away."

"I've got a READ board meeting, remember? It's our year-end presentation for Mr. Honeywell."

"Yeah, but I'm *working*." There is a long silence.

"Fine. I'll walk over." Kate hangs up. *Why is it that I can keep soccer schedules, violin practice, vet appointments and campus office hours in my head, but no one can remember the one day of the week when I have an appointment?*

OK, don't panic. I can still make it if I hurry. She makes the ten-minute walk to the university, moving as quickly as she can without breaking into a full sweat in her best suit and blouse. She arrives at Andy's office and slips out of her jacket, feeling the perspiration settling on her back. She knocks, then opens the door. Andy's six-foot-four frame is hunched over his desk alongside a long-limbed coed wearing low-slung jeans and a small T-shirt exposing her flat stomach. Her hair is cut in long golden layers and her skin is dewy. Her slender arm is gesturing to some point on the page in front of them.

"So then doesn't this new calculation need to take into account the systems change in Group A?" she is asking.

"Absolutely," Andy says.

Kate clears her throat and they both look up.

"Hi. We were just finishing up. Tara, this is my wife." Andy pushes back his chair, brushes a lock of sandy-brown hair from his forehead and nods in Kate's direction.

"Hi, Mrs. Thompson . . . nice meeting you," the co-ed says flatly. "So I'll make that change and get it in by Monday," she adds, gathering her notebooks and adjusting her jeans as she glides toward the door.

"Nice meeting you, too, Tara." Kate turns to watch her leave.

As Tara passes, she pauses, waving her hand vaguely over her shoulder. "Uh, looks like you've got something on your shirt."

Kate reaches toward her shoulder and, to her horror, peels off a small dingy tube sock. "Mmm. Thanks."

Tara, barely acknowledging the response, makes her way down the hall. Kate watches her go. Her legs are beginning to itch in her stockings, and the control top is pulling at the waist where her shirt has come slightly untucked. *Was I ever that young, that thin? She probably thinks I look like her mother. Who am I kidding? . . . I could be her mother.*

Kate turns back to Andy. "I need the car keys," she says briskly.

"Why are you so tense? You're not stressing over this Honeywell thing, are you?" Andy asks.

Clueless. "No, I'm stressing over the fact that I should have left twenty minutes ago . . . *And,* I'm stressing over the laundry, which has apparently broken free of the kitchen and is now following me around town." She tosses the sock on his desk.

"I'll take care of the laundry when I get home," he says.

"Thanks, anyway," Kate says, remembering the last time Andy did laundry. Henry had to wear pink underwear to school for a week until she could buy him some new ones—though why a boy who puts his shirt on inside out half the time without noticing would be upset about pink underwear is beyond her.

"For God's sake, Kate, it's laundry. Not finding a cure for cancer."

"OK, fine. Just sort out all the dark things and wash them in cold water with a cold rinse. I'll handle the rest."

"No problem. I'm a rocket scientist, remember?"

"All right, thanks. Look, I really have to run," she says giving Andy a grudging peck on the cheek. He hands her the keys and tells her where the car is parked. Kate walks toward the faculty lot, past clusters of students crowding the sidewalk, laughing and holding books to their chests.

Kate thinks back to the conversations she and Andy used to have when they were students together—intense late-night talks about Freud, the merits of Realism versus Cubism, the Marx Brothers and the big bang theory. Kate was working toward her PhD in psychology then—until she found out she was pregnant with Henry. *Whatever happened to those days? Now all we talk about is soccer schedules and laundry.*

Kate pulls out of the campus parking lot and turns right, heading for the main road that will eventually take her up into the beautiful rolling mountains surrounding the town. *If I don't hit any traffic, I might still make it on time.*

Easton is a typical New England small town, saved from the typical small-town mentality by the three colleges that anchor it, and its proximity to Boston and New York. Not for the first time, Kate feels as if she's driving through a modern-day Norman Rockwell painting. Main Street is bustling at this hour: moms pushing strollers out of Starbucks, on their way to playgroups and craft sessions; college students hanging around outside the Internet café; workers changing the title of the featured films on the marquee of the art movie house. She cruises down a wide street, bordered by ancient elms, past the stately Victorian homes that herald the gracious family neighborhoods within walking distance of the town center. Five minutes later, she's trying to make up for lost time by driving too fast on Route 7 as it winds up into the hilly stone-walled countryside surrounding Easton.

Kate reviews her presentation as she drives. She's written out a short speech but she's still nervous about getting up in front of the board, especially Gerry Honeywell. He's one of those second-generation, old-money types. He's the kind of benefactor you see on those news magazine shows, the kind who builds museum wings and puts entire high-school classes through college.

Kate hopes she isn't so nervous that she misses any of the details of the Honeywells' house. She knows Dani will kill her if she doesn't file a full report. The Honeywells have their "summer cottage" in one of the small, rural towns surrounding Easton. Rumor has it that, come summertime, there are more New York City millionaires hiding out in the rolling hills and valleys of Goshburg than are left in Manhattan. It's not exactly the social circle you'll run into on a Saturday night at the local Mexican restaurant. These people are more likely to hop their private plane for a quick lobster dinner in Nantucket than venture down to Nelson's Fish and Chop House. This is her big chance to see how the really rich live, and she is not going to let stage fright dull her powers of observation.

Kate feels a twinge of anxiety and then thinks of a quote from Dr.

Mia. She bought her book last year, *Drawing the Map of Your Life,* and must have read it five times by now. She can almost recite it by heart. *When facing a challenge, remember it is there because you have created it. No challenge exceeds your ability to meet it.*

She runs through her speech a few times, speaking aloud to the rearview mirror, and is actually feeling pretty confident as she approaches the mile-long driveway that leads to the sprawling stone house. The gardens lining the drive are resplendent in their late-summer bloom. In the distance an automatic sprinkler soaks a great expanse of emerald grass. At the circular drive in front of the house a valet takes the keys to Kate's rental car–blessedly free of sippy cups, used paper towels, crushed Goldfish crackers and dog hair. Kate smiles graciously, accepting a tall glass of lemonade topped with a sprig of mint from the white-gloved waiter who greets her at the bottom of the steps leading up to the house. *Now here's something I could be grateful for,* Kate thinks as she enters the tall, cool foyer, where a huge crystal chandelier casts rainbow prisms on the ivory walls.

She eases her way through the crowd, soaking up the posh atmosphere of the mahogany-paneled library. The turnout for last year's meeting in the Florentine Room of the Easton Grille wasn't even half this size. She guesses no one wanted to pass up a chance to check out the Honeywells in their native habitat.

The imposing leather chairs and couch have been pushed to the back of the room, and rows of folding chairs have taken their place on the crimson Oriental carpet. At the front of the room, a long table set up in front of the huge gray-stone fireplace serves as a podium. Above the fireplace is a gold-framed portrait of Honeywell and his third–and current–wife, Sunny. He's posing in a dark suit, a serious expression on his chiseled face. The artist has kindly thickened the graying hair at his temples and only hinted at the emerging paunch beneath the fitted suit. Sunny poses on a chintz sofa, wearing a yellow suit, an enormous diamond and ropes of pearls. Her elaborately coiffed pale blonde hair frames her narrow, tan face. Even seated, it's clear she's much taller than her husband. His hand rests on her shoulder, as if to make sure she doesn't stand up. Kate wishes Dani were there with her. She can imagine her running commentary: *That's a Chanel suit in the por-*

trait, for sure, about two seasons old; check out the rock on her finger–I heard it's Harry Winston. How much work do you think she's had done?

When Kate tears her gaze from the portrait, she notices Sunny gesturing for her to come to the front of the room. Everyone finds a seat in the rows of rented chairs as Sunny steps to the microphone and smiles at the crowd.

"Thank you all for coming today. It's always a pleasure to see the faces of the volunteers who work so hard to fulfill READ's mission of keeping literacy alive in our community. I'd like to introduce Kate Thompson, our part-time director in charge of outreach programs at READ. Kate has . . ." Sunny falters and narrows her eyes at Gerry, who is seated in the front row and making a slashing motion across his throat. ". . . graciously offered to update us on the organization's activities over the last year." She finishes in a rush of words and hurries to her seat at the edge of the room.

"No one's here to listen to you," Kate hears Gerry mutter and for a minute she thinks he means her.

Her palms already sweating, she freezes, halfway to the microphone. Suddenly she realizes that he meant his wife. She starts moving again, reminding herself to breathe and resolving to make her speech as quick as possible. She reaches the podium and spreads her notes out in front of her with shaking hands.

Fear can be a catalyst for growth. You are capable of anything you desire.

Dr. Mia's words are reassuring. Kate takes one more deep breath and begins.

"Thank you all for coming today. I'm very proud of what READ has accomplished. Over the last year we've raised enough money to hire reading specialists who rotate through the libraries in our state. We've developed a list of books designed to appeal to delayed readers of all ages. We've even had enough money to advertise our programs in local and community papers, bringing more kids into the libraries, where we give the librarians some training and tools to start–and keep–them reading."

Kate looks up at her audience, which is smiling and nodding in agreement. This is going better than she expected. She glances at her notes again and is about to continue when she sees Gerry Honeywell standing up and moving toward the front of the room. "So, uh, thank you all for coming and for your continued support," she says, crumpling her speech into a sweaty ball. She makes her way over to an empty seat, to a scattering of applause.

Gerry Honeywell makes his way to the podium.

"Thank you, Kate, dear. It's been a wonderful year for the organization, indeed. And I have a special announcement to make. I have just returned from California where in addition to shooting just four over par at Pebble Beach"—he smiles modestly at the polite applause—"I accepted an award on behalf of READ from the National Education Community Council for . . ."—he clears his throat as he pulls a piece of paper from his shirt pocket—"for 'a dedicated vision of community service and commitment to inspiring lifelong learning.' I'm delighted to tell you that the state of California has decided to adopt our library program. This is the beginning of the national recognition that has been my goal for this organization from the start."

An award? Kate thinks. *I didn't know READ got an award . . . I wouldn't have minded a trip to California to accept it . . .*

He gestures in her direction. "And I really have to thank Kate, here. Without her great office skills, we never would have gotten this idea out to the award committee on time." He smiles broadly. "Thanks for all those long hours at the computer, Kate."

Kate's face grows hot. *It sounds as if all I did was type up some forms. He's totally stealing the credit. That library program was my idea.*

Everyone is standing and applauding. Honeywell holds a hand up until the applause dies down, then he steps back into the crowd. Kate follows in his wake as he accepts congratulations from those assembled. As she watches the handshakes and backslaps, it occurs to Kate that they should be for her; then she immediately feels selfish and petty.

Of course he deserves the credit. Without his money and name, none of this could have happened in the first place. Really, when you think about it, my role was mostly organizational. Why would anyone send a part-time glorified secretary to California to accept an award?

Kate is considering making a break for the nearest bathroom to pull herself together when someone lightly touches her arm.

She turns to find Sunny Honeywell. Up close, Sunny is even more angular than in her portrait. Her nose is a perfect ski slope, her teeth unbelievably white, and even and her skin is smooth and wrinkle free. Her bright blue eyes are evaluating Kate shrewdly.

"Kate, I want to congratulate you personally."

"Excuse me?" Kate says.

"The award. I know that program was your idea, Kate," she says softly, her direct gaze kind and knowing. "This is what Gerry does . . . Trust me. I doubt he ever even read the proposal. But I know how hard you worked for this."

Kate manages a weak smile.

"Really, Sunny," she says feebly. "It's no big deal. I mean, without Mr. Honeywell's support for the program I would never even have been able to get the proposal off the ground."

"That's bull and you know it," Sunny responds, flashing her perfect smile and giving Kate a little squeeze on the arm. Kate begins another protest but Sunny moves smoothly away, floating through the crowd to her husband's side.

It's not public recognition, but still, Sunny's words make Kate feel a little better. Reminding herself that she doesn't volunteer at a non-profit for the glory, she pushes the award to the back of her mind and even manages to enjoy the catered tea sandwiches. *When was the last time I had poached salmon with dill sauce on fine china with crisp table linens and fresh flowers?* she thinks. *Shouldn't this be reward enough?*

—

That night Kate lies in bed and imagines that she's at the award ceremony in California. "Oh, I'm just your average small-town mom," she says modestly as she accepts the award. "It's just a matter of juggling priorities." The perfect California sun shines down from a perfect blue sky. She is standing at a podium, under a striped canopy, before a sea of smiling faces. She is still dreaming of the California sunshine when she feels someone tugging back the covers.

"Mommy, Chancey peed on the kitchen floor." Charlie is standing next to her in his dinosaur-print pajamas, his hair sticking straight up.

She nudges Andy awake.

"Did you let the dog out last night before you went to bed?"

"Oops. I'm sorry, Kate, I forgot."

"Then the puddle is yours, my friend." Problem solved. She rolls back over, hoping to catch just fifteen more minutes of that glorious California dream.

"Mom, I don't have any shorts for soccer." Henry wanders in, wearing socks, Spider-Man underwear and his soccer T-shirt. "I need my team shorts."

He stands at the edge of the bed, an expectant expression on his freckled face as he stares at her with his unblinking blue-green eyes. His blond hair is slicked down with water and carefully parted to one side. "I don't want to be late, Mom," he says.

Kate groans and swings her legs over the edge of the bed.

At least Andy did the laundry.

Yep, Kate thinks with satisfaction, *I may not win any awards, but I can still get things done. I can delegate with the best of them.*

She goes downstairs, swerving around the puddle on the kitchen floor, and heads down to the laundry room.

The pile of clothes definitely looks smaller.

She checks the dryer.

Empty.

Her heart sinks. In all their years of marriage, Andy has never taken the clothes out of the dryer and folded them.

She looks at the washing machine. The lid is up.

"Mom, do you have my shorts?"

Kate peers into the machine. There are Henry's shorts, all right. Sitting in a tub of soapy water.

She closes the lid and the washer clicks on.

As she digs through the dirty laundry trying to find a pair of shorts that won't embarrass Henry (or her) on the soccer field, Kate tries to summon the confidence of this morning's dream.

Who am I kidding? I don't deserve to run an organization or receive any special awards. I should stick to doing laundry.

The sun is just breaking over the trees when Dani finally falls into a fitful sleep. She dreams that Mayor Giuliani has just slapped her with a $250 fine.

"What's this for?" Dani asks him.

"You've been spending insufficient quality time with your child and it is my duty as mayor to fine you."

"Hey, wait a second," Dani protests. "You can't fine someone for that! I mean, can you? Anyway, I spend plenty of quality time with Brianna. It's not my fault that I work for an inconsiderate bastard who has no respect for my personal life. Don't you see I have to keep this job to be a good mother to Brianna? This is an outrage! And by the way, I don't even live in New York City now . . . And, come to think of it, you're not even the mayor anymore!"

She wakes with a start. Her T-shirt is damp and twisted at her waist. Sunlight is creeping around the edges of her room-darkening shades. Yesterday's skirt and blouse hang over the rail of the treadmill in the corner. Magazines are stacked haphazardly on the nightstand next to a glass of water.

She hears a faint chatter in the next room.

She looks at the clock: 7:58.

I must have shut off the alarm. Oh my God. Brianna has to be at soccer in half an hour. Dani heaves herself out of bed and grabs a pair of sweatpants.

She walks down the hall and pokes her head into Brianna's room. Her daughter is already dressed in her soccer shorts and team shirt and is sitting cross-legged on her bed, surrounded by a mound of stuffed animals. She is wearing a stethoscope and has the flat end pressed to the chest of a purple hippopotamus. She looks stern. "Don't worry. I will take care of this," she tells the animal.

"Hey, Brianna. Sorry I slept late. What are you doing?"

Brianna looks up, her expression serious. "Playing veterinarian."

"Looks like you're doing a good job . . . very busy practice. Is the hippo going to be all right?"

Brianna brushes her wispy bangs out of her eyes and nods. "I think so. He's got hemproids but I think it can be treated."

"What? Do you mean hemorrhoids? Where did you hear that word, honey?"

"Daddy told Allison that he needs to go to the doctor because his hemorrhoids are killing him."

"Oh, did he now?" Dani stifles a laugh. For a second she's pleased. *Won't be so easy cruising on that new three-thousand-dollar mountain bike you just bought, will it, Brian?* Then the thought hits her: *I am a mean, terrible person.*

"Honey, maybe you can take care of Hippo later. We've got to get a move on. What do you want for breakfast? Eggo blueberry?

"I can't take care of Hippo later. I need to take care of him *now*."

"Brianna, we don't have time to play. You can take care of him later."

"I can't. I won't be here later." Brianna's face suddenly falls and she looks like she's about to cry. Her hands clench into fists and she presses them into her skinny thighs.

Dani fights a lump in her own throat. "You can bring him to Daddy's if you want."

"He needs to be *home*. He's sick, Mommy!"

"Tell you what, sweetheart. Before we leave, you tell me what to do and I'll take over until you get back."

"You can't. You're not a vet."

Dani considers pointing out the fact that Brianna is not a vet either but says instead, "Vets have helpers. They're called 'veterinary technicians.' So how about I fill in until you get home?"

This seems to satisfy Brianna. She carefully tucks the hippo in under her lavender flowered bedspread. Grabbing her soccer cleats from under her bed, she knots the laces and slings them around her neck—just like on her poster of Mia Hamm—and follows her mother down the hall.

By the time Dani pulls her battered white Volvo into the parking lot, Brianna's team is already starting to form a huddle around the coach. One short, red-haired boy is furiously chasing a ball. His shorts look about two sizes too big and his socks sag around his ankles. When he tries to stop the ball with his foot, he falls face-first into the wet grass.

"Oops," Dani says aloud.

"Oh, jeez," says Brianna. "That's Calvin Betts. I hope he stays on the bench. We'll never win if they let him in. He trips everyone and kicks the ball the wrong way down the field."

"Now, Brianna, everyone needs a chance to play," Dani says, trying to be diplomatic. "Some people learn faster than others."

Dani's phone rings right in the middle of her inspiring lecture on good sportsmanship. She checks the caller ID: Bryce.

Brianna stares at her, then at the phone in her mother's hand. "You've gotta take that, right?"

"I'll be quick. I promise. Run ahead and I'll be right over."

Brianna stares at her.

"I promise I won't miss any of your game." Dani meets her gaze.

Brianna throws her a look that says, "Yeah, right, heard that before," but doesn't say anything. She grabs her water bottle, opens the car door and slides out, slamming the door behind her. Dani watches her lope across the field, then punches the TALK button on the phone.

"Hello?"

"You're not answering your office phone," Bryce snaps.

"I'm answering my cell," she retorts.

"I need you to pull a file."

Like hell you do. You're probably calling from the golf course clubhouse.

"I'm not at the office," Dani is forced to admit.

"Well, I'll call you at the office in about . . .."–he pauses, no doubt calculating the amount of time he needs for his lesson with the golf pro, a sauna and lunch–"two hours. Have the Holskin file on your desk."

The phone goes dead and Dani's snappy retort dies on her lips. She settles for a fierce glare at the phone.

Her gaze flicks up to the rearview mirror. Her mother's face stares back at her. Not her mother in her Subway Queen of Brooklyn days but closer to Mom of hair-so-red-it's-the-loudest-thing-in-Coral Gables-and-that's-saying-something days. The lines around her eyes look like crevices in the broad daylight. She didn't have time to put on any makeup and she's overdue for an appointment with her hairdresser. Flecks of gray appear at the roots where the color is growing out.

In fact, Dani thinks bitterly, she probably doesn't even look as good as her mother these days. Her dad's been dead nearly fifteen years, and Dani's mom, Bebe, is doing fine. She's the queen of the Bird of Paradise home for active mature adults. She's got her early-bird dinners, her apricot toy poodle, Baby, her "gentleman friend," Mort, her classes and lectures, her line-dancing on Saturday nights—she's in her element.

This wasn't supposed to happen for another couple of decades, was it? Dani thinks of the *New York Times* article she read about women who throw Botox parties. "Here, doll, have a glass of Chardonnay and a couple of injections in your forehead." *Why don't I ever get invited to any Botox parties?* Dani asks herself only somewhat facetiously. She grabs her hair and pulls it back in a high, tight ponytail; it hurts, but she thinks her eyes and brow are lifted—slightly less saggy. She fumbles in her pockets, pulls out one of Brianna's ponytail holders and twists it into her hair.

As she gets out of the car and walks toward the field, the coach shouts to Brianna's team to get into their positions. Dani is taking in the coach's very broad shoulders and nice, well-developed calves when she feels a nudge.

"You made it," says Kate. Her hair is pulled back in a sloppy braid and she is wearing an oversized sweatshirt and baggy jeans. Her eyes are a bit puffy.

"Just barely," Dani says.

"Me too," Kate sighs. "Charlie was up in the middle of the night. He had that horrible monster dream again."

"It could have been worse, it could have been Rudy Giuliani."

"What?" Kate asks, distracted.

"Never mind. Poor little guy. So you and Andy spent the rest of the night getting kicked in the head by a three-year-old."

"You got it." Kate rubs her eyes and yawns. "What's with the hair?"

Dani's hand shoots up to the bushy ponytail sprouting out of the top of her head. "It's straightening out the forehead wrinkles," she says lamely. "Not working, huh?"

Kate shakes her head sympathetically. "Afraid not. The effort is admirable, though."

"Where's Charlie?" Dani asks.

"I didn't have the energy to chase him around the soccer field this morning. He's home with Andy, probably watching videos like he's been doing since he got up at six a.m. Is seven hours of video too much?"

"Nah, sounds all right to me." Dani pictures Brianna in her favorite spot on the couch in a trancelike state watching endless reruns of *The Croc Files* on Animal Planet.

"I mean, shouldn't I be making papier-mâché dinosaurs or pipe-cleaner sculptures with him or something?" Kate asks, a weight in her voice.

"Don't ask me, I hate arts-and-crafts projects. I cringe at the sight of glitter glue. Hey, how was the Honeywell shindig?"

"Oh, it was fine . . . nice spread, you would have loved it. The house is unbelievable and Sunny was wearing this huge emerald ring. I wish you'd been there to see it."

"How did your speech go?"

"Pretty good, I think. The real glory went to Gerry Honeywell though. READ won an award for its library program."

"Kate, that's great. Congratulations—what do you mean Gerry got all the glory? That program was your baby. You worked so hard."

"Well, Gerry went to California to accept the award. He practically finances the whole thing, after all. I'm just a volunteer."

"Kate, you've got to stick up for yourself. You deserve credit for what you do."

"The point is getting the program out there. I'm sure Gerry Honeywell appreciates what I've done. It's not a big deal—really," Kate says unconvincingly and turns her attention to the soccer field. "Way to go, Henry," she shouts.

"For what it's worth, it's a big deal to me," Dani tells her. "C'mon, let's do something to celebrate."

"Well, maybe we do need to do something. We're feeling a bit down in the dumps, right? You're stressed. You need a vacation but won't take one. And I could sure use . . . something. Well, you know, like Dr. Mia says, "*If you don't like your attitude, change your circumstances.*" If we're not feeling fabulous, we can change our circumstances. Let's have a party. Let's have a fabulous party."

"Who's Dr. Mia and does she do Botox?" Dani asks, only half kidding.

"She's not that kind of doctor. You know, the lady on *Oprah*. She wrote that book I gave you. C'mon, Dani. Wouldn't it be fun to push all of this work stuff aside for an evening? Get dressed up? Talk about something other than what brief you need to file next, who sat next to who on the bus or whose weekend it is with Brianna? One night. We need this." Kate looks at her, pleading.

Dani thinks about a night of adult conversation that does not revolve around who's suing who. A night of crudités and elegant chatter. It doesn't sound half bad. Maybe they need to shake things up a bit.

"Sure, why not. Count me in. I haven't thrown a decent party since the Reagan administration."

"We can do it at my house," Kate volunteers. "And it will not be one of those hummus and dried-beet affairs this town is so good at. We will allow no complaining about lawns, talking about the new sink that's been installed or griping about your child's teacher. We will create an atmosphere so dazzling that we will all communally transcend the dreary."

"Hey, at this point, I'll settle for a decent crab dip and wine that's not served in a Dixie cup."

"Then it's a plan," Kate says firmly. "Good going, Henry. Nice play!" Kate claps her hands, smiling.

Dani turns her attention back to the mass of disorder that is a coed soccer game of seven- and eight-year-olds: swinging sneakers, flailing limbs and ponytails. Technically, this is "no score" soccer, fostering a modern parent's dream of healthy, noncompetitive youth. But most of the kids keep score as though their lives depend on it. Her daughter is no exception.

They lose when Calvin Betts inadvertently but quite efficiently assists the winning (and only) game goal. Calvin is clearly the MVP of the opposing team. Too bad he plays for their side. Dani herds Brianna into the car. Brianna's face is flushed and bright. Her silky, light brown hair is escaping from her braids.

"We stink," Brianna announces. "We never win."

Dani knows how she feels. She hates to lose, too. But somehow it seems wrong to be promoting the killer instinct in a seven-year-old. She wracks her brain to recall what the parenting book she just read said about children and competition.

"This is about doing your best and everyone getting a chance to play," she tells Brianna, pleased with her politically correct take on sports.

There is a long, unsatisfied silence.

"Mom, did you see Henry's kick? We've been working on that," Brianna says brightening.

Dani admires her daughter's ability to find the good in a bad situation. She certainly didn't get it from her.

"That was great, Brianna. You both did a great job. What do you say we make a quick stop at Friendly's for lunch?" Dani asks her.

"I thought I had to be at Dad's at twelve o'clock. I thought you had to work," Brianna says looking out the car window. Dani thinks of the pile of paperwork on her desk. Another gorgeous day and she is going to spend it indoors staring at a pile of papers and a computer screen. She glances in the rearview mirror, at the small girl kicking the back of her seat.

"Right," Dani says finally. "Another time."

～

When they pull into the driveway, Dani can see Brian and Allison in the backyard. Allison is in tennis whites and is rolling an oversized, multicolored beach ball toward Connor, their eighteen-month-old son. The baby smiles with glee, flops on the ball and promptly rolls over on the grass. Brian scoops him up and heads toward the driveway when he sees the car. He gives a wave. *What a picture of domestic tranquillity,* Dani thinks. *Wouldn't I like an afternoon tennis game and nothing better to do than to aimlessly throw beach balls around on my back lawn?*

When she looks over at Brianna, her daughter's face is shining. She grabs her backpack and throws open the door. "Hi, Daddy!"

Brian puts Connor down and the baby comes toddling over, hands flailing wildly, while Allison, carrying the beach ball, trails close behind.

Brianna turns back to Dani and for a moment the smile is gone. "Bye, Mommy, don't work too hard." She pauses, looking serious.

"Oh, don't you worry. I love you, sweetheart. You have a good time. I'll pick you up after school on Monday." Brianna grins and, in a flash, dashes off, giving the beach ball a big kick.

Dani pulls out of the driveway. In her rearview mirror she can see Brian and Allison, shoulder to shoulder, their blonde heads glowing, the baby waving obliviously at her. *Don't worry, I'm leaving,* she thinks. Brianna has already raced around the corner of the newly painted Victorian house. There are already bunches of dried corn and pumpkins decorating the front porch. Perfect. And Dani has to admit, it kills her.

Chapter Three

The house is quiet, which in and of itself is a minor miracle. Charlie is at his friend Ben's house. Henry won't be home from school for two hours.

Kate scans the place with new eyes. It's as if she hasn't really looked at it in years. She glances at the sofa, and even from across the room she can make out the faint grease stains on the right arm where Charlie massaged in a handful of mac and cheese. *No problem. Nothing a decorative pillow and dim lighting can't fix. Candles are key. Lots of candles. I need to rearrange some furniture, hang the drapes I just picked up from the dry cleaners. OK, so the major cleaning can wait until tomorrow. Right now, I just need to get organized. There is serious work to be done.*

She makes a list and then organizes it into separate lists. Dani's dealing with invitations and ordering food from the caterer: a smoked salmon, grilled filet mignon with a delicious horseradish and herb sauce, hors d'oeuvres and fresh-baked rolls. Kate pulls the wrinkled, maroon tablecloths out of the hall closet and puts them aside to press. She counts chairs. She crafts the centerpieces for the tables, in her mind. She remembers how on the Home and Garden channel the other day, the craft lady spray-painted chestnuts, almonds and a variety of other unshelled nuts gold for a decorative fall touch. When she lay them in simple wooden bowls with her large, sure hands, they shone like the sun. That would be easy enough, Kate decides. She refuses to be deterred by the memory of her last spray-paint attempt in which, while coating a small wooden race car for Henry in the garage, she miscalculated the aerosol's range of fire and speckled their black minivan cherry red. Henry thought it looked cool. Andy was less pleased.

Think positive and you will attract positive circumstances into your life.

Glancing around the room, Kate imagines heaps of sparkling gold chestnuts glinting in the candlelight. Then the room comes sharply back into focus—golden dog hair glistening on the carpet. *Who am I kidding?*

She grabs her keys and shoves the lists into her handbag. As she heads for the door, the phone rings.

She considers ignoring it but instead doubles back and grabs the receiver.

"Hello."

"Hello, there. You sound out of breath. Is this a bad time?"

"Hey, Mom. No, not at all." Kate is struck, as she so often is recently, by how her voice sounds like an echo of her mother's in the receiver. They have the same inflection and the same timbre. Kate wonders if her mother hears it, too. "I'm just getting some things together for this weekend. Dani and I are throwing a party. We're celebrating the end of drudgery and the blahs."

"Sounds like fun. No doubt, you're just the gals to do it. How are the boys? Andy?"

"Everyone's fine, Mom. How are you feeling?"

"Oh, not too bad."

Her mom's idea of not too bad is your average Joe's idea of code red.

"What's going on? You haven't had to see Dr. Wilson, have you? You're not due for your checkup until December, right?"

It's been almost two years since her mom had been feeling a bit achy and tired and her dad insisted she go see the doctor. That alone alarmed Kate because her father is not too keen on the medical profession.

The doctor didn't seem concerned at first. But, three days later, the universe was realigned: breast cancer.

Her mom sailed through the surgery. She bonded with the radiation and chemo nurses. They greeted one another like old friends. She knew all about their families and sympathized with them about their work schedules. Hauling Charlie with her, Kate flew down to Pennsylvania as often as she could, while Henry started kindergarten without her. By the end of the year, Eve was back on her feet and redesigning her gardens; Andy and the boys were back in their routines and glad to have Kate home with them full time; everyone was back to normal. Everyone, that is, but Kate. It was as though in the blur of activity she'd lost sight of something essential but what that was, she couldn't quite say.

"You're sure you're feeling OK?" Kate persists.

"I'm sure, I'm just a bit behind on sleep," Eve insists.

"Why aren't you sleeping?"

"Oh, well, your father's had a bit of insomnia. I was up playing hearts with him last night. The night before that, your brother woke me up just after I went to bed. You'd think that after ten years in LA he'd remember the time difference. Or maybe he just thinks I always stay up until two a.m."

"Mom, you have really got to take care of yourself. Dad will just have to learn to watch late-night movies like the rest of us. I may have to have a word with Chris. I owe him a call, anyway."

"It's just a few hours' sleep, Kate." Her mother sounds bewildered. Kate feels a vague sense of panic. Her mother has always been so busy doing things for others, but who's looking out for her?

"So you promise you'll get to bed early?"

"I will if I shut the TV off before that O'Reilly character comes on," her mother says. "He just gets my blood boiling. Did you hear what he said the other night about the glass ceiling? Someone should take that fellow over their knee. He needs a good spanking, that one."

Kate laughs. It is not the first time she's heard this tirade.

"Anyhow," her mother continues, "you better get going. I'm fine, darling. Truly. Listen, you and Dani have a good time. I'll give you a call to see how it went. Bye, bye. Love you."

"Love you too, Mom."

As always, Kate marvels at her mother's strength and her ability to handle anything life throws at her. Eve wouldn't be intimidated by throwing a neighborhood cocktail party. Kate feels a surge of optimism as she stuffs her to-do list into her bag and heads out the door. *Fabulousness, here we come.*

⁓

"Matt, hold my calls for the next half hour, OK?" Dani takes her finger off the intercom button and slides the manila folder out of her brief-case. She opens it to the checklist inside. There is a satisfying row of checks next to the neatly typed list:

Order flowers–check
Take red silk dress to dry cleaners–check
Call Value Wines, 10 red, 10 white, 1 bottle Veuve Clicquot (*Hey, the hostesses deserve a little something to get in the mood!*)–check
Call caterer–

The number for the caterer, Best Kept Secret, the town's finest, is at her fingertips and she's ridiculously happy as she dials, anticipating a pleasant conversation in which she simply tells someone exactly what she wants and they cheerfully comply. A nice change from her usual discussions with the people around her. She is worried that the defensive tone she uses at work with Bryce is finding its way home with her. Lately, whenever she says anything to Brianna it turns into a contest of who can have the last word. *Drawn down to the level of a seven-year-old, that's what I've come to,* she thinks. Maybe that's why she's so excited about this party–it's a chance for some meaningful adult interaction.

It's not like Dani totally gave up her social life when she moved to Easton from New York. She's had Friday-night pizza parties with the parents of Brianna's friends. She's had Kate and Andy over for a grown-ups-only dinner party. *Yep, I am the hostess with the mostest.*

The truth is, Dani loves parties. She loves the organizing, the ordering, the planning. She and Brian used to throw parties all the time and everyone clamored to be invited. And why wouldn't they? Brian was the acknowledged star in the real-estate department of the firm. A six-foot-three smoothie with perfect blond hair and even more perfect teeth, he could charm a potential client into retaining the firm in just one lunch. And Dani? She was the other half of the team. Respected in the litigation department for her killer instinct and refusal to be intimidated. Tall and thin enough to look good in a power suit, her dark hair a foil to his sunny good looks. What a shock it was to find out that Brian didn't want a teammate. He wanted a cheerleader.

He used to say that since Dani was so good at giving parties, she should give up the lawyering and go into business as an event planner. A nice part-time job she could hold down once she had the baby. Dani used to laugh. She really didn't see why having a baby would change her goal to make partner at the firm–maybe it would take a year longer, but nothing more. Her daughter would grow up knowing that her mommy was a successful businesswoman, too.

Turns out, Brian was serious. Once Brianna came, he was even more insistent that Dani should become the perfect housewife and mother. Brianna had a fever? She had to call in. Nanny out sick? Another sick day for Dani. And, eventually, she started to feel like a bad mother if she even considered that maybe it didn't always have to be she who stayed home. After two years it became clear that Dani was slipping off the partnership track. Then Brian decided it would be better to raise a child outside the city. The next thing Dani knew, he had left the firm, bought a beautiful old home in a picture-book neighborhood far from New York and started his own law office.

Brian never even asked her what she wanted; he just assumed that she'd agree the move was the best for their "family." That's when Dani understood that what she had thought was an equal partnership, Brian had simply considered a cute phase of her being a career woman while waiting to reach her true potential as the mother of his children and the keeper of his castle. For a while, Dani even convinced herself that he was right–that it was selfish of her not to want what he saw so clearly as best for all of them.

So there they were, living Brian's picture of the perfect life: He, the benevolent provider, and she, the dutiful wife and mother. He worked long hours during the week, building his practice and unwound on the weekends by taking up tennis. Dani did her best to enjoy cooking dinner each night and keep a big house running smoothly. She filled her schedule with Mommy and Me music classes and Splash 'N Swim at the Y. But she missed the excitement of the courtroom and the satisfaction of writing a solid brief. She loved Brianna; she loved being a mom. But she loved being a lawyer, too. The only thing she didn't love being was the kind of wife Brian seemed to want.

Dani spent a long time trying to be what her husband wanted her to be, and nearly as much time wondering why she couldn't get it right. The day she stopped by the country club and saw him with his tennis instructor, Allison, she finally realized that she could never be what he wanted at all.

Everyone was impressed with how amicably they split as Dani kept a stiff upper lip. She found a job again, in a town not far from Brian. She told Brianna that she was lucky to have two houses. She told Kate that she was doing great. She told herself that now she could be *the real her*. She didn't have to answer to anyone.

We've been divorced for three years now, Dani thinks, *and Brian's got the life and the wife he always wanted. And me? Well . . .*

"Best Kept Secret, may we help you?"

Dani presses the mental pause button on the video of her-marriage-gone-wrong and places the order for the party. Finishing the call, she adds another satisfying check mark to her list.

She moves her fingers down to the next line:

Invite guests–

Here's where her future career as a party planner gets a little shaky. Her current social circle is not the biggest or the most glamorous–primarily because she doesn't have a social circle. Between work and Brianna there's no time for anything else. *So, OK, let's start at work: my assistant Matt and his boyfriend, Oliver.* Dani writes their names on the pad then puts down her pen. She's reached the limit of people from her office with whom she's willing to freely associate.

She grabs the phone and dials Kate's number. Kate picks up on the first ring.

"It's me. The catering is all set and I'm working on the guest list."

"Dani, you're so efficient. I can't believe you can get all this done while you're working."

"Well, the efficiency stalled a bit on the guest list part. I can't think of anyone to invite. Who've you got so far?"

"I was just about to call and tell you," she says, rattling off a bunch of names. Kate's invited a few of Andy's colleagues from the university, a couple of parents from school, some people from the neighborhood.

"Good mix," Dani tells her encouragingly.

"But guess who else?" Kate sounds like she's scored a major social coup and Dani's curious.

"Brad Pitt and Jennifer Aniston?"

"A little older—well one of them is at least."

"Harrison Ford and Calista Flockhart?"

"Close. Gerry and Sunny Honeywell." Kate says, triumphantly.

"You didn't!"

"I did. I just ran into her at the post office of all places and she was so nice and asked what I was up to these days and it just slipped out."

"And they're coming, for sure?" This is a social coup, indeed.

"She said they wouldn't miss it."

"And Gerry's clear that the party is your idea?"

"Cut it out, Dani," Kate's voice becomes tentative. "Do you really think we can pull it off? I mean, that tea I went to at their house . . ."

"Of course we can pull it off," Dani reassures her. "You've just raised the bar."

After Dani hangs up, she considers the names on her notepad, then hits the intercom button on her phone.

"Matt, could you come in for a minute, please?"

Matt strolls into the office carrying a box of hand-dipped chocolates from a small specialty store downtown. He slides the chocolates and the *New York Post*–thoughtfully opened to the gossip section on Page Six–onto the corner of Dani's desk. Then he pulls the leather club chair out of the corner and settles his tall frame into it.

"So? Time for a little break from the drama of apportioning Emily Peterson's estate?"

"Besides you and Oliver, who should I invite to this gala Kate and I are throwing?"

Matt frowned. "Bryce?"

"No way, no how. This is supposed to be a civilized evening. C'mon, help me think of someone who is not going to discuss personal injury tort or troll for clients all evening."

Matt is silent a little too long.

"Matt, please, tell me I know some people."

"What about the handsome and athletic Michael O'Grady?"

"O'Grady . . . O'Grady . . . I'm drawing a blank. Is he a client?"

"Think shorts, not torts, boss."

"Oh—yes! Brianna's soccer coach? No way."

Matt leans out of the chair and across the desk.

"I've been to Brianna's games. I've seen him . . ." he raises his eyebrows and nods knowingly.

"Matt! I can't invite the soccer coach; this is a big, fancy, grown-up shindig. Not some postseason pizza party. Kate's invited the Honeywells, for God's sake."

"Well, you're the one desperate for party guests," Matt sniffs, standing up and sliding the chair back into its corner.

"Desperate for party guests?" Bryce strides into the room. "I'll invite Hal Baskin—you've met him—my friend in insurance, he's been after the Honeywell account for years. Can't seem to get close to the guy. Where and when do the festivities start?"

"Around seven o'clock at my friend, Kate's," Dani says weakly, glaring at Matt's back as he beats a hasty retreat to his desk. "It's sort of a formal event."

"Seven it is." Bryce was already heading for the door. "I'll be sure to wear something swell. Tell your friend to wear that tight pink sweater she had on at last year's holiday party. She looked hot."

Invite guests—check.

Chapter Four

"Dani, you look gorgeous." Kate tells her. And she does, wearing a dark red silk halter dress that's kind of clingy, yet makes her look curvy and softer. Her hair is loose and her wild curls give her an exotic look that's completely out of place in Kate's imitation French country kitchen.

"A leftover from my former fabulous life. And I see you're wearing the pink sweater."

"What's wrong with this pink sweater?" Kate looks down at her mohair-blend sweater and gray silk pajama-style pants.

"Bryce was hoping you'd wear it."

"Eeewww..."

"Besides, we're supposed to be glamorous, remember? You're just wearing a dressy version of your usual uniform." Dani hands her a bottle of champagne.

"C'mon, we're going to review your party clothes."

Dani grabs two wineglasses from the counter and heads for the stairs, Kate close behind.

"Adjusting your appearance to reflect your desired self can elevate your sense of well-being." Dr. Mia's words float through Kate's head.

"Where's the family?" Dani gestures for Kate to tear the foil from the neck of the champagne bottle as she heads up the stairs.

"Andy took the boys for pizza. He promised to be back in time to shower and change."

"Will the wonderfully competent Claire Howard be riding herd tonight?"

"Sadly, no. She's selfishly watching her grandchildren. Jenna's coming instead. Henry really likes her."

"Wasn't Jenna on duty when Charlie committed the great haircut caper?" Jenna is a redheaded tenth-grader with a new belly ring who lives around the corner from Kate and enjoys hanging out in the pizza parlor downtown refining her video-game skills.

Kate shoots Dani a look. "It'll be fine. We'll be right downstairs."

Pushing the crumpled sheets to the foot of the unmade bed, Kate sits down and gestures to the closet. "Enter at your own risk."

Dani opens the door. "Jeez, Kate, your wardrobe could use a little editing." She nods toward the champagne. "Hand me some inspiration and step back!"

Kate hands her a glass and watches as Dani begins digging through her closet. A hand soon emerges, dangling a pair of canary yellow velour stirrup pants. "These are cute . . . Don't tell me–there's a matching top and you're going to be Big Bird for Halloween."

"Present from the in-laws . . . and there is a matching top," Kate says laughing.

"I thought they liked you," Dani says.

"They do. Andy's mom got herself a set in orange. She thought they were 'peppy.'"

"Aha!" Dani reappears from the depths of the closet. "Put this on." She hands Kate a simple black skirt with a high waist that she had forgotten she even owned. The knee-length skirt that had always looked so dowdy to her is suddenly more flattering when paired with her only dressy shoes: black high-heeled sandals.

Dani disappears into the closet again. When she comes out she's holding up a silky black wrap blouse that Andy had bought Kate for an anniversary gift. She thinks she wore it once. In fact, Charlie may have been conceived that night.

"Oh, no, Dani. That's too much."

"Too much what, Kate?" she says, pouring herself another glass of champagne. "Too much black?"

"Too much cleavage," Kate says, digging through her bureau drawer for a black bra.

"Mmmm, sexy lingerie, Kate. I think Granny Strauss had a bra just like that."

"Shut up and give me the blouse." Kate prays that Dani will see the error of her ways and realize that she has dressed her like some porno version of a widow. Kate thinks back to the first time they met at a now-defunct afternoon playgroup. Dani seemed so stylish and self-possessed—everything Kate was sure she'd never be. There was Kate, in her applesauce-splotched sweatshirt and jeans while Dani looked great in a chic turquoise shell, black capris and impeccable accessories. But somehow, their connection was immediate. Dani laughed at Kate's jokes that drew blank stares from the other mothers. On some primal level, even on that first day, Kate knew she'd made a lifelong friend—in fact, a best friend. There was nothing she wouldn't do for Dani and, just as surely, she knew that Dani felt the same.

"Don't look yet," Dani says. "You just need a little something . . ."

Kate feels her fasten a necklace around her neck.

"And *voilà*!" Dani spins her around to look in the mirror.

Kate does a double take. The faux diamond necklace, offset by the dark blouse, shimmers against her chest. The skirt flares slightly at the knee in a way that minimizes her full hips. She doesn't look half bad, emerging grays and all. Dani steps up beside her and drapes her arm around her shoulder. "Let's hope this town can handle a little glamour."

Kate raises her glass of champagne. "To us!"

"To us!" Dani says as they clink glasses.

───

Kate is not sure if the warm glow she is feeling is from the champagne or from the many candles strategically placed on tabletops and windowsills throughout the house, but she's actually anticipating the evening ahead with something akin to pleasure. The burgundy tablecloths and delicate crystal bowls, some filled with floating candles and others with gold-coated almonds, look elegant in the dim light.

At six forty-five, the doorbell rings. Dani and Kate are still arranging the food on the buffet. Dani has cued up the CD player and Louis Armstrong's growly drawl fills the room.

"Yikes," Kate says. "Well, ready or not!"

"Who shows up for a cocktail party fifteen minutes early?" Dani asks.

"And if you are fashionably late, what do they call you if you're early?" Kate wonders.

"Annoying," Dani says with a laugh as the doorbell rings insistently, and Kate rushes to get it.

As she opens the door, Joy Harvey and her husband, Chad, are locked in verbal combat on the landing. Joy was class mother with Kate last year when Henry was in first grade.

"Then next time *you* pick up the damned babysitter!" Joy hisses. Her head snaps forward when the door opens, cheeks jerking, as if airlifted, into a too-bright smile. Chad, for his part, looks beaten down.

"Hi, Katie!" Joy practically screams. "Don't you look *gorgeous!*"

Kate winces. The only person who's ever called her Katie was her Aunt Helen, who, come to think of it, Kate never liked.

Joy steps inside, removing her magenta trench coat. She is petite and her black hair is cut in a perfect bob. Her large gray eyes, which look as though they might pop out of her head at any moment, are fringed with mascaraed lashes that could put Liza Minnelli to shame. Chad is wearing a shockingly bright striped sweater that Kate would bet her last dollar his wife picked out. As Joy lands in the foyer, she thrusts a large glass plate covered in clear plastic toward Kate. On it jiggles an atrocious, intergalactic green mound with large chunks of unidentified objects floating at various heights in it. "How *are* you, Katie? It's so nice of you to do this. We just don't get out that much anymore. Everyone's so *busy.* Isn't that right, Chad? Yoo-hoo, earth to Chad?! Katie, you remember Chad, don't you?"

From what Kate can see, Chad has built up some seriously bad marriage karma. Maybe he was Henry VIII in a past life. He holds his hand out to her. Kate is reminded of a kidnap victim trying to signal for help without tipping off his captor.

"Of course. Hi, Chad. So nice of you to come."

Kate reaches for Chad's hand and it is limp in hers.

"Nice seeing you, Kitty,"

Just then Andy appears and offers to get them both drinks. He herds them into the living room while Kate heads back to help Dani put the finishing touches on the buffet. Kate sets Joy's glass plate down and Dani gasps.

"Joy Harvey's famous Alien Jell-O mold?"

Kate nods.

"Well, *this* goes in the kitchen for later. *Much* later." Dani whisks the Jell-O away, returning with the last two platters of cold hors d'oeuvres. "I think we should congratulate our fabulous selves. We may actually pull this off." Dani is glowing.

The doorbell rings again and Kate runs to get it. *This going to be great. Let the fun begin,* she thinks. She glances through the peephole and sees the Rudlings on the steps: all five of them. *What are the children doing here? I know the invite said adults only* (which Kate thought suggested an orgy but Dani overruled her). Three more kids. And the *Rudling* boys, no less. They're notorious. Rudy Rudling was in Henry's class last year and was an utter terror. He made a gun out of hardened Play-Doh and tried to stick up a classmate for his Ring Ding. His younger brothers are supposed to be even worse. Kate cannot bring herself to open the door. The bell rings again.

Andy appears at her elbow. "Aren't you going to open the door?"

"I can't believe it," she whispers. "The Rudlings brought all *three* boys."

"Oh, right. I forgot to tell you." Andy smacked his forehead. "She called and said they couldn't find a sitter, so I told her to bring 'em over. I figured Jenna could watch them, too."

Kate stares at him in disbelief. "They can't find a sitter for a reason," she says.

"Oh c'mon, Kate. It's just a few more kids. Two, five, what's the difference?"

Dani joins them at the door. "What are you waiting for? The secret password?"

"Andy told the Rudlings to bring their boys," Kate tells her.

Dani turns and stares at Andy with a look that sends him scurrying over to check on the ice at the bar.

Kate clutches her arm. "What should I do?"

Dani shrugs. "He's your husband . . . But I'm going to get another glass of wine."

The doorbell rings again and for a brief second Kate, irrationally, considers not answering. Then she sees Betty Gilligan and her husband, Harold, making their way up the walk, and she concedes to the inevitable and opens the door.

"Hi!" says Rita Rudling, stepping inside along with her husband, Ronald, and their three bad seeds. "How *are* you?"

The boys are lined up in matching sweaters and corduroys. Their dark brown hair is cut in identical bowl cuts; their faces are blank. Kate chastises herself for judging them. *They're just children. Look how sweet they are.* Then the middle boy glances up at her, scowls and sticks his tongue out.

"Ralphie! Remember what we discussed about manners. Kate, so sweet of you to let us bring the little guys along! We just couldn't get a babysitter. You know how it is," she says, lowering her voice in a conspiratorial tone.

"Oh, no problem," Kate manages. "Here, let me take your coats and we can just take the boys upstairs to play with Henry and Charlie."

When Kate heads back downstairs, the foyer is filled with newcomers. Bryce and his playboy junior associate Cuomo are hanging their coats in the closet. Kate sees Gerry Honeywell decked out in a gorgeous navy suit and silk periwinkle tie. Though barely five foot eight, Gerry commandeers the hallway as though the house were a ship and the rest of the guests his crew. Sunny has on a bright red tailored dress and her blonde hair is swept back in a perfect chignon that exposes the collar of diamonds around her neck. Kate can't believe they actually showed up.

"Hello, Kate," says Gerry. "Don't you look lovely this evening."

"Hi, Gerry. Sunny. So glad you could make it!" Kate points the Honeywells in the direction of the bar.

By seven thirty the house is full of people. Kate takes a quick inventory of the buffet table. She refills a couple of dishes and brings out a few replacements.

"For you!" Dani hands her a big glass of Merlot. "Hey, relax, everything's fine. Enjoy yourself a little, hostess extraordinaire. Check out Olga Finch in that purple number. She looks like Stevie Nicks caught in a shredder."

Dani motions to the corner of the room. Kate sees Olga draped, quite literally, in head-to-toe purple fabric with faint sparkles in it. The fabric falls in strips from the large sleeves. Olga is not a petite woman. Long panels overlap and sweep nearly to the floor.

"Wow. At least she dressed up. You got to give her that. Betty Gilligan is wearing her usual Easton Co-op T-shirt and jeans."

Olga sees them looking at her and gives them both a wave. She makes her way over in an undulating, sparkling sea of purple.

"Hi, Kate. Hi, Dani!" Olga exclaims. She has twinkling blue-green eyes accented with purple shadow, to match the outfit, no doubt.

"You really dressed up," says Dani.

"Well, it's funny," says Olga, motioning with one arm and sending her streaming muumuu into a frenzy. "I got this in Santa Fe last year. It's what they call wearable art. And I thought, my word, when in the world will I have occasion to wear such a thing? And then when I got your invitation, I thought—perfect."

"It's stunning," Kate says truthfully. Olga is approached by Joy Harvey who loudly admires her garment and launches into a discussion about Sante Fe being a hotbed of creativity and design innovation.

"Who's the buff guy in the black slacks?" Dani says suddenly, sounding a bit breathless.

Kate turns to see Michael O'Grady pouring himself a glass of wine at the bar. He is wearing a crisp blue dress shirt and dark pants. A woman next to him says something and he smiles warmly in her direction and hands her the glass in his hand.

"Dani. That's Michael O'Grady. Your daughter's soccer coach . . . the one you've seen every Saturday for the past year."

"Jeez, I didn't even recognize him. He cleans up well. Anyway, I mostly just see the back of his head."

"I hear he's single. I've always thought he was a catch," Kate says encouragingly. "What do you say, Dani, shall we, I don't know, discuss the lineup for next week's game?"

"No meddling, Kate. Remember the last time you fixed me up—with your tax attorney—the one who cost me another twenty-three hundred dollars in taxes I never should have known I had to pay. I mean, yeah, O'Grady's cute, but I'm sure we have nothing in common. Looks aside, he's clearly not my type."

"Oh, right, your type is rich, handsome, smart, funny, sexy, socially appropriate, incredibly indulgent, and oh, did I mention rich?" Kate ticks each point off on her fingers.

"That's the guy for me," Dani grins. "Did you invite him?"

Kate waits a beat. "Couldn't," she says. "He doesn't exist."

"He may not be in this room," Dani says, finishing the last of her wine. "But I can assure you he's out there somewhere." She taps her empty glass and heads toward the bar.

Sunny Honeywell appears with Gerry in tow.

"Kate, it was so sweet of you to invite us," she says. "It's not often we get into town to socialize."

Kate pictures them sitting in the library of their huge home, surrounded by acres and acres of quiet wooded land.

"Quite the turnout," Gerry agrees heartily. "So glad we were free tonight."

"Well, I'm delighted you could come," Kate says. "Please, help yourself to something to eat."

Gerry and Sunny turn and take a few steps toward the buffet table.

"What am I supposed to find to eat here?" he says, not bothering to lower his voice. "It looks like they cleaned out the deli department of the local supermarket."

"Hush, Gerry," Sunny says. "We can get a bite later if you want."

"What the hell are we doing here, anyway?" he says.

"We were invited, I accepted, and it would have been rude not to come," she whispers back. "Besides, I'm enjoying myself. I've met quite a few interesting people."

"Of course you'd find them interesting," he says. "If not for me, you'd be throwing the same kind of dull gathering with a roomful of nobodies drinking wine from a box and thinking they were somebodies."

"Gerry!" Sunny's voice is quiet but sharp. "That's enough. We don't have to stay long, but you're here now, so make the best of it." She hands him a plate filled with food.

Kate's ears are burning, and her eyes are starting to sting as well. *Dull? A roomful of nobodies?* She hurries away from the buffet table, unwilling to let them know she's overheard.

Kate looks around the crowded room, searching for Dani. She knows she'll say something sharp and funny that will make her feel better. She doesn't see her as she scans the party. In each room, groups of people are talking and laughing, balancing plates of food and glasses of wine. They don't look bored—or boring. She studies the groups again—on the lookout for anyone who might not be having a good time.

Dani materializes at her elbow. "Ooh, Hal Baskin seems to be enjoying the spread, especially the inedible part."

She nudges Kate and gestures toward Hal, who is shoving his fist into one of the centerpieces and retrieving a couple of the gold-coated almonds. He cracks one in his teeth and chomps on the meat inside without missing a second of his chat with Merl Boman. By the bar, Chad Harvey is gulping down a glass of Chardonnay. When he finishes, he pours himself another without ever letting go of the bottle. Just then, Kate hears a low rumbling, like a stampede, overhead.

"What was that?" Dani asks.

"I don't know but I think it's time to check on the kids." Kate quickly makes her way upstairs and is practically flattened by a mob of wilding boys with Jenna on their heels. "Rudy, Henry, please come back in here," Jenna calls. The boys stop when they see Kate.

"Hey guys, let's put on a video," Jenna says.

"Good idea," Kate agrees. "Boys, I really hope that you're not giving Jenna a hard time. No running around. I could hear you from downstairs." The video idea seems to go over well and, satisfied, Kate freshens her lipstick and heads back to the party.

Andy sees her come downstairs. "Everything OK?"

"Yeah, I think it's under control." She exhales. "You having fun?"

"Yeah, but I got cornered again by Phyllis Merkin." Phyllis is their neighbor two doors down; she's eighty if she's a day. Her hips have been bothering her so Kate's been taking in her mail. She thought Phyllis might enjoy a night out. "She was looking for advice about her arthritis," Andy continues. "She's still got the MD/PhD doctor thing a bit confused."

"What did you tell her?" Kate asks.

"Oh, I prescribed Valium, threw in some antipsychotics. That's all those MD doctor guys do."

"Glad you took care of it," Kate says, giggling, and kisses him on the lips.

"Hey, hey! Get a room, you two!" It's Hal Baskin. His cheeks are rosy and plump. He looks a bit like an aging Fred Flintstone with all of the requisite social grace.

"Kate, where's that Honeywell fellow? Someone told me he was coming. I think he *just* may be in the market for some life insurance, and Hal Baskin is *just* the man to set him up." He says it in a laugh that comes only from his throat and makes a vague honking sound.

"Uh, Hal. Well, to tell you the truth, I think Mr. Honeywell is pretty well set up." Kate says, trying to be delicate.

"*I'll* say he's pretty well *set up*! Three and a half billion *dollars* worth. I saw it on that . . . er, uh . . . Ford's list."

"Forbes's," Andy says helpfully.

"Yeah, whatever. That guy's loaded and *someone* better make sure he's thought ahead. No paperwork in the Great Beyond, I say. Don't take care of it now, it's too late!" The man is runaway steam engine. There will be no stopping him.

Just then Phyllis Merkin approaches, looking up at Andy.

"Dr. Thompson, I am so sorry to trouble you. You have been *such* a help already, but I just had one more teensy-weensy little question."

"Excuse me, Phyllis, first, have you met Hal? Hal Baskin?"

"Why, no. Hello, Hal."

"Phyllis, is it? Hello, Phyllis. Why we were just talking about the importance of good medical care and insurance policies. Of taking care of your personal affairs before it's too late. Making sure that all of the i's are crossed and the t's are dotted, if you know what I mean . . ."

At eight thirty the party has achieved critical mass. Bryce is in the corner plying Sunny Honeywell with his own greasy brand of charm. Kate sees Ashley Peterson and Nicky White, neither of whom she's talked to in ages, on the other side of the room. Nicky's son, Liam, is in Henry's class this year. Kate always liked them both. She heads toward them. She is actually starting to relax and have fun.

Then she hears it. A loud scream from the other room. Kate hurries in to see Dani and another guest throwing glasses of liquid in the direction of the source of the scream—Olga Finch. She is jumping around waving her arms, the huge purple panels of her dress flapping up and down. Finally Kate notices that one of the panels is smoking, as is the back of the dress.

"WATER! We need more WATER!" shouts Dani.

Kate races back to the bar, grabs a bottle of seltzer and begins to splash its contents on Olga's backside. She sees a small flash of a flame and continues to throw water at the moving target. There is some sizzling and more smoking but Olga stops flapping around.

"I'm OK, I'm OK," Olga says her eyes fluttering. "Oh, *my!*"

"Olga, you must have backed right into that candle," Dani exclaims, pointing toward the thick red taper set on the windowsill.

"You sure you're OK?" Kate asks, truly appalled.

"Yes, I'm fine. *Really.* It's out. You can stop throwing that water!" Olga nearly shouts.

Kate is not throwing water, and it is then that she sees it: a thin stream trickling through a crack in the ceiling directly over Olga's head. *Oh, no.* She barely registers what's happening when a torrent gushes from a light fixture directly over Gerry Honeywell's head. Betty Gilligan and Ruth Ward are next to him and they, too, get drenched. Both women are fifty-something with wide hips and even fuller chests. Betty's white T-shirt is soaked and in a flash Kate sees more of her than she wishes. Ruth Ward pulls her damp shirt away from her body but not before Kate confirms that, like Betty, Ruth is not wearing a bra. The water keeps coming. Kate races upstairs.

"WHAT IS GOING ON?!" Kate shouts. Jenna appears, looking frantic. "Rudy," Jenna says, "I'm going to ask you one more time: *Where are the faucet handles?*"

Kate runs into the bathroom to find both faucets on full blast, the water pouring like a river over the sides of the sink. Jenna's right; the handles are gone. Kate finds Henry in the hallway and grabs him by the shoulders. "Henry, listen to me, *Do you know where the handles are?*"

"We were playing hide-and-seek and Rudy told me to hide the handles and so I put them in the toy box. Am I in trouble?" He promptly burst into tears.

Kate runs to the toy box, rummages through the Lego's and stuffed animals and, sure enough, sees two silver handles lying on the bottom.

She runs to get Andy, but he is already bounding up the stairs. Kate hands him the two silver handles. "Two, five, what's the difference?" she chokes out.

"Oh, boy," Andy says. "OK, you just go downstairs. I've got this."

Kate makes her way downstairs and sees that Michael O'Grady and Matt have sprung into action clearing the room and trying to stave the torrents of water that continue to pour through the light fixture and ceiling. Matt has positioned large plastic wastebaskets under each water source. All of a sudden the water stops.

"OK, *so* sorry about that," Kate says to the small drenched group. "We had a little plumbing problem upstairs. Can I get you some paper towels?" Dani appears with three rolls of paper towels, dispensing them all around. People are in the foyer claiming their coats and slipping out the front door. Some are still pitching in to help with the aftermath. Most people make a swift exit, including the Rudlings and their evil brood. Rita Rudling catches Kate's eye as she's dragging Rudy out the door. Kate can see his boot repeatedly kicking his mother's ankle as they walk.

"Thanks, Kate. Sorry about the sink. Ron and I call Rudy our little engineer! You should hear what he did to our plumbing. Oh, boys will be boys!" she says cheerfully.

Matt glides by. "I think we got it pretty well mopped up in there. Thanks, it was a great party. Really. Memorable." He gives Kate a wink and a warm smile.

She gives him a hug. "Thanks for all you did. I really appreciate it."

Kate settles up with Jenna, who has put the boys to bed, haggard and looking ten years older than she did when she arrived. Kate pays her double her usual rate.

There are still a few people milling about in the kitchen and dining room. Andy and Michael have managed to get the living room pretty much under control. Kate goes upstairs to check on the boys. Henry, miraculously, is asleep. Charlie calls out to her when he hears her in the hallway. "Mommy. *Mommy!*" he says emphatically.

"What is it, sweetheart?"

"The monster is in my closet," Charlie says.

"Honey, there are no such things as monsters, remember?"

"But I know he's in there!"

Kate defaults to the logic of a three-year-old. "Well then, why do you suppose he's hiding in your closet?"

"I don't know, but I heard him in there," Charlie insists.

"Fine, I'll show you that nothing's in there. Look: there's no monster in the closet." Kate walks over and opens the door. A man's leg falls forward, and his large black shoe thuds to the floor. She yelps.

She throws the light on and the large body doesn't budge. Kate thinks she recognizes the sweater.

"Chad. Chad Harvey?!" Kate calls.

Nothing.

She grabs onto a limp leg and shakes it. "Chad! What are you doing in the closet?"

"Oh, hello, Kitty. I must have just dozed off." There is some shuffling and then Chad is sitting upright. His face is half visible behind the low-hanging clothes; the pant leg of a red snowsuit is draped over his head.

He scrambles up from amid the pile of tennis shoes and abandoned laundry. Kate helps him, catching him as he nearly teeters over.

"We don't need to mention this to Joy, do we?" Chad says, slurring his words a bit. There is an imprint of a sneaker tread on his cheek.

"See Mommy, *I told you* he was in there," Charlie calls out as Kate leads Chad out toward the stairway.

When they get to the top of the stairs, Joy is at the bottom, glaring up, holding Chad's coat.

"Chad, I think we best be going." Joy eyes Kate suspiciously as she helps her husband with his coat and they head out the door.

With that, the house is silent. The place is a disaster. Without hesitating, Kate turns and heads back upstairs to her bedroom.

About twenty minutes later she hears a knock. "*Kate?* You OK?" It's Andy.

Kate sits in the dark. The silence and the pitch black is perfect.

"Kate. Come on. Everyone's gone. It's OK."

Kate doesn't want to move. She stares into the darkness and sees nothing. The past two hours are nearly erased. Maybe this is how Chad Harvey felt. Maybe he just wanted to get away from it all.

"Kate, please come out of the closet. Look, I'm really sorry about the Rudlings."

Sorry. I know he's sorry. Isn't he always sorry?

"OK, I'm coming in," Andy says finally.

He gently opens the door and a shaft of light washes over her. Kate, sitting sideways, is propped on a pile of winter boots and a couple of shoe trees but doesn't seem to notice. Andy scoots over toward her, moving the boots and trees out of the way.

"I told Dani to go home," he says softly. "She insisted on helping, but I told her we'd deal with it in the morning. She says she'll call you first thing. I am sorry about the boys. I never should have . . ."

"Andy, this was really important to me." She sniffles, wiping a tear from her cheek.

"I know. Well, next time, no midgets, I promise."

"Next time? I can never show my face in this town again," Kate stammers.

"Honey, it's not your fault. You threw a fantastic party. Really, I'm sure people had a good time."

"Until the monsoon," Kate adds.

"Yes, I admit that the monsoon was unfortunate. C'mon." He extends a hand in her direction. Kate hesitates and then reluctantly lets him help her up. Her skirt is twisted so that the back is now in the front.

"I love you," Andy says, taking her in his arms. "Let's get some sleep."

Chapter Five

Sunday Morning

What a disaster, Dani thinks. *Like the* Titanic *on dry land. We would have been better off at Chuck E. Cheese's. At least there would have been an intact plumbing system and live entertainment. Well, it wasn't dull, especially once the water started pouring down from the chandelier. I guess that's the closest the world will ever come to seeing Ruth Ward and Betty Gilligan in a wet T-shirt contest.*

Dani thought she was going to bust a gasket watching Hal Baskin bite into the gold-covered nuts out of Kate's centerpieces. *Clueless.* He spent the rest of the night yammering on about the Red Sox with chips of gold glitter on his lips and chin. *Damned if I was going to tell him. I'm surprised he didn't take a bite out of a floating candle while he was at it.*

Dani is sitting at her kitchen table in a pool of sunlight, a cup of coffee at her elbow. But instead of the Sunday papers, there's a stack of file folders and legal pads in front of her. The first message on her machine this morning was from Bryce. The jerk must have called on his way home from the party. The second was from her mom. Dani glances hopelessly from yellow-lined notepads to telephone and back to notepads and sighs. There's no putting it off. She glances at the clock: just past nine. Maybe Bebe is still asleep. Dani picks up the phone and dials her mother.

The phone rings five times and the machine picks up.

"You've reached the home of Bebe and Baby (yip, yip). We're not here right now, but please leave a message for your favorite girl after the tone. . . ."

Dani lets out a sigh of relief. As she waits for the beep, she contemplates leaving a message of a few yippy barks herself. Maybe Baby the poodle would be glad to hear from her.

Beeeeeep . . .

"Hi, Mom, it's me. Just returning your call. I'll try again . . ."

"Darling!" Her mother sounds breathless. "I'm just running in from yoga. Hold on while I turn the machine off."

"I didn't know you were taking yoga," Dani says, though she's not surprised. If it's young and trendy, Bebe is going to try it.

"It's just wonderful. Makes me feel ten years younger. You should take it up, Dani." Her voice is girlish but hasn't lost the slightly nasal tone of her years on Long Island. "It's important to exercise as you get older, you know."

"I know, Mom. I exercise regularly," Dani lies.

"Not that running you do, dear. It's too hard on your knees as you age. And of course, once you've had a child, it's just not good for your . . . well your *feminine parts* . . . to be bounced around all the time."

"That's absurd, mother. Running doesn't bounce around any of my parts." Dani realizes that she's getting sucked into the conversation. Always a mistake with Bebe.

"I'll send you a video. I have a wonderful tape that combines yoga and Pilates. The instructor is the most energetic young woman."

"Really, Mom, thanks. But I don't have much time to do exercise videos. Work is crazy and Brianna's schedule is . . ."

"Oh, darling, that's right. That's why I called. I just went to the most fascinating lecture on sex roles in children, and I wanted to talk to you about Brianna and that horrible tomboyish tendency of hers."

"It's not horrible to be a tomboy, Mom."

"Well, Danielle, she just doesn't seem to want to do *anything* lady-like. All that interest in basketball and soccer and such. The last time I called all she wanted to know about was whether I could get her tickets to see the Miami football team if you visited. According to the brilliant young doctor that gave the lecture, she's a prime candidate for gender confusion. Does she even wear the dresses I send her?"

Dani pictures the dresses–velvet with lace and bows, silk with embroidered flowers and full skirts, dresses perfect for a New York City child who goes to the ballet and French restaurants with her doting parents–hanging in the back of Brianna's closet.

"She loves them," she lies again.

"Well, I just think you need to be careful. According to this doctor, who is very cute–and available, I might add–sex roles are determined at a very young age, and since you're always running off to work in those masculine suits, I just worry about Brianna's perception of womanhood."

"Mom, I'm a perfectly feminine woman, Brianna's a perfectly normal seven-year-old. There's no need to worry." Dani tries to think of a way to end the call without seeming abrupt.

"This doctor, Danielle, he's from the New York area. Maybe you should make an appointment to take Brianna in."

"Brianna doesn't need to see a therapist."

"Maybe you could just schedule an appointment to just talk to him; he's really *very* approachable . . ."

Dani mentally curses herself for giving her mother the room for this segue.

"You're trying to set me up with the sex doctor, aren't you, Mother? Listen, I'm just fine. Brianna's just fine. Life is good, just busy. I take care of work. I take care of Brianna."

"But, honey, who takes care of you? It's like I was saying to my gentleman friend, Mort, the other day: It's just a shame that that handsome ex-husband of yours remarried. I always thought that you two could work things out." Bebe says this as though she's just thought of it; not as though it's something she says every time they talk.

Dani realizes that she's got to end the call. And soon. Bebe's coming dangerously close to sensitive turf. Dani knows her mother–if she senses weakness, she'll move in for the kill and the next thing she knows, she'll be dating some sex therapist from New York.

"Actually, Mom, I've met someone that I think is just perfect. He's a lawyer from Boston. Big money. Very powerful. I'm sure the next time I talk with you I'll have more news."

"Danielle! That's wonderful. I'm sure he'll adore you. Well, I'm so glad everything is going well. I've got to run. I've got my book club this afternoon and I just want to review for it. Give Brianna a kiss for me. Bye-bye, darling. Don't work too hard."

Dani hangs up with the usual mix of exasperation and depression that commonly accompanies a conversation with her mother. Luckily, after years of dealing with this, she knows just what to do. Misery loves company. She dials Kate's number. As she listens to the phone ring, she gazes out the kitchen window.

Brianna is outside, dribbling a basketball in the driveway. With one hand she brushes the hair out of her eyes and stops, squinting in the sun, poised ten feet from the basket. She heaves the ball high into the air. It drops, bounces on the rim and then teeters on the edge before falling through the net. She throws both arms up in the air and then dashes in for the rebound.

The phone rings five times and the machine picks up. Kate is a serial screener, but Dani can't blame her this morning.

"Yo, Kate. If the phone is still above sea level, pick up." Nothing. "Maybe you're out."

Dani knows that Kate will be taking this hard. Kate, who is always thinking about how to make other people feel better (something Dani would like to work on in herself), must be mortified at inflicting such a bad time on her guests—not to mention the humiliation and property damage. Dani is weighing the options of how she might cheer Kate up when she hears a loud *beep* and then, "Hello."

"Hey there. It's me."

"Yeah, I know. I was hoping that it was all just a bad dream. I'm dodging Joy Harvey. Apparently she left her plate. She called when she got home last night and said she'd be over today to get it. I can't face anyone."

"At least you've got the Jell-O." Dani hopes for a laugh.

She gets silence. Then, "Dani, where did we go wrong? . . . At least people liked the food, right?"

"Yeah, they even started on the centerpieces."

"Then there was the Great Flood. We would have been safer sitting on lawn chairs eating Cheez Whiz and Bugles."

"Hey, at least we tried."

"I am a wreck. Can you be hungover from half a glass of Merlot?"

"It's the humiliation hangover . . . without the anonymous sex. The worst kind."

"And Gerry Honeywell was there with his perfectly coiffed wife. How horrifying. He didn't even want to be there. I heard him. And Sunny—she probably thought it would be nice to hang with solid, small-town folk and instead she got the Beverly Hillbillies on acid. I want to die."

"So he got a little wet. So his pricey tie got ruined. It's not like he can't buy ten more. It's not so bad." This is what Dani says, but she knows if she were Kate she'd be crawling into the nearest manhole.

"Oh, what can you do anyway," Kate sighs deeply. "Charlie, hey buddy, where are you?"

Dani can hear the yipping of a dog faintly in the background, but it doesn't sound like Chance. The yipping grows louder.

"Sounds like you have to go," Dani offers.

"Charlie, come in here . . . Yeah, this kid is going to drive me to an early grave. Oh, jeez, the glass door's open . . . How the heck? I thought we fixed that. Call you later."

Dani hears a click. She doesn't know what she would have done if Brianna was like that. She's always been active, sure, but nothing like Charlie. That kid makes Houdini look physically challenged. Charlie can get out of anything—anytime, anywhere.

The back door swings open and Brianna bounces in, basketball balanced on her hip.

"Can we go to the new indoor ice-skating rink? I want to try out my new skates. Can we? *Please?*"

"Oh, Brianna, I've got to get to some of this work."

Her face falls.

"Why don't you watch a video while I do some of this? Then maybe we can go to the park. I'll run and you can Rollerblade."

Her face brightens a bit. "Can I watch *Mulan?*"

"Sure," Dani says with false heartiness.

Brianna skips off to the TV room and Dani pops a Sam Cooke CD into the boom box. She pours another cup of coffee and, pushing aside all thoughts of parties and mothers, failed and otherwise, she begins shuffling papers again.

~

"CHARLIE!" Kate's heart is pounding and now she's in full panic mode. She races to the front gate and looks down the street–nothing. *Good. At least he hasn't gotten out of the fence.* Kate turns around and then she sees it: a lump under the swing set. The small body in the red sweatshirt and blue jeans is completely still.

She shrieks and runs to his side. "ANDY!" Kate yells like the madwoman that she is. "ANDY!" She wants to scoop Charlie into her arms but despite her panic realizes she shouldn't move him. He's breathing and his pulse is steady. Kate bursts into tears just as he raises a small fist and starts rubbing his eyes, then scratches the top of his head.

"Charlie, Charlie, listen to me . . . Are you OK? Charlie, look at me."

His body tightens and he suddenly sits up, wobbling a bit. Kate holds him to her. Andy comes racing from the house. Kate's impressed. She can't remember the last time she's seen him move faster than a slow lope.

"What's going on? I heard you shouting." Andy's face is white.

"Charlie was just lying here when I found him. He must have passed out or something."

"What happened? How did he get out?"

"I thought he was upstairs with you."

"Hey, big guy, you OK?" Andy squats down in front of Charlie. "Can you tell us what happened?"

Charlie still looks a little dazed.

"My head hurts . . . I was swinging . . . My head hurts."

Tears are running down Kate's face now, tears of relief and fear. *He's talking, how bad can it be?*

Charlie fixes his gaze on her. "I'm OK, Mommy, don't cry."

"I'm so glad, sweetie. You just scared Mommy." Kate wipes her wet cheek. "Let's go inside. I think Dr. Hilton may want to take a look at you."

"Do you think it's OK to move him?" she asks Andy.

"Well, he seems all right. He sat up easily and, really, he couldn't have fallen too far. You OK, sport? Will you let Daddy give you a ride into the house?"

Andy gently scoops Charlie up and walks him toward the back door.

Kate watches the broad shoulders of her husband as he carries the small frame of her son. She hears them laughing about something and then it comes over her, first in slow sobs, then in quick convulsions.

I am a terrible, terrible mother. He could have died. He could have broken his neck and I would never have known until it was too late. Where was I? What was I doing? How did I not notice he was gone? This is the only thing I'm doing that really matters—being a mom. And I can't even do that right. I should get a pink slip.

Andy calls out the back door.

"Coming," Kate shouts.

She pulls herself together and quickly walks inside.

～

Dr. Hilton isn't very concerned. In fact, it's Henry who is most worried. "How many fingers do you see, Charlie?" he asks, holding his hand up in front of his brother's face. Charlie is too busy playing with the doctor's stethoscope to answer.

"Probably a mild concussion," Dr. Hilton says. "But there's no need for us to keep him. He'll be much happier at home. Keep some ice on that spot if he'll let you, and keep him quiet for the rest of the day." He gives Henry the sheet with information about blows to the head. "I hope you're considering medical school, young man."

Henry beams.

Kate feels so guilty that she makes them stop at the local toy store on the way home. Charlie scores a new dinosaur coloring book and four Hot Wheels cars, and Henry chooses a model of the human skeleton. If only Kate knew what it would take to make her feel better.

MONDAY AFTERNOON

The sky has been overcast all morning, the Indian summer of recent weeks has passed and the late-afternoon air is damp and raw. As Kate drives down Grove Street on her way into the office, drops of rain begin to pat against the windshield. She cruises past the building, its drab stucco exterior gloomy against the gray sky, hoping to find a spot out front. She has to settle for a spot three streets away. She's forgotten her umbrella so she rests the manila folder she's carrying on the top of her head, and scurries down the street as the rain falls.

The READ offices are on the second floor, over a florist shop. The narrow stairs are worn and the beige hallway could use a coat of paint. Kate unlocks the front door and peers in through the paned glass before entering the large room that is their office. It's dark, despite the windows overlooking the street. She welcomes the empty space and the quiet. There are no volunteers in today so she is hoping that she'll be able to get a jump on organizing the carnival fund-raiser they'll be throwing in a few months. She goes to the back of the room, weaving around the tables stacked with literature and paperwork to be filed. Her workspace is a small cubicle, separated from the rest of the room. She's tacked up pictures of the boys and Andy on the inside walls and brought in a small green plant that looks as though it could use some water. She turns on her desk lamp. There is a stack of unopened mail and a Staples catalog on her chair. On the desk is a single white envelope with her name on it, no stamp, no address. It looks like a greeting card. She opens it up and a folded check falls onto the floor. The card is one of those fairly sappy numbers: sweeping, well-flowered landscape pictured on the front, large flowing script inside:

You make it all possible, thank you.

Then handwritten: *All of your hard work and dedication to READ is deeply appreciated.*

Regards,

Gerry Honeywell

Kate cringes with renewed embarrassment as she leans over and picks up the check. This is odd. Honeywell just sent in his annual contribution a month ago. Could he have forgotten? Must be tough to keep track of the millions tossed in every direction.

She gasps. The check is made out to her: Kate Thompson. *What the . . . ?* She looks more closely: $1,000,000. She looks again and counts the zeros. Clearly, there is a mistake here. And a big one at that. The note section reads, *for a job well done.* Kate stands there for a moment in stunned silence. Then she bursts out laughing. *Jeez, lucky this is made out to me and not someone who'd just take the money and run.*

She'll just call Gerry Honeywell and let him know about the error. It's probably meant to be a check for READ. Perhaps he decided to increase his donation. He's been donating for years, though, and his checks always come made out to READ. Kate wonders who left the card on her desk. Honeywell's checks are usually mailed. She picks up the phone and dials the foundation number. She gets a recording. "This is Kate Thompson calling from READ," she begins when the phone beeps and someone picks up. It's Sunny.

"Hello, Kate. What can I do for you? Lovely party," she says.

Kate winces. "Oh, thank you. We appreciated your coming. Errr . . . sorry about the shower." She feels like a complete idiot all over again. "Well, I'm actually calling because I think there has been a mistake with Mr. Honeywell's most recent contribution. The check was made out in my name. I also wanted to remind him, I mean, I'm sure he keeps track of these things, but he did make a very generous donation already for next year and . . ."

"No, darling, there was no mistake. Gerry specifically requested that the check be made out in your name. As you know, he was very impressed with the library curriculum you created. He's not good at giving up the spotlight, but he knows what you've brought to the program. Good work should be well compensated, is what he told me."

Kate doesn't believe what she's hearing. "I truly don't know what to say. I really can't possibly accept such a generous gift. Not that it isn't appreciated. But the card was truly thanks enough."

"Well, you'll have to take it up with Gerry. Not that I think you'll get anywhere with him. He's off on a business trip until next week."

"Well, thanks. Thanks so much for your help with this. Please let him know that I called and would love to speak with him when he has a moment. I understand he's very busy."

"Will do. Bye-bye."

This is totally bizarre, Kate thinks. *Well, I'll just have to wait until he gets back.* The check feels heavy in her hand. What is she supposed to do with it? She tucks it carefully into the corner of her purse. For a split second, her mind races. *I could jet off to Tahiti this very afternoon. I could be skiing in the Alps tomorrow.* She catches herself. *Jeez. Get a grip.* She opens her purse to make sure that the check is still there. OK, so she'll just straighten it out with Honeywell when he gets back.

Wait until Dani hears about this.

⁓

"This afternoon was so fun, Mom. We couldn't go outside because of the rain, so Ms. Crandall made an obstacle course in the gymnasium and we all got to swing on the ropes like Tarzan . . ." Brianna barely stops to take a breath as she expertly unlocks the door to the house and heads toward the television, leaving a trail of backpack, lunchbox and outerwear.

Dani is ten paces behind her as they return from their respective full days. Dani barely got any real work done—what with Bryce popping in every five minutes to drop another file on her desk, accompanied by rude remarks about the party.

"Hang up your jacket, Brianna."

Dani goes from the kitchen into the tiny TV room.

"Take your shoes off the couch, please."

Brianna is flopped on the couch, remote in hand. Using the arm of the sofa, she kicks her shoes off. They fall to the floor with a thud. Dani resists the urge to tell her to pick them up. She's trying to learn to choose her battles. Lately it seems like Brianna's in training to be opposing counsel.

"Can I watch *Rugrats*?"

"You know I don't like those smart-mouthed brats." *You've learned too much from them already,* she thinks.

"Please, Mom. Talia gets to watch them."

Dani is too worn out to mount a good argument. "You can watch one episode. One half-hour episode."

Brianna's already mesmerized.

Be grateful she's sitting still, Dani consoles herself.

Back in the kitchen, she hangs up her jacket, grabs a Diet Coke out of the fridge and snags the *Vogue* out of the pile of junk mail and stacks of bills on the kitchen table. She heads for the dining room that serves double duty as her home office. She just needs fifteen minutes to herself, then she'll start supper.

The light on the answering machine is blinking like a firefly on speed. She hits the play button.

"Dani, ohmigod, Dani, call me right away. You will not believe this."

Beep.

"Dani? Where are you? I tried your cell. Why aren't you answering? Call me."

Beep.

"I'm at the READ offices and I have to talk to you before I go home. You won't believe what's happened."

Beep.

"I'm staying here until I hear from you."

Dani peeks around the corner at Brianna. She is totally zoned, staring at the set. Dani grabs the phone and heads to her bedroom.

"Dani?" Kate picks up on the first ring. "Why didn't you answer your cell?"

"I haven't checked messages in two hours. I couldn't stand the barrage from Bryce." Dani digs her cell phone out of her bag and checks the display: five voice messages. "Why? Are you all right? Is it Charlie again?"

"Not Charlie. Gerry. Gerry Honeywell." Kate sounds vaguely hysterical and short of breath.

"Is he hassling you about what happened at the party? Breathe, Kate, just take a deep breath. Don't worry—I'll take care of it. What's his number?" *That bastard,* Dani thinks, *so what if his Hermès tie got ruined, I'm sure he's got a closetful.*

"He's not suing me, Dani. When I got to the office today I found—

I mean, he had . . . he . . ." Kate is beginning to laugh—or cry—Dani can't tell which.

"He came by the office and made a pass at you, didn't he? I saw him leering at you in that blouse. I'll slap a sexual harassment suit on him so fast his head will spin." Dani's blood is boiling, *What kind of small-town hicks do he and his pampered lapdog of a wife think we are?*

". . . so much money." Kate is still talking.

"Whoa, Kate, we can get a lot of money. I guarantee it. I mean, you're a volunteer for one of his pet charities. He'll probably want to settle."

"Dani, shut up and listen: He sent me a check. A personal check. For a whole lot of money. A ridiculous amount of money. So much money I can't even say the number. Clearly it's a mistake, but still . . . There was a card on my desk when I came in today. It's for me. Not for READ. *For me.* For a job well done."

"So we're going to be able to escape our social humiliation by jetting off to a tropical island until the scandal dies down?"

"That's right, Dani, you've just won an all-expenses-paid vacation to Tahiti with your best friend." Kate sounds giddy. "And if you correctly identify the amount of money involved, we'll throw in some nice new luggage."

"A hundred?" Dani guesses.

"Add zeros," Kate says.

"A thousand?"

"*Zeros,* plural."

"Good joke, Kate. You almost had me there." Dani starts to flip through the pages of *Vogue.*

"Dani, it's a check for *a million dollars.* There. I said it."

Dani opens her mouth. Closes it. Finds her voice. Shrieks.

Brianna appears in the doorway. "Mama? Are you OK?"

"I'm fine, honey. Kate just told me something funny."

"My show's over."

"You can watch an extra little bit," Dani says, magnanimously.

Brianna sprints back to the couch.

"No way, Kate." Dani keeps her voice down. "You're rich. You are totally stinking rich."

"I guess I am, on paper, anyway."

"What do you mean 'on paper'? It's a cash gift, Kate. Oh my God, a million bucks." Dani feels a twinge of envy. OK, more than a twinge. A big, huge, *why-couldn't-it-have-been-me?* wrench.

"Earth to Dani: You realize that it's some kind of accounting mistake, right?

"Possession is nine-tenths of the law, Kate. It's your money now. Run—do not walk—to the bank and put it in your account. He won't even miss it."

"I can't do that, Dani. I have to talk to him, but Sunny said he's away on business."

"You talked to Sunny? You asked her about the money? What did she say?"

"She said the check was *supposed* to be made out to me."

"You heard her. No mistake. I'll meet you at the bank tomorrow."

"C'mon Dani, get real. This is not some fairy tale. I've got to give this money back."

Dani decides to play dirty. "Don't you think you deserve it, Kate? Haven't you worked your ass off at that unpaid volunteer position? Don't you think the big national award Honeywell collected on behalf of READ for innovation in reading curriculum was really *your* award?"

Silence.

"What would Dr. Mia say?" Dani is merciless. "Really, c'mon, Kate."

"She would say that there are no mistakes . . ." There's a thoughtful tone to Kate's voice and Dani's encouraged.

"You can give it to me if it'll make you feel better." Dani is not kidding. Not kidding at all. She enjoys a brief daydream in which Brian pulls up to her beautiful brick colonial with its well-manicured gardens, but Brianna doesn't want to get out of the big in-ground swimming pool to leave for the weekend. Dani comes around the corner in her casual little Ralph Lauren golf outfit, a basket of freshly cut peonies and roses from her garden on one arm. "Don't worry, Brian," she says, "I'm off all this week. Maybe Brianna can spend the next rainy weekend at your house."

"Honestly, Dani, what should I do?" Kate interrupts her beautiful fantasy.

"I told you. Take the money and run."

"Dr. Mia also says you can't run from what's in front of you."

"Dr. Mia has a point. This isn't a mistake, and you shouldn't try to avoid your great good fortune." Dani is actually starting to get irritated. Does Kate really believe she should give the money back?

"You're not in court, Dani. Stop twisting Dr. Mia's words around to fit your argument." Kate sounds vaguely irritated, too. Dani can't figure out why. She's the one with all the money.

"I told you what I seriously believe you should do," Dani says. "And now we know what Dr. Mia would tell you to do. Make it unanimous: what did Andy say?"

There's a long silence on the other end of the phone.

Brianna appears in the doorway again.

"Is it supper yet?"

"In a minute honey."

"But I'm huuunngry . . ."

"Kate, I gotta go. You know what Brianna gets like when her blood sugar drops. I'll call you back later at home."

"It'll probably be crazy tonight. I'll call you tomorrow, OK."

"OK, Mrs. Moneybags," Dani says, trying to lighten the tone. "I'll talk to you tomorrow." She hangs up the phone.

Dani heads to the kitchen and begins hunting through the fridge for the makings of dinner. *A cool million. What I would do with that kind of dough . . . And Kate's going to give it all back.*

Then it hits her. Kate hasn't told Andy about the money.

Very interesting. Very interesting indeed.

Chapter Six

Kate doesn't go straight home from the office, calling Andy and asking him to put the boys to bed. She's surprised he doesn't ask questions. She drives around aimlessly, ending up in the neighborhood surrounding the college. Lamplight turns the windows of the stately brick houses golden as she drives past the manicured lawns and fading gardens of the nicest part of town. She touches her purse on the seat beside her and lets herself fantasize. *We could buy a new house and fix it just the way we wanted from the very start. The boys wouldn't have to share a room, and I wouldn't have to negotiate for every new piece of furniture I want.* She sighs and reaches blindly into the box of cassettes in the passenger seat. *I don't want to think about this anymore*, Kate thinks. *There's been a mistake. I'm not the type of person this happens to, and there's no point in pretending I am. The money goes back to the Honeywells, and I go back to my regularly scheduled life.* She pops the cassette in and turns up the volume, ready to drown out her thoughts with whatever Raffi tape she's grabbed.

Dr. Mia's low persuasive voice fills the car. This is her most recent audiobook: *Drawing the Map of Your Life.*

"We draw the maps of our own circumstances. The route to our future is the net effect of our thoughts and actions. By studying the maps of our daily lives, our futures are revealed: We arrive where we deserve to be. Reality is our own creation. We cannot ask directions of anyone if we wish to reach our own true destination."

Kate pushes the eject button and the tape pops out of the dashboard. *What if this is the destiny I've created? What if Sunny's right? What if Gerry really does want to do this? Those kids he put through college probably didn't believe it either. Is Dr. Mia right? Maybe this is the map I've created. Is it possible that I am actually meant to be sitting in my car with a ton of money stashed in my purse?*

Lost in thought, Kate drives past her driveway. When she realizes what she's done, she slams on her brakes and is jolted by the insistent blare of the horn of the car behind her. With an apologetic wave in the rearview mirror, she swings on to a side street, turns around and heads for home.

She pulls into the driveway and parks in front of the garage. She can see the television on in the family room, a blue glow against the half-drawn curtains; the rest of the house is dark. *Andy's never going to believe this*, she thinks. She reaches across and gingerly picks up her purse. Her hand rests on the door handle, but she doesn't get out. *What will Andy say?* Suddenly she's got a funny feeling in the pit of her stomach and it takes her a minute to name it. She feels guilty. She didn't call Andy first. *Why?* She asks herself. *Because you knew he'd tell you to return the check. That's why you called Dani. Because just for a minute you wanted to pretend you could keep this money. Because you had a selfish impulse and Andy doesn't have a greedy bone in his body.*

Kate opens the car door. *I'll just march right in the house and tell Andy. We'll have a good laugh and tomorrow I'll go drop off the check with Sunny. There's no point in holding on to it for a week, pretending that it's really mine.* She walks slowly toward the house, her purse cradled under her arm.

The porch is dark and she stumbles over Henry's soccer cleats and Charlie's Big Wheel trike, banging her arm against the door frame as she catches her balance. She turns the doorknob. Locked. Kate fishes her house keys out of her purse and pushes the door open. The kitchen is dark, except for the light coming from the open refrigerator. Flicking on the overhead lights, she sighs. Dishes overflow from the sink, a pot of macaroni and cheese sits congealing on the stove, sections of the newspaper and half-finished glasses of milk obscure the tabletop.

Andy's in front of the TV; the Patriots are on.

"Hey, honey." He tears his gaze away from the screen. His face is relaxed, a faint stubble visible on his chin. "Boys are in bed. Made 'em dinner, gave 'em a bath and everything." He smiles proudly, then frowns. "You OK? You look beat."

"Just a long day," Kate says, thinking of the mess in the kitchen behind her.

"Well, you should hit the sack, then." Andy turns his attention back to the game.

"Just thought I'd tidy up a bit first—no, no, don't get up," Kate says, trying for sarcastic.

"OK, well, see you in the a.m., then," Andy says distractedly, watching an instant replay. So much for sarcasm.

It takes forty-five minutes, but finally the kitchen is under control and Kate is heading upstairs. As she dodges the trail of dirty socks, underwear and wet towels leading from the bathroom to the boys' bedrooms, she realizes that her purse is still tucked under her arm. She also realizes that she still hasn't told Andy about the check.

~

Kate doesn't sleep well and by the time she heads downstairs Tuesday morning to get everyone breakfast, she's already exhausted.

"Mom, where's my permission slip for the field trip?" Henry's voice has an edge of hysteria.

"What permission slip? What field trip?" Kate gulps her second cup of coffee while starting to rifle through the stacks of paper on the counter.

"To the pet store. We're going today. They're gonna have ferrets." He crosses over to the counter and starts pulling sheets of paper out of piles.

"I wanna see the ferrets." Charlie pulls stacks of paper off the kitchen table, pretends to read each one and drops it to the floor.

"You and I will do something special today, bud," Kate tells him. She turns to Henry. "What color was the permission slip?"

"Blue. No, yellow." Henry redoubles his efforts to dig through the paper.

"I wanna see ferrets." Charlie is clinging to Kate's leg and she drags him across the floor to the kitchen table where she sees a slip of yellow peeking out from under the fruit bowl.

"Here we are, Henry. And look, it's already signed."

"It's got *stains* on it." Henry snatches the paper from her hand, accidentally tearing it in half. Tears well up in his eyes. "It's no good anymore; I'm not gonna be able to go."

"It's OK, pal. I'll drive you into school this morning and sign another slip right in front of your teacher."

Leaving Henry to pack his backpack and Andy to dress Charlie, Kate heads upstairs to get dressed. She pulls a pair of khakis from the laundry basket, rubbing her hands down her thighs in a futile attempt to press out the wrinkles. She digs a bra out of the dirty laundry pile and throws a clean T-shirt on over it, then runs a comb through her hair. She glances at the clock. No time for makeup if she wants to get Henry to school on time—no matter how much she needs it.

"Mom, we're gonna be late," Henry hollers from the kitchen.

Sighing, she heads back downstairs. Biting back a comment on Charlie's dashing outfit of bright green corduroys and an orange-and-brown-striped rugby shirt, she grabs her car keys. "Let's get moving, boys."

"Bye, hon." Andy is sipping coffee, the newspaper in hand. He looks up long enough to give Kate a halfhearted peck on the cheek.

"See you," she says. *Oh, and by the way . . . someone gave me a check for a million dollars—what do you think I should do with it?*

Kate herds the boys into their car seats and fastens their seat belts. She tries not to think about the check. Besides, what is there to think about? She already knows what she's going to do.

~

"All set for the big field trip, Henry?" His teacher, Ms. Abrams, gently spins him around and gestures at his cubby. Henry begins to unload his backpack.

"I wish we could have scheduled this trip for earlier in the day; I don't know how I'll be able to keep all their excitement in check until this afternoon." She smiles at Kate, as if the challenge of controlling eighteen frenzied seven-year-olds is going to be the highlight of her day.

"I need to sign a new permission slip," Kate says. "The last one had a bad run-in with some salsa or something."

Ms. Abrams hands her another yellow sheet. Kate puts Charlie down and he makes a run for the class guinea pig. Kate glances at Henry's sullen expression, at Charlie's ragtag outfit and at her own wrinkled khakis—and suddenly she gets a vivid picture of what Ms. Abrams must see: an out-of-control, harassed, frumpy-looking, middle-aged housewife.

Ms. Abrams feels sorry for her, Kate can tell. And suddenly, she feels sorry for herself.

～

"But the guinea pig *wanted* to come with us." Charlie's been working up to another crying fit since they left the classroom.

"I'm sorry." The multipierced twenty-something leans across the counter putting herself at Charlie's eye level. "But guinea pigs aren't allowed in Starbucks." She lowers her voice to a whisper. "They poop all over the carpet."

Charlie squeals with glee. *The magic effect of the word "poop" on a three-year-old. Why didn't I think of it myself?* Kate wonders. She orders drinks and snacks for the both of them, and then she and Charlie settle into a pair of upholstered chairs near the front window. Kate has just taken a huge bite of a chocolate croissant when someone says her name.

She looks up, croissant crumbs spilling into her lap. Martha Wilson, one of the READ board members, is standing in front of her, folding her *New York Times* into her briefcase. Martha is a tall, angular woman with well-disciplined hair and the no-nonsense air of a high-school English teacher—which is what she used to be until budget cuts forced her into early retirement and a second career in real estate.

Kate takes a gulp of coffee, trying to wash down the half-chewed croissant.

"Martha, hi. How are you?" she says, wiping her mouth.

"I heard READ won a national award. I'm so sorry I missed the meeting. Was it nice?"

"Not as nice as the Honeywell homestead," Kate says.

Martha smiles. "Yes, some place. It's nearing the end of the year. Has Honeywell given you the check yet?"

How could she know about the check? Kate hoped she sounded nonchalant. "What check?"

"Oh, the one he gives his volunteer directors every year."

"Um, yes, actually, he did. But—you know—I've really got to give it back."

"Give it back? Don't be silly, Kate. He can spare it and you certainly deserve it. I'm sure Lelia Kelly never thought about giving it back. Seems to me she was off to Italy so fast you'd think she'd just robbed a bank."

"So she used her check to go to Italy?" Kate wants to ask more, but Charlie is worming himself into her lap, splashing now-cold hot chocolate on his pants, her arm, the chair.

"She's coming home next week. You can ask her yourself." Martha glances at her watch. "I've got to run; great to see you."

"You too," Kate says, mumbling around the muffin Charlie is trying to stuff in her mouth.

~

The day continues its downward slide. Charlie's mood never improves and Henry comes home with a ferret bite that necessitates an emergency call to the pediatrician to make sure his tetanus is up-to-date. Between Charlie's ferret envy and Henry's frantic insistence that he needs a rabies shot, Kate can't even manage damage control around the house. For the rest of the afternoon, while the laundry and dishes sit, she mediates, medicates and cajoles.

They finally settle on a project that delights both boys: constructing a ferretproof (Henry's idea) fort under the dining room table. By the time Kate gathers all the necessary sheets, blankets, pillows and gear to make the fort as homey as possible, it's dinnertime. Andy comes home from work and immediately folds his tall frame under the table with Henry and Charlie. Kate's still mustering up the energy to tackle the sink full of dirty dishes left from breakfast.

When the inevitable question *What's for dinner?* comes up, Kate offers to go get takeout. *Why not?* She rationalizes. *I've got a check for a million bucks in my purse* . . . While the boys large and small celebrate the thrill of midweek pizza, Kate celebrates the thrill of twenty minutes alone in the car.

"I didn't call ahead, so this might take awhile," she warns.

"No problem." Andy's voice is muffled under the dining room table. "Just don't forget to order extra pepperoni."

Kate grabs the car keys and exits to the sounds of high fives being exchanged. Sitting in the car, she allows herself to relax for the first time all day. Without the boys as a distraction, however, her thoughts go right back to the check in her bag. She hasn't talked to Dani today. She's almost afraid that her friend was right about what Dr. Mia meant. *How ironic is that?*

Kate doesn't want to think about the money anymore. She decides to use this time in the car for her and her alone. She pops in Dr. Mia's tape.

"You must accept circumstances before you can fully realize the life you are meant to have. Everything happens for a reason. You must embrace the reality in front of you. Accept it. It is the map of your life. This is Dr. Mia, reminding you that only you can "Drive Yourself.""

Abruptly, Kate swerves into a gas station and pulls to a stop. A silver minivan sits next to a pump where a woman is swiping her credit card. Kate reaches into her purse, pulls out her phone and dials Dani's number. She picks up on the second ring. Kate starts to talk before Dani can even utter hello.

"Maybe you're right."

"Kate? Of course I'm right. I'm always right." Dani pauses. "About what?"

"Maybe this is all meant to happen. We've been saying we need a break. Maybe this is it. Maybe we need to go—get away. It's destiny."

"Kate, I don't have any idea what you just said. I don't know anything about destiny. I agree we need to get away. Maybe we could go to New York or something. Just for a couple of days. This is a long weekend, remember? Brianna's spending all three days with Brian. I'm sure he'd take her for an extra day or two on top of that. Maybe Andy can watch the boys for a couple of days."

"New York sounds great. You know what? Let's just do it. I'm driving this car. This is the map of my life . . ."

"Kate, you're losing me again."

"Never mind. Let's just talk in the morning. And be ready."

Kate has to drive two towns over, but she finds a bank that is open until 6 p.m. She circles the block twice before she gets up the nerve to drive into the parking lot. *This is where I am supposed to be,* she thinks. *It's a necessary stop if I am going to continue this journey.* Kate gets out of her car and heads for the entrance to the building. It's not the branch where she has a checking account, but she thinks that's better somehow.

The bank is empty; it's nearly closing time and the tellers are all standing around chatting with each other. Kate goes up to a window and quietly waits for someone to notice she's there. When the young girl comes over to help her, she can barely croak out the words: "I'd like to make a deposit please."

Kate's hand is shaking as she signs the check and hands it over to the teller. The teller's eyes go wide.

"One moment please," she says.

Kate stands frozen at her window. Her knees are shaking and her stomach churns. The teller's gone for what seems a very long time. When she comes back, she's on Kate's side of the window and there's a distinguished-looking man in a dark suit beside her.

Oh my God, it's the bank security, Kate thinks. *I'm going to jail.*

"Kate Thompson?"

You're under arrest, Kate adds silently. *Just like in the movies.*

"Paul Gamble, president of North River Savings Bank," he says clasping her hand. "Please, won't you come join me in my office?"

"We're are so delighted you've chosen North River as your bank, Ms. Thompson," he says, gesturing to the chair in front of his huge oak desk. Kate sits, her head spinning. *Is this how they treat you before they haul you off to prison?*

"Now usually, we can't process such large amounts this quickly," Mr. Gamble is saying, "but Mr. Honeywell is well known to us and his checks are always good here. We can have all your documents ready shortly. Will you need business checks? Temporary cash cards? A line of credit?"

In a daze, Kate nods. Suddenly she has an inspiration.

"Would you mind, please, that is, I'll need them for my, uh, associate, Danielle Strauss, too." She manages to get the words out. "She'll need . . . she'll need . . . whatever it is you're giving me."

Mr. Gamble looks even more pleased, as if he's just figured something out. "Ah, is Mr. Honeywell perhaps an investor . . . ?" he asks delicately.

"Yes, yes, you could say that." The words just roll off her tongue. "We'll need the cash cards immediately. You can mail business checks to my attention at the office." She gives him the address for READ. "I don't expect we'll need a line of credit just yet. But we can keep that option open." It's as if she's stepped outside herself and is watching some Kate Thompson she doesn't even know.

"Very well," he murmurs. "If you could just sign these forms."

Kate signs the paperwork in the folder in front of her. In a few moments, the teller who first took the check comes in and hands him an envelope.

"Your temporary cash cards. The permanent cards will arrive within seven to ten days. The checks will go in the mail tomorrow. It's been a pleasure to do business with you." Mr. Gamble hands Kate the envelope. "Thank you again for choosing North River to meet your banking needs," he says.

"Thank *you*," Kate says, slipping the cards into her coat pocket. She pushes herself out of the wingchair and locks her shaking knees as she stands. Mr. Gamble escorts her to the front door and holds it open. She steps out into the cool night air, and just like that, she turns back into the Kate Thompson she knows: just a mom, heading out to pick up pizza for supper.

That night before bed, Kate tells Andy that she and Dani are thinking about getting away for a girls' weekend. He's all for it, and somehow, Kate never gets around to explaining how they're paying for it. He doesn't ask and Kate has to admit, she knew he wouldn't.

When the phone rings early Wednesday morning, Dani is in the middle of getting Brianna's stuff together for school. For a moment, her stomach clenches. Early-morning phone calls rarely bring good news.

"Hello?"

"Dani, it's me."

"Kate, why are you whispering?"

"I'm hiding in the bathroom. I've got to be quick: listen, can you really get free this weekend?"

"Well, I was going to go into the office and try to clear out . . . Brianna's off from school because of the holiday, so she's spending the long weekend with her dad."

"Forget about work, we're getting away."

"Getting away? What are you talking about, Kate?"

"You were right. Dr. Mia is right. I deposited that check."

Dani is speechless.

"We're going to New York. Tomorrow." Even though Kate is whispering, there is a tone to her voice that Dani is not inclined to argue with.

"Sure, no problem. I'll tell Bryce that my millionaire girlfriend is taking me away for a weekend in the lap of luxury."

"I'm not taking you—we're taking each other. Look in your . . ."

Kate's whisper is drowned out by a banging on her end of the phone.

"I'll be out in a minute," she calls in a normal voice.

"Charlie spilled his juice." Dani can hear Henry's voice, muffled through the door.

"Henry took my Pop-Tart."

"I'm in the bathroom, boys," Kate says. "What's the rule about disturbing people in the bathroom? Can't Daddy help?"

"He's busy," Henry says.

"Doing what?"

"He's in the bathroom."

Dani cracks up.

"For Pete's sake," Kate mutters. Her voice drops to a whisper again. "Dani, just look in your mailbox. I dropped off a cash card last night.

We're in this together, and we're leaving for New York tomorrow morning before I lose my nerve."

The banging on the bathroom door has resumed.

"Count me in," Dani says loudly. "Count me in."

Thursday, Early Morning

Woooooweeee . . . Dani's hair is swept back in a startlingly white scarf, her oversized Jackie O black shades are perched on the end of her nose. The wind whips through her flowing scarf as she screams down the turnpike in her white convertible Mercedes coupe. Just ahead, she sees a minivan broken down on the road's shoulder and a blonde woman—it's Allison—tiredly raising her hand in Dani's direction in the blazing midday heat. The minivan's door is ajar and inside Dani sees eight toddlers strapped in car seats crying uncontrollably. Allison's waving her hands now and shouting, as Dani's little white convertible zooms by, her eyes fixed on the road in front of her, both hands on the wheel . . .

~

It takes Dani a moment to realize that the ringing she's hearing is her cell phone. She looks at the clock: 7:30 a.m. *Oh, for God's sake.* She leaps out of bed and snatches up the phone.

She looks at the screen: BRYCE. *Is there no limit to his rudeness? He knows I am off until Tuesday. I wrapped up every last detail of the case we're working on and referred all questions to Cuomo.* The phone rings and rings. Dani stares at it. It looks like a small bat in her hand. She turns it off and puts it in her bureau and closes the drawer. *No way* is she taking it on the vacation of a lifetime. She sifts through her drawers and closet, pulls out some clothes. She is going for chic and sexy. She sorts through the options. Dani's closet is filled with dark suits, a veritable rainbow of navy to gray to black and back again. She realizes to her horror that her most cutting-edge clothing items are now about ten years old. She randomly tosses a few things in a suitcase. *Whatever.* She calls Kate. It's 8:15 a.m.

"I'm packed . . . You?" Dani asks.

"Uh, pretty much. What do you think? There's an Amtrak that leaves at 10 am. And gets into Penn Station at . . ."

"Wait. I have a much better idea. You be ready at nine o'clock. I'm picking you up."

"Uh, OK."

"Hey, where are we staying by the way?" Knowing Kate, Dani thinks she's probably (responsibly) gotten them a two-night special with continental breakfast at the Budget Lodge.

"I'm not saying, but you'll like it. Let me put it this way. It's no Budget Lodge."

—

As Dani sits at the curb outside Kate's house, she can hardly contain herself. She checks her watch: 8:59. The front door opens. Kate takes one look in Dani's direction and stops. She squeals. "Dani! What in the world?"

Dani is sitting in a sparkling, jewel red Cadillac convertible. True, she is wearing her T. J. Maxx bargain rack shades instead of the Jackie O's, and there is no flowing white scarf, but it's close enough for her.

"Dani, where did you get this?"

"Well, I went to pick up something at the Stop & Shop and it was just sitting there in the parking lot with the keys in it and I thought, Hey, it's fate!"

Kate looks stricken.

"I'm kidding. You know that place in Hadley, Bob's Auto? They own a couple of vintage cars and rent them out. Anyway, it's all ours 'til Tuesday morning. Get in."

Kate throws her tote bag in the backseat and slides in to the front. She glances in Dani's direction and a huge smile breaks over her face.

"Well, what are we waiting for?" Dani slams her foot on the accelerator and peels out like a sixteen-year-old. They both howl with laughter. Dani sees Mrs. McNair peeking through her curtains next door, scowling. Dani gives her a big wave and they're off.

Part II

~

"The more you know, the less you need."

—Aboriginal proverb

Chapter Seven

Not long after they pay the toll at the Henry Hudson Bridge, the road swings out and the water opens up to the right. It's a balmy day for October, the Indian summer is back, and even with the convertible's top down on the open highway the temperature is perfect. The Hudson River sparkles in the midday sun. Kate gazes out over the open water. It looks so tranquil and bright. It seems impossible that the river holds any dark secrets, much less the secrets of a city of millions.

Dani has the CD player blasting with Smokey Robinson seconding that emotion. She bobs her head in time to the music and her mouth traces every word, though Kate can't hear her over the noise of the road and the stereo. They stay in the left lane, flying past the other cars and trucks until the traffic slows approaching upper Manhattan. The traffic is bumper to bumper and Dani turns the music down a bit.

"So, are you going to tell me now?" Dani asks with a big smile. Her hair looks like it's been in a blender and Kate can only imagine what her own looks like.

"Tell you what?"

"What fabulous place you've booked us into?"

"Nope. It's a surprise."

"Well, you'd better at least give me a hint–like the address maybe– because we're already at Ninety-sixth street."

"OK, it's midtown. Let's see . . ." Kate pulls the little scrap of paper she'd jotted the information down on out of her purse. "Well, sort of midtown. Forty-second and Broadway"

"Forty-second and Broadway?"

"I was sure you'd guess from the address, *Ms. New York.*"

"I know, it's probably one of those swanky new boutique hotels. Ian Schrager, here we come!"

"Wasn't he in *Star Wars?*" Kate asks excitedly.

"You're joking right? . . . You've really neglected your Page Six and *InStyle* magazine. Don't worry, I won't tell anyone."

Without taking her eyes off the road, Dani reaches back and pulls a CD case out of her bag. Kate is guessing maybe the Supremes to usher them into midtown. Expertly, Dani cracks the case with her fingernail and slides the CD into the player. She cranks up the music. A slow bluesy number. It sounds somewhat faraway, like an old recording, like the Little Rascals intro Kate remembers from her childhood. A trumpet wails and then a woman's voice booms through the speakers. It is big and haunting. Kate's never heard anything quite like it. *I hate to see the evening sun go down . . .* the voice declares.

"Hey, DJ Jazzy Dani. What's this? Not Motown."

"It's Bessie Smith, Empress of the Blues."

"She sounds so sad. Like the world is about to end."

"Well, it's the blues, baby. But believe me, Bessie was no sad sack. The woman was a force. She was one of the first black singers to break through to the mainstream. But she was also this larger-than-life personality. As the story goes, she once single-handedly told off a group of Ku Klux Klan members who were trying to collapse the tent on her show."

"When was this?" Kate sees a huge tower with the gold Trump logo on it looming in front of them as they creep along.

"In the twenties. They used to do these tent shows in the South, traveling by train from town to town doing song and dance. Kind of like the circus. Apparently Bessie was taking a break during one and went outside to get some air when she saw a group in white hoods start pulling up the tent stakes to collapse the thing on her and everyone inside. She called to her bandmates, who stepped out of the tent, took one look at the group and ran back inside. Who could blame them, really? The Klan was at its peak back then. Anyway, Bessie was having none of it. She marched right up to them, and with one hand on her hip, proceeded to chew out the whole lot of them. They stood there stunned for a moment, then fled into the night. She went back to the tent grumbling about how useless her chicken bandmates were."

"That's pretty amazing. She could have been killed."

"Yeah. It seemed she pretty much did and said what she wanted. If something wasn't right, or she wasn't getting the respect she deserved, she'd let it fly. She once decked this high society white woman who'd been rude to her. Bessie was pretty crazy but she did it her way, did what she thought was right and didn't suffer fools. It's hard not to admire her spirit. Sometimes, when Bryce is giving me grief, I think, what would Bessie do? Then I think: Bessie didn't need to hold on to her day job."

"From what you've said, I'm not sure I could picture Bessie in an office job. What happened to her?"

"She was huge in the twenties and thirties, then the Depression hit and no one wanted to hear sad songs anymore."

"*I've got the St. Louis Blues, I'm as blue as I can be,*" Bessie roars. Dani cranks it up. And then it registers for Kate. Dani looks different, and it isn't the Don King hairdo. It's almost as if Kate is looking at an old photo of her friend even though she's right there in front of her. The pinched expression, the hardened look are gone. Dani looks relaxed, happy. And Kate realizes how long it's been since she's seen her this way, if ever.

"What the . . . ?" Dani stammers and her relaxed look disappears the minute they pull up in front of the hotel.

They are parked in front of a massive building that could pass for a rehab center. Kate checks the paper against the number on the building. *Nope, this is it,* she thinks.

"Kate, where have you taken us?"

"It's the Plaza, you know, high tea, old-world glamour, where that little character Eloise ran around . . . It looks really different from the books."

Dani bursts into laughter. Tears begin to run down her face.

"What?" Kate asks. "It looks like it's fallen on hard times. We can try some place else. I did get a great deal though. I was surprised."

"Kate, this is the *Times Square* Plaza! . . . Drug den, streetwalker central. No wonder you got such a good deal. OK, sister, let me show you the way. And forget those bargains. Have you forgotten? *We're richer than God.*"

Kate's face begins a slow burn; *I am such a hick*, she thinks. "OK, give me your cell phone and I'll call someplace else."

"I left the phone at home." Dani waves her hand dismissively. "No way Bryce is going to be able to find me this weekend."

"No phone?" Kate can't believe it. "You really are living on the edge."

Dani hits the gas, lets out a hoot and in the process almost side-swipes a yellow cab. The cabbie slams on his brakes and leaps from his car, shouting and pumping his fists in the air. But they are already on their way uptown.

—

"Now *this* is more like it!" Dani announces, plopping herself into one of the richly upholstered Louis XV–style armchairs in their suite at the Plaza Hotel. The *real* Plaza. The living room is palatial, with antique furniture and exquisite walls. An entire family could live in the lap of luxury in the bathroom alone, with its sweeping mirrors and plush towels. The windows offer views of Central Park and Fifth Avenue. Kate half expects to see the Queen Mother in the next room sipping out of a china teacup.

Kate throws her bag on the floor. "I'm going to check in at home, let them know we got here."

After five rings, the machine picks up, and Kate figures the boys are outside playing. She leaves a message with the hotel phone number and room number. As soon as she hangs up, she feels inexplicably free. Dani picks up a phone in the sitting room. "I'd better give Brian the number here, too."

Moving around the suite, Kate drinks in all the details. She's almost afraid to touch anything for fear of leaving fingerprints. The place is immaculate. There is a faint scent of lilies in the air from the arrangement on the cherry dresser. She wanders into the bedroom and falls back onto one of the king-sized beds. She rolls to the middle of the mattress and stretches flat out on her back, her arms and legs reaching for either edge. *A huge bed, all to myself. And nothing to do in it but sleep. I could get used to this*, she thinks.

The next thing she knows, someone is gently shaking her shoulder. "Not now, honey," Kate mutters automatically. She rolls on to her side. "I'm exhausted."

"I can see that that Andy is a lucky man," Dani drawls sarcastically.

Kate snaps awake. Remembering where she is, she forces herself up on her elbow. "Was I sleeping?"

"Like a baby. I could barely bring myself to wake you. But just consider it a quickie."

"A quickie?" Kate flushes guiltily, not wanting to admit how happy she is to be in a hotel room without feeling like she has to rekindle the passions of her youth.

Dani grins as if she's reading Kate's mind. "Yeah, you remember those from the pre-kid days, right? A little afternoon delight?"

"It was a nap," Kate says.

"Haven't you heard? Sleep is the sex of the new millennium."

Kate starts to giggle. "Guess which I'd rather have . . ."

"Well, nap time is over, we've got work to do!" Dani pulls her to her feet.

"This is a vacation, remember?" Kate protests. "This is the first nap I've had in seven years that didn't involve a couch, a video and sleeping with one eye open."

"C'mon sweetie. This will be fun—and trust me, we need it. If you don't believe me, go take a look at yourself in that mirror."

Kate walks into the bathroom and lets out a small yelp. Her hair is doing things that defy gravity. Her blouse is rumpled and stained with the coffee she spilled when Dani made one of her now famous, quick getaways.

"Which way to the spa?!" Kate shouts.

Dani has a five-minute conversation with the concierge while Kate browses the jewelry store conveniently located in the lobby.

"Let's go," Dani says, prying her away from the display cases. They move soundlessly over the red floral carpet to the elevator. All around them are sweeps of white and gray marble. Gold chandeliers the size of small cars descend from the high ceilings.

"We're set for a facial, massage and exfoliating scrub–then we're off for hair, nails and makeup," Dani announces. The elevator door opens in front of them and two slim blondes with flawless skin and stylish outfits step off.

"So, if this is what life in New York is like, how'd you ever leave?" Kate asks.

"Trust me, Kate. Everyday life in New York isn't quite like this."

The spa is an oasis of ivory walls and aqua tiles. Voices murmur from private treatment rooms and the occasional guest drifts by looking more relaxed than anyone has a right to be.

Minutes later Kate is lying on a heated table, her body wrapped in warmed towels. Cool compresses cover her eyes and a young woman in a pristine white lab coat and with what Kate thinks is a Russian accent is gently rubbing potion after potion onto her cheeks and forehead.

"Your skin is lovely," she tells Kate reassuringly. "You will look so rested after the treatments, yes?"

Kate stops worrying about the fact that she's naked under the towels. She's not sure, but she thinks she stops worrying altogether. Hot towels follow cool lotions and the scent of lavender fills the room. On the table next to Kate, Dani sighs deeply.

Too soon, the facial is over. Kate glances over at Dani, too relaxed to even utter a word.

"You think this is good, just wait," Dani says as two other women enter the room.

"I am Irina," one of them tells Kate, flexing her arms to reveal biceps that could put Vin Diesel to shame. "She is Oksana." The other woman is standing near Dani's table. "We will do scrub, then massage. Please, I will start with your back."

Without waiting for Kate to answer, Irina reaches one hand under

Kate's elbow and the other under her hip and flips her over in a smooth motion. She grabs Kate's ankle and begins to scrub her calf with a loofah. When Kate tentatively reaches a hand back to replace the towel that is slipping off one hip, her hand is slapped back down and the towel whisked away.

Ten minutes into the scrub, Kate again forgets that she's naked in front of strangers. She forgets that her thighs jiggle with each stroke of the loofah. Any worries, cares or self-consciousness seem to be sloughed off along with the top layer of her skin. Irina motions her to hop off the table and she obediently complies. She steers Kate to the shower and briskly instructs her to rinse off and return for the massage. The hot water feels wonderful, and when Kate emerges, the massage table has been covered with fresh, thick towels. She hops back up and Irina begins working on her aching shoulders and neck.

Time goes by in a blur of strong hands and fabulous-smelling oils. By the time Irina claps her on the shoulders and announces, "Done!" Kate has all but forgotten her name.

Irina helps her down off the massage table and points her in the direction of the showers. Kate wobbles out the doors with Dani right behind her.

"That was the most amazing experience," Kate calls out to Dani. She is standing under a showerhead as big as a dinner plate. "My skin is so soft."

Dani laughs. "I think Oksana exfoliated places where no loofah has gone before! And the massage . . ."

By the time Kate has changed back into her clothes, she's bursting with energy.

"Why haven't we done this before?" Kate asks. "How could I have gone for so long without exfoliating?"

Dani snorts.

"So this is what it feels like to be full of energy, yet relaxed."

"Look at you," Dani laughs. "You're a spa junkie already."

"You know who would just love this?" Kate asks thoughtfully. "My mom. I bet a massage would be great after a day of gardening."

"Yeah, your natural aversion to pampering does seem to run in the family," Dani agrees. "It's a good bet Eve's never had a spa day."

"Well, everyone should," Kate says firmly. "I mean just look at us. We look radiant."

"You ain't seen nothing yet," Dani says gleefully. "Let's get moving. My buddy the concierge scored us appointments at the hottest salon in New York."

Kate glances around the spa longingly. "Do we have to leave? I was hoping for the peppermint foot treatment . . ."

"We can't keep Larry waiting."

"Larry?" Kate trots behind Dani out of the hotel and down the street.

"Laurent Loget, master of the hair universe. Larry works magic. Believe it or not, before he got his hands on Julia Roberts, she was constantly mistaken for Wallace Shawn."

Kate laughs.

"OK, I made that up, but trust me, he's just what we need, if the state of our hair doesn't scare him off first. Of course, we won't get the hair god himself–he's probably busy touching up Julia's roots or something. But the concierge booked us both in. We'll get one of his wizards."

Kate follows Dani down Fifty-seventh Street past windows full of beautiful clothing on stylized mannequins.

"Here we are!" Dani announces, stopping in front of a discreet doorway next to a high-end designer. "The salon's on the top floor."

The salon is like another planet. The elevator deposits them into a vast, blond-wood wonderland. Where the Plaza Spa was the picture of old-world opulence, this salon is the epitome of minimalist chic. Everything smells great. Everyone looks great. Even with foil wraps and towels on their heads.

"Psssst." Kate feels a sharp elbow in her ribs.

"Ouch. What?" Kate flinches and jumps back, slamming into a dashingly handsome, dark-haired gentleman. "Excuse me, I'm sorry." She gasps.

"Not a problem. You are here for an appointment, *oui*?" His accent is killing her. So is his smile. Kate's knees feel a little wobbly.

"Mr. Loget, a pleasure," Dani says.

"The pleasure is mine, no doubt. Who are you here to see?" he asks.

"Gee, umm," says Dani, rummaging in her pocketbook for the concierge's instructions.

"Come here, this young lady will help you." The hair god himself walks them over to the receptionist and personally locates their names on the schedule. "Kate, Dani, right this way." He guides them toward the waiting chairs and disappears like a vision into thin air.

"Cute, huh?" Dani giggles. "Do you believe we are on a first-name basis with Laurent Loget?! I knew all my hours of studying *InStyle* magazine would pay off someday."

Dani is escorted to her private treatment room as Kate dutifully climbs into her chair. "So what are we doing today?" asks Kate's wizard Olivier. He is tall, with short-cropped, salt-and-pepper hair and bright green eyes. *Is this the land of pods?* Kate wonders. *How did everyone get to be so beautiful?*

"Well, I definitely need a cut. What would you recommend?"

"Yes, a cut and perhaps a little color as well?"

"Color?"

"Oh, yes. You have gorgeous hair. You must touch up some of this gray here and perhaps some golden highlights. While you wait with the color, a manicure and pedicure, yes? And for a cut . . . I think some layers around the face. A nice shape, no?"

"No—yes. Definitely, yes. Whatever you think." Kate decides to let this wizard do his thing.

She can't believe the sight taking shape before her. The gray is gone. The ragged edges are gone. In their place are long, tousled layers of gold that fall around her face.

"See, it brings out your eyes. Gorgeous. Did anyone ever tell you that you look like Meg Ryan?" In fact, she had heard that—but not in a very long time.

"Thanks. Maybe Meg Ryan after sixty days in the outback. I could use a little makeup, couldn't I?"

"Darling, your skin is beautiful, so young—glowing. But if you like, we have wonderful artists here," Olivier says discreetly, not answering her question directly. " Let me check for you."

Dani emerges from the room next to Kate's. She shuffles over wearing the same adorable beaded flip-flops that came with Kate's pedicure, sporting a red on her toes that is so bright it's hard not to look away and a broad grin on her face. Her hands are extended, revealing an immaculate French manicure.

She looks stunning. Like a movie star. Her hair has been given a slightly auburn cast and her curls have been ironed into a silken sheet that reaches her collarbone. Kate is seeing her cheekbones for the first time.

"You look incredible," Kate gasps.

"You too." Dani stares back.

"Ladies, the makeup artists are available for you now," Olivier says as he reappears in the room. With one last expert fluff of Kate's hair, he takes her elbow and steers her and Dani toward another secret, glorious corridor. By the time the makeup woman has had her way with them, the transformations are complete. Kate can hardly believe it. For the first time in as long as she can remember, she actually likes what she sees in the mirror.

They pay up and Kate has to muffle a scream when she sees the grand total. Then it occurs to her. *This is not a problem. This is my life. The one I have created. I have not just sentenced my family to ten years of Kraft macaroni and cheese: I can do this.* Dr. Mia's voice sounds in her head:

Where there is a wish, there is an ability to make it come true. The Universe has unlimited abundance. We limit ourselves and accept less than what we truly need to be happy. Put your desires out into the Universe, and the Universe will supply.

Kate has always wanted to believe her, but until today it seemed like Dr. Mia was talking about everyone else. A world of unlimited happiness and supply *was* out there, Kate had believed that part, but it always felt out of reach. Those things didn't happen to her. They weren't there for her. But maybe she was wrong, maybe the Universe was about to start supplying . . .

~

By the time they exit the salon, it's dark, but the streets are still humming with activity. The stores are still open and well-dressed couples are beginning to fill the tables at the windows of restaurants. Dani and

Kate walk for a bit, enjoying the city's energy. They pass a French café where a few men in suits sit at an outdoor table. One raises his martini glass in a toast as they pass. "Good evening, ladies."

Dani smiles back.

Kate eyes the breadbasket on the table. "Is it really seven o'clock? No wonder I'm so hungry." She says.

Dani puts her hand up for a cab. "Do you realize it took nearly seven hours and about fifteen people each to get us looking like this?"

"I'm seriously considering building an extension onto the house and inviting them all to come home with me."

They hail a cab and are whisked back to their new temporary home in no time. They glide through the magnificent Plaza lobby as though it is their living room. As they approach the elevator, Kate sees a flash of navy to her right, feet in the air and then Dani is standing again, arms overhead, looking triumphant.

"*Ta da!* I didn't know I could still do that!"

"Dani, are you crazy? A cartwheel in the lobby?! You're gonna get us kicked out," Kate says in a hushed tone, but she is about to laugh.

"Hey, this place has had Johnny Depp throwing lamps out the window and rock stars making floats out of their mattresses. We're fine."

As they walk by the concierge desk on the way to their rooms, Kate sees a brochure for the spa.

"Go on up," Kate tells Dani. "I'll be up in a second."

Dani follows Kate's gaze to the desk. "Booking more treatments already?" she says. "I'm so proud of you."

"Something like that."

Dani continues to the elevator and Kate approaches the desk. She is not sure that the concierge will be able to do what she wants, but he listens to her requests and assures her confidently that "Anything is possible here at the Plaza." Kate heads back upstairs with a spring in her step.

Up in the room, she raids the minibar. "Mmmmm, Toblerone *and* macadamia nuts," she sighs.

"Nectar of the gods," Dani agrees, laying her clothes out on the bed.

Kate pulls out a little black cocktail suit she's had for five years. It still fits her but it's snug. The neckline plunges, revealing enormous cleavage.

"Look at you! You're a bombshell." Dani has on one of her sleek black suits, but somehow it doesn't look corporate or stuffy.

"If I can just get these things back into their little linen cage," Kate says, taking off the jacket and pushing her heaving breasts deeper into her bra.

"Ooh look, the Granny Strauss bra gets another outing," Dani teases. "Remind me to make sure you buy some new lingerie on this trip."

Kate frowns at her and pulls a camisole on over the bra. The view is still impressive, but at least she feels more covered up. Dani watches her fool with the neckline of the jacket.

"Relax, Kate, movie stars bind themselves in rolls of tape to get a neckline like that. Remember Uma Thurman at the Oscars? Va va va voom. You look great."

~

They descend to the Oak Bar in the Plaza lobby. It boasts an enormous old-fashioned curved bar lined with high stools, all of which are occupied. Men and women in business suits crowd around the bar and mingle at the small tables that fill the rest of the large space. Kate and Dani spot an empty table and quickly grab it. Everything is done in dark wood; large delicately painted murals adorn walls that overlook the large banquettes. They've already had a couple of vodka martinis and several bowls of pretzels when Kate looks at her watch: 9:15. With a start, she realizes that she hasn't called Andy. She goes to the pay phone, feeling a little light-headed and woozy.

"Hello," a bleary voice answers.

"Hey, honey, how are my guys?"

"Oh, I must have fallen asleep . . . How are you, darling? How was the trip? Get there OK?"

"Yeah, it was great. We're just heading out to a late dinner and I wanted to check in."

"We're good. We had a real bachelor's night in. Kegs, skin flicks . . .

Well, actually it was more like pizza and *Toy Story 2*. The boys sacked out early. I guess I did, too. We're fine, don't you worry about us. You just have a wonderful time. Love you."

"Love you, too. Kiss for the boys. Oh—and did you let the dog out?"

"Oh, right. I'll do that now." Andy hangs up and Kate sighs and heads back to the table. Dani is chatting up a couple in a neighboring booth. The couple is laughing hysterically. The woman slaps her hand on the table and almost tips over her water glass.

Dani stands up when she sees Kate and waves good-bye to the couple.

"We're all settled up. Where to?" Dani asks.

"Oh, I don't know. I'm still hungry. I'm not so sure those martinis on an empty stomach were such a good idea."

"Let's go eat. We can ask our new best buddy, the concierge, what he recommends."

They get into the elevator. Kate watches the numbers light and then pass "G."

"Whoops. Better press the button."

Dani laughs. "Wow, I admit, I'm a bit tipsy."

"Me too. It feels great . . . it feels like fun. Remember what that is?"

The elevator stops on the third floor and the doors open slowly.

They are staring into a sea of men in black tie. They are grouped in clusters throughout an incredible ballroom with high ceilings and gorgeous moldings. Most are sipping from tall fluted glasses. A couple of gentlemen by the elevator glance in their direction. The one nearest them nods his head. Kate looks at Dani,.

"What do you say we skip dinner and go straight to dessert?" Dani says. Without another word they make their entrance.

~

They step off the elevator and are met by a wave of black suits and crisp white shirts. Dani freezes for a moment, flashing back to every holiday party her former law firm ever threw. Through martini-blurred eyes, Dani thinks she sees Brian coming toward her and she spins hard to her right and walks blindly forward. Out of the corner of her eye, she sees Kate hang back, and for a minute she thinks Kate's going to turn around and run for the elevator.

"F-U-N," Dani mouths silently in Kate's direction.

Kate nods and then flashes Dani a wicked grin as she's whisked toward the bar, a tuxedo-clad escort on either side.

"So what's a nice girl like you doing in a place like this?" Kate is swallowed up in a sea of testosterone and Dani turns in the direction of the question.

"Who says I'm a nice girl?" Dani says, tilting her chin down to gaze upon a glaring bald spot with a bad comb-over.

"Bad girls are even better," her munchkin friend says with too much sincerity for her liking.

Dani snorts. *I don't have to stand here listening to bad pickup lines. I am sensational in my new hair and makeup, and I am enjoying all the freedom that money can buy.* She looks across the room teeming with dozens of big bellies and bigger wallets and almost feels pity. She doesn't need any of these men.

Without a word she spins on her heels and heads to the bar. She decides she's getting Kate and they're getting the hell out of here for some serious female bonding. That's what this weekend is all about anyway.

Dani finds Kate in the center of a group of guys, like Marilyn Monroe in *Diamonds Are a Girl's Best Friend.*

"Hi, Dani," she says, swaying a little on her heels as she gestures around her with a half-empty glass of champagne. "Meet my new friends: Bob, Ed, Dave and Ralph. They're CPAs. They're at a convention here at the hotel. This is their big banquet night."

Kate fills Dani in on their wives, kids, neighborhoods. They're already like old college friends.

"Well, Dani, you can see that Kate knows all about us," a tall skinny guy with glasses–Ed, Dani thinks–says, as he leans toward her. "Now maybe you can let us in on her little secret."

Oh, Kate, you didn't tell them about the money did you? Dani thinks. *We'll be stuck here all night talking retirement accounts and tax shelters.*

"Yeah, our beautiful mystery woman won't reveal her last name," Bob says.

Kate shakes her head at Dani ever so slightly.

"Well, it should be obvious," Dani says, accepting a glass of champagne and deciding to play along. "Doesn't she remind you of someone?"

The four of them stand gaping at Kate as she does a slow twirl, arms upraised.

"That girl from that movie with, you know, that guy–Bill Crystal." Ralph is wracking his brain.

"Meg Ryan?" Ed says.

"Very good, Ed," Dani says. "Gentlemen, meet Kate Ryan."

"Are you really her sister?" Ed can't believe he's guessed. Kate nods modestly.

"Are you an actress, too?" Ralph says.

"Oh, I guess I can act," Kate says. Four jaws drop. Dani can see them mentally debating whether it would be cool to get her autograph or ask for a photo.

"What about you, Dani," Bob says, moving closer to Dani. "Are you an actress, too?"

"She's my lawyer," Kate says.

"Beauty and brains," Bob says.

"An unbeatable combination," a new voice says from behind Dani.

"Guy!" Bob says with a forced heartiness. "Come and join our little group. Dani. Kate. This is Guy." Dani turns and finds herself nose to bowtie with what turns out to be the most gorgeous man she has seen in quite some time. Lifting her gaze, Dani locks into incredible green eyes.

"Dani's a lawyer and Kate is Meg Ryan's sister," Bob finishes his introductions.

Dani wrenches her gaze away from the eyes and drops it to the full lips, the strong jaw. In a glance she takes in the impeccably tailored tux, the expensive-looking watch, the lack of a wedding band . . . She's in love.

"Pleased to meet you both," Guy says, nodding to Kate and reaching his hand out to Dani.

Dani's knees go weak as he grips her hand and she tells herself to slow down on the champagne.

"So, you're an accountant." *Jeez, nice opening conversational gambit, Dani!*

"Actually, no. Bob's my accountant."

At the sound of his name, Bob tears his gaze from Kate's cleavage.

"That's right. Guy here's our biggest client. And his company is our second biggest client." Bob guffaws like he's gotten off the greatest one-liner. Guy gives a fake smile, as if he's heard it a thousand times before.

"He's a social incompetent but a great numbers guy," he whispers in Dani's ear. Her knees buckle again and she puts her empty champagne glass down on the bar.

"What can I get you, Dani?" The skinny guy, Ed, puts his arm around her waist.

"I'll take care of whatever the lady needs," Guy says coolly. Ed yanks his arm back as if he's stuck it into a nest of fire ants.

The lady can take care of herself, Dani says. Only it comes out as, "I'd love another glass of champagne."

Guy moves between Ed and Dani and leans in toward the bar. As he signals for another glass of champagne, Dani takes a good long look: about six feet tall, prematurely gray hair and the body of someone who doesn't sit around at a desk all day. Plus he gives off that aura of power she's always been a sucker for. *Yep, just my type. Once I marry him, Kate and I can be millionaires together.*

"So you're a lawyer?" Guy says, handing Dani a full glass. "I'm glad Shakespeare's argument wasn't widely acted upon."

"First thing we do, let's kill all the lawyers," Dani beats him to the punch line. "*Henry VI,* act 4, scene 2."

"Let me guess. You're a criminal defense attorney?"

"Why do you ask? Are you a criminal?"

"Naw." He smiles a slow grin that starts her heart racing. "I was just thinking that if you're as smart as you are beautiful, you probably never lose a case."

Keep breathing, Dani. Remember this guy doesn't know about your ex-husband, your lame suburban life or your bad hair days.

"I mostly handle Kate's affairs now," Dani says, remembering that she's supposed to be the personal attorney of a famous-by-relation person.

"Well, Kate's mighty lucky. I need someone like you." Guy touches her arm.

"I hope we're not talking about work anymore." Dani meets his intense gaze. She feels an electric connection to this man. He steps closer; she doesn't move away.

Dani's real life, the teeming party, even Kate and her harem of penguins fade into the background as Guy regales her with stories of private jets, yachting parties and polo matches. She's mesmerized by his slow drawl—and her vision of herself at his side in Cannes.

"Dani," he is saying. "Sometimes you don't know what you need until you hold it in your hand." He takes her chin in his palm and tilts her face up toward his. "Would you agree?"

"Earth to Dani . . ." Kate is tugging on Dani's arm. "Are you up for going out some more?"

Dani doesn't even look at her. "Oh, I am so up for it," Dani says, not knowing—or caring—what she's signing on for. Guy continues to stare into her eyes.

"Is everyone coming?" Dani asks Kate, tearing her gaze away. Without waiting for an answer, she turns back to Guy. "Are you coming?"

"I'd follow you anywhere," he says, putting an arm around Dani's waist and steering her toward the door. "My car's just outside."

Five minutes later they're all settled in the back of the biggest limo Dani's ever seen. She looks over at Kate and they both grin like idiots. *I could get use to living like this,* Dani thinks.

"It's one of the new SUV models," Ralph is saying excitedly. He slides over closer to Kate, effectively trapping her between him, Bob and the minibar.

"Where to?" Bob asks Kate. "You probably know all the best places."

"Uh, well . . . surprise me," she says. "I mean, Meg's so busy—she never takes me anywhere."

There's a brief conference among the CPAs; Bob leans up and says something to the driver, and fifteen minutes later they pull up in front of Light, reputedly the hottest new club to hit the New York scene.

"Let's party!" Four middle-aged men leap out of the limo, pulling a laughing Kate along behind them.

"Shall we?" Guy leans across Dani to open the door.

No, let's just sit here with your leg pressing up against mine in that incredibly suggestive way, and while you're so close, how about locking that door and taking me off to your penthouse where we can plan the rest of our lives together.

"Let's party," Dani says, swinging her legs out of the car.

The dance floor is noisy and crowded, and Dani keeps catching glimpses of Kate being swirled around like a sorority sister at a kegger. Dani had always been skeptical about Kate's tales about her wild college days, but right now she sure looks like she knows how to cut loose. Dani turns her full attention back to Guy. Unfortunately, the backbeat-heavy dance music is terrifically loud. Fortunately, that means Guy has to keep his mouth right next to Dani's ear for her to hear him.

"How long are you in town for?" he's saying.

"Just the weekend."

"Me too. I've got to be back by Monday. I'd love to show you my ranch, though. Why don't you come back to Texas with me?"

"Well, I do have some other commitments." Dani stalls for time. *Like a seven-year-old and a job where I'm the only competent person in the office.*

"Well then, we'll just have to make the most of this time we have, won't we?" He pulls her in closer as they dance.

Dani rests her cheek on his shoulder. Her head is reeling—and it's not from all the drinking. Now she knows how Kate felt when she opened the card from Honeywell. This guy has dropped into her lap, just like the check dropped into Kate's. She's won the love lottery. The music shifts to an up-tempo tune and suddenly Kate is beside her, pulling on her arm.

"C'mon, Dani. We're going to another bar. Ed says it's really wild."

"Great," Dani mutters "A CPA's version of a wild bar."

"No, really, he says it's crazy."

Kate is flushed from the dancing and her new hairstyle is tousled, but she looks more carefree than Dani's ever seen her. So who is Dani to spoil her big night out?

"Let's get crazy, then," Dani says, taking her arm.

Chapter Eight

"Are you sure this is the right place?" Kate says, squinting through the tinted windows of the limo. The bar they've stopped in front of looks like a Hollywood version of a biker bar, complete with Harleys parked outside. One of the accountants—Ed, Kate thinks—leans across her lap toward the window and she shrinks back so his outstretched elbow just misses its target of her breasts. *Sorry, Buddy. I'm drunk, but not that drunk.*

"Yeah," he says. "Hogs and Heifers."

Dani catches Kate's eye and cocks an eyebrow. "Oddly appropriate."

They crack up and Kate is relieved. Dani's been so wrapped up in Mr. Ken Doll on the ride over that Kate's worried she's forgetting the whole point of the evening: girls' night out.

"Who you callin' a heifer?" Kate says. But she's lost her again. Dani's mesmerized by her smooth-talking, tuxedo-wearing version of Mr. Right. The driver opens the door and Kate steps out, followed by her entourage of middle-aged men.

"Shots of tequila for everyone," Ralph shouts as he shoulders through the door.

"Set 'em up," says Dave, as Kate is swept into a smoky, crowded room.

"I'm not much of a tequila drinker," Kate says weakly, realizing how drastically out of place her black cocktail suit looks among all the low-rise jeans and baby tees.

"C'mon, Kate, isn't this what it's all about?" Dani joins her at the bar. "Living someone else's life for the weekend?"

Dani raises a shot glass. "To money and all it can buy." Kate raises her glass and slugs down the drink. She coughs as the tequila burns a trail to her stomach. The sensible mommy voice in the back of her head is saying: *Take it easy, dear, you'll have a terrible headache tomorrow . . .*

Kate tells her inner wuss to be quiet and slams her glass down on the bar.

"So whaddya think of this place?" Ed puts his glass down next to Kate's and gestures to the bartender.

"Well . . ."

"It's totally famous. I mean, Julia Roberts, Drew Barrymore, they've all been here. Even your sister."

The bartender, who Kate imagines is probably a Victoria's Secret model by day with a cascade of red ringlets to the middle of her back, expertly slides two beers and two more shots in their direction.

"Meg Ryan's been here, right?" Ed's shouting over the music.

The bartender nods and gestures back over her shoulder. "That's hers right up there."

Kate looks up and sees a line of bras hanging above the bar.

"Women leave their bras?" Kate wants to know more about this, but feels a heavy tap on her shoulder.

"Let's dance, beautiful."

Kate turns to see a huge guy in a leather vest and red bandanna holding his hand out in her direction. He's built like a bulldog, with a massive chest and short, bowed legs. Tattoos of naked women and motorcycles twine their way up his beefy arms. Kate thinks she sees a silver stud glinting from the center of his tongue when he opens his mouth.

The sum of our experiences is our essence. Dr. Mia's voice in Kate's head sounds slurred, but she figures the good doctor's got a point. Ed's backed off and joined Dave, Ralph and Bob in a huddle, probably debating whether or not to rescue her. Kate is staring at the outstretched hand, trying to think of a polite way to decline the invitation, when the music kicks in. She hears the first few guitar chords and recognizes them instantly. AC/DC's "You Shook Me All Night Long" is booming out of the speakers. *What the heck*, Kate thinks as she shimmies away from the bar.

"She was a fast machine, kept her motor clean.
She was the best damn woman that I ever seen . . ."

Kate is shakin' it. *When was the last time I had this much fun dancing?* The crowd clears a space as her dance partner drops to his knees. Kate raises both arms above her head and sings out the chorus as she swivels her hips and bounces away.

The music ends and Kate's dance partner whips his bandanna off his head and mops his face. The tiny white Christmas lights strung across the ceiling reflect off his shiny shaved head. He returns Kate to her bar stool with a kiss on her hand and a courtly bow.

"You can really dance," the bartender says admiringly as she puts a cold glass of ice water down in front of Kate, who gulps it gratefully.

"Thanks," Kate says, realizing that she's having a blast. She also realizes that she hasn't seen Dani in a while. She hopes Dani didn't miss seeing her get her groove on with a Hell's Angel.

Kate gets one knee up on her bar stool and checks out the room.

"They're over in the corner playing tongue hockey." Now that Kate's dance partner has returned to his table on the far side of the room, Ed materializes at her side. She follows his gaze and sees Dani and Guy in a dark corner, making out like teenagers.

"Looks like they're hitting it off," Kate says, keeping it casual.

"Oh, Guy hits it off like that with some woman at every party he goes to," Ralph says, joining their conversation. "And then drops her like Enron stock."

"He's a total dog." Ed confirms.

Kate looks over at Dani again and quickly weighs the options: 1) She's totally into him and this is going to break her heart; 2) She's not into him at all, just having a great time with no strings attached; or 3) maybe he thinks she's different. Maybe she's the one for him.

Ralph and Ed are trading anecdotes about Guy's way with the ladies, and Kate quickly rules out option number three. Just as she's decided to go over and save Dani from herself, her friend strolls out of the darkness.

"Come to the ladies' room with me."

They crowd into a tiny room about the size of a closet, Kate leaning against the door to hold it closed.

"He's too good to be true," Dani says, trying to clean up her smeared lipstick.

"He might be."

"Kate, he's perfect. Smart, handsome, rich . . ." Dani takes out her lipstick, begins to reapply it, laughs and puts it back in her bag. "What's the point? I'm heading out there to wear it off again anyway."

"You certainly seem to have a chemistry."

"Oh my God, Kate, I'm pretty sure he's the one."

"Actually, according to Ralph, Guy's a bit of a ladies' man."

"I know exactly what you're going to say," Dani holds up a hand and cuts Kate off. "Guy brought it up himself. Sure he's played the field. Look at him—he's gorgeous, he's rich—why wouldn't he? He says the women he usually dates aren't interested in their careers, that they can't meet him on an intellectual level. He says he would never have pictured himself falling for someone like me. But you know, Kate, sometimes you don't know what you need until you hold it in your hand."

The words sound a bit canned to Kate, but Dani looks like she's about twenty and without a care in the world. So who is Kate to spoil her big night out?

"He's totally hot," Kate says honestly.

Dani grabs her hand and makes a beeline from the bathroom to the bar. For a minute Kate thinks she's being dragged over to bask in the perfection that is Guy, but he holds out his hand to Dani who instantly slips her hand out of Kate's and is gone.

As she watches Dani go, Kate thinks of Andy and she is suddenly, intensely grateful for her sweet, comfortable marriage and her gentle, easygoing husband. Dr. Mia's voice slurs in Kate's head again: *When we are certain of what we have, we are free to explore who we are.*

That's what this weekend is all about, she reminds herself. *I'm ready to explore who I am. All the possibilities of Kate Thompson.* Kate leans up against the bar and the bartender slides another Corona her way.

"You ready to shake this place up a little?" she asks.

"Uh, what do you have in mind?" Kate isn't sure she wants to explore *all* the possibilities.

"Climb up," she says, gesturing as she hops nimbly onto the bar.

Kate stares at the bartender's outstretched hand for a minute and then figures, *What the hell?*

"Hit it," the bartender says and suddenly "Born to Be Wild" is blasting through the bar. The next thing Kate knows, the bartender's dancing and she's dancing. The crowd roars as the bartender slithers her little red lacy bra out from under her sleeveless T-shirt and whips it around over her head. She motions to Kate, who slides out of her suit jacket and drops it over the bandanna-wrapped head of her dance partner who has suddenly appeared, clapping worshipfully at her feet. The bartender is hiking her T-shirt higher. A smooth expanse of tight abdomen flashes above her low-rise jeans. Kate thinks of her soft belly, the extra skin that never went away after Charlie was born.

But the crowd is roaring and cheering and she doesn't stop dancing. Kate scans the bar. Where's Dani? She should be up here with her. Kate watches the bartender do an amazing swivel-hipped turn, wispy lace underthing waving like a flag. She lets it fly and it lands on Ed's head.

"Woooo-hoooo!" Ed shouts.

The strap of Kate's camisole has slipped down off her shoulder, but she's done with modesty. Kate hooks her thumb under her bra strap. *I'm an Amazon, I'm an amazing woman reveling in my sexuality. I'm . . . Oh my gosh, I'm wearing the Granny Strauss bra. I'm . . .* Her concentration momentarily broken, Kate takes a step forward . . . *falling off the bar.*

Her dance partner catches her from her less than graceful dismount and gallantly hands Kate her suit jacket.

She has the feeling that this would be a good time to make a getaway. Dani materializes beside her and Kate thanks God for telepathy.

"Jesus, Kate," Dani says as she pulls her through the crowd toward the door. People are smiling and giving Kate high fives as she passes. A greasy little guy with a cigar and bad hairpiece grabs Kate's arm. "Baby, you got what it takes. Call me." He tries to press his business card into her hand, but Kate waves it away. He pats her back instead.

"No, we'll just catch a cab," Dani is saying over her shoulder. "You all go on without us. I think we're done for the night."

"It made sense at the time," Kate says, slipping her arms into her jacket as they hit the sidewalk. The night air is brisk and soothes Kate's hot face.

"I'm sorry if I pulled you away from Guy. I hope . . ."

"Kate, that was outstanding!" Dani is whooping and hollering and holding Kate's hand up for a high five. "You were *hot!* None of those CPAs is ever going to forget you! Not to mention that biker in the leather vest . . ."

"You're not mad you had to leave Guy?"

"As my good friend and go-go dancer, Kate Thompson, says: 'Always leave 'em wanting more.'" Dani opens the door of a cab that's pulled up to the curb and waves Kate in with a flourish, slides in beside her, then starts talking about Guy.

". . . And he's got a ranch in Texas and a house in Malibu and he loves to view movies in his private screening room and he collects paintings and Arts and Crafts furniture . . . He thinks I should be doing something more challenging with my career; that I'm perfect for mergers-and-acquisitions-type work . . . He said he loved the way I dressed; he even noticed my shoes–said they were sexy . . ."

She goes on without taking a breath the whole way back to the Plaza.

"So you kind of like him, huh?"

"Mark my words. I will become Mrs. Guy De Varen."

The cab pulls up in front of the hotel and Kate gives the driver an extra-big tip. Partly because–hey, she's rich. And partly because she's too foggy to do the math.

"So you really like him, huh, Dani?" Kate asks in the bright light of the elevator.

"Why?" Dani looks at her suspiciously.

"Well, maybe it was just, you know, kind of an in-the-moment thing."

"Why? You don't think this could ever happen for me? You don't think someone like Guy . . ."

"Whoa, easy," Kate says. "You don't understand. I just hope he's good enough for you."

"What are you saying? That he's not good enough? What could possibly be wrong with a package like that?"

Kate fumbles with her purse and after a few clumsy tries manages to get the security card into the lock. Dani stalks off in the direction of her bed and falls across it.

"Why can't I be lucky, too?" she asks. The room is dark and Kate can hear a sniffle from the direction of Dani's bed.

"You're my best friend, Dani," is all she can think of to say. Kate peels out of her suit and lets it fall to her feet. Across the room, the sniffle turns into a gentle snore.

It takes about forty-five minutes under a steaming shower before Kate's ready to pull back the heavy brocade drapes in the room and face the day.

"Thought you'd drowned," Dani says when Kate comes out.

"It hurt to shampoo," Kate explains, pouring coffee into the delicate china cups on the room service cart. "Bless you for ordering."

"I don't know how you faced getting wet before coffee." Dani picks up her cup and heads toward the bathroom. "I'll be out before lunch."

Their clothes are scattered all over the room. Kate's first attempt to bend over and pick up her skirt results in an increased pounding in her head. She manages to snag her jacket, attempts to shake the wrinkles out and throws it over a chair. A white card flutters to the floor. Kate stares at it until curiosity gets the better of headache and she bends over and picks it up.

She sees the back first. In black ink is a handwritten message: "Call me—I'll make you a star" and a phone number. For a business card, the paper is heavy and expensive-looking. Kate flips it over.

"Waldo's World Adult Entertainment—XXX Satisfaction." There's a street address and a name: Waldo Woods, President. Kate flashes back to their exit from the club, the greasy little guy trying to press his business card into her hand.

"Eeeewww," she screams.

Dani sticks her head out of the bathroom. "What's wrong?"

"That guy last night, with the business card?"

"Scary, just thinking about him, huh?" Dani nods sympathetically.

"He's some kind of porn impresario." Kate walks over to the bathroom door and holds the card up for Dani to read.

Dani takes a good look and laughs so hard she has to sit down on the floor.

"What? Like I couldn't be a star?" Kate says, starting to giggle herself. Kate nudges Dani back into the bathroom and closes the door, but she can still hear her laughing hysterically. Suddenly feeling modest, Kate pulls the plush terry robe tightly around her, sits on the edge of the bed and picks up the phone.

"Hello, Thompson residence, who's calling please?" Her throat tightens up at the sound of Henry's voice.

"It's Mommy, honey, how are things going?"

"Great, Mom, we're having pizza for breakfast. It's left over from last night and Dad says it's better cold. Then we're gonna fix the toilet. Charlie really did it this time. But Dad says that we'll be able to find your . . ."

"Hi, honey." Andy's voice replaces Henry's.

"What's this about the plumbing?"

"Not to worry, it's all under control. How's your little getaway to the big city?"

Kate has a sudden vision of herself up on the bar flashing bikers and CPAs alike. "Pretty different from home, I'd say."

"Well, we miss you. Want to say hi to Charlie?"

"Hi, Mama."

"Hi, bud. What's new?"

"Daddy's fun. We broke some stuff playing. When are you coming home?"

"Soon, baby. Put Daddy back on the phone, OK?"

"We're fine, Kate. Really. You and Dani enjoy yourselves. We'll see you in a few days. Charlie, put that down! Charlie! I gotta go, honey. Love you."

"Love you, too," Kate says to the dial tone.

She puts the phone down and lies back against the pile of pillows on the bed. She can hear the sound of a blow-dryer coming from the bathroom. She's sipping her coffee and admiring her pedicure when Dani comes out of the shower.

"Everything OK at home?"

"They're surviving. I think."

Dani brings the coffeepot over and refills Kate's cup.

"I'm sorry if I upset you last night," Kate says. "Really, Guy seems like a nice, uh–guy."

Dani waves her hand. "I overreacted. If he calls he calls. If not, there are plenty of fish in this big pond."

Kate tries to get a good look at Dani's face, but Dani makes a show of intently studying the selection of pastries on the room service cart. Then she turns away and butters a roll. "Really, Kate. It was no big thing. So what's on the schedule for today?"

"No more alcohol, that's for sure." Kate says. "If rich women party like that all the time, I'm ready to give all the money back."

"Rich women don't just party," Dani says.

"No?"

"No."

"Well, I'm manicured, my hair is fabulous and I've had just the right amount of breakfast. So what do they do?"

Dani smiles. "They shop."

<hr>

The phone rings and Dani, sorting through her clothes for a suitable outfit, jumps for it. But Kate, from her sprawled position on the bed, lazily reaches toward the nightstand beside her and picks up the receiver first.

"I'm sorry, you must have the wrong room," Kate says. "Yes, this is room 351 but we didn't order a car." She shoots Dani a look, takes in her friend's expression–raised eyebrows, wide, hopeful smile–and continues. "But of course, I misunderstood. Please tell the driver we'll be down shortly."

"So? I put in an early-morning call to our pal at the concierge desk, just in case. We can't possibly tote around all those enormous bags and bundles in our new Jimmy Choos."

"You have a point. Just one question." Kate looks at Dani sideways, "Who or what is a Jimmy Choo?"

"Jimmy Choo. The shoe guy. You know, everybody is wearing them—OK, everyone who has a minimum of five houses or has starred in a major motion picture in the past two years."

Kate stares at her blankly.

"So that ten-pound fall issue of *Vogue* I gave you is being used as doorstop, isn't it? Clearly, we have our work cut out for us."

Kate throws on some clothes, applies her lipstick, picks up her bag and crosses the room to get her coat, which is lying on a chair near the windows. She gazes out across the city. "Kind of a change from my usual morning madness," she muses. "It's a luxury just to be able to pause and admire the view."

Dani joins her at the windows. Central Park spreads out beneath them, a patchwork of gold and red. Dani sees a footbridge gracefully arching over the lake. In the distance, the roofs of the buildings at the zoo are barely visible through the trees. Dani thinks about the long Sunday afternoons she used to spend in the park with Brianna. They would visit the zoo, ride the carousel, stop by the boat pond. Dani would push the stroller while Brianna explored. Sometimes Brianna would take a nap and Dani would find a quiet spot and leaf through the Sunday *Times*.

She has a flash of her usual morning routine, if it can be called that—slurping a half-cold cup of coffee while she slaps together Brianna's turkey sandwich and tosses it in her Powerpuff Girls lunchbox; the rush to pack Brianna's backpack: *Did you remember your homework?*; the frantic dash to the bus stop on the corner. She pictures Brianna, backpack bigger than she is, shuffling to take her place in line with the other kids. For a second, Dani misses her daughter more than she can bear. She reaches in her purse for her cell phone. *Oh, yeah, right*, she remembers, *no phone*.

Kate throws her coat over her arm and begins to head toward the door, when Dani blurts out, "Hey, do you mind if I make a quick call before we go down?"

Kate, looking relieved, falls flat on her back on the bed, with her head sinking into the pillows. She is a bit pale. "No problem, take your time. They know we're coming. Do you have any Tylenol?"

Dani tosses her a container from her bag.

She dials Brian and Allison's number. On the third ring, she hears the machine pick up and the lilt of Allison's voice, "Hello, you've reached the Saunders's residence, I'm sorry but we can't . . ." *Beep.* Then the real Allison interrupts. "Hello?"

"Oh, uh hi, Allison, it's Dani. Is this a bad time?"

"Oh, no, sorry we were just out collecting leaves in the yard. Bree and I were going to make a collage of fall colors. Do you want to speak with her?"

Brianna. Bri-an-na. She's a child not a cheese, Dani thinks, irritated.

"Yes, I'd love to speak with her," Dani says, a bit too cheerily.

"Hi, Mommy," Brianna says out of breath. She sounds happy.

"Hi, sweetie, I'm just checking in. You having fun?"

"Yes, Mommy. We carved a pumpkin last night and it had a big nose and a wart on its lip and Dad said it looked like my teacher, Ms. Crandall. Then we made a really pretty one and I told Dad that it looked like you."

"Oh, did you now?" Dani smiles. "Well, you have a good time. I'll see you on Monday night. Love you."

"Love you, too, Mom." And she's gone, just like that. Dani keeps the phone to her ear, listening to the dial tone as if to hold on to Brianna just a little bit longer. She hangs up, knowing her daughter is happy and safe. For the first time, it doesn't make her feel bitter. In fact, she feels strangely light.

Grabbing her bag, Dani gives Kate a nudge. "What?" Kate practically shouts.

"Oh my word, Katherine, are you asleep again? Up, up . . . No rest for the weary. We've got some serious shopping to do."

~

"Good morning, ladies. Where to?" Their driver looks like Gabriel Byrne if he had been born on Long Island and had a few more gray hairs. He is standing out front next to a shiny black sedan.

How about your place? "Saks would be great," Dani says instead. "I'm Dani," she babbles, "and this is Kate."

"Max Myers," he says, opening the car door with a flourish.

"Has anyone ever told you that you look a lot like Gabriel Byrne?" Dani asks.

He laughs. "I guess I've heard it once or twice. Who wants to be an overpaid movie star when you can sit in Manhattan traffic and breathe in exhaust for a living?"

Staring at Max's handsome profile from the backseat, Dani wonders how much limo drivers make and suddenly she is thinking of Guy. She can practically hear his voice as she stares out the window, watching the throngs of people on the sidewalks: "Call you tomorrow, Dee."

One evening together and he already has a nickname for her. Dani remembers his hand on hers. The way he smelled. The way he looked at her. Maybe fate has finally shown some mercy. *Danielle De Varen. It has a nice ring to it . . .*

"Earth to Dani," Kate says amused, shattering her reverie. "Come in, Dee Dee."

"Shhh. It's Dee, anyway, and I wasn't thinking about him . . . please."

"Thinking about who?" says Kate.

"No one."

"Uh huh . . ." She smiles.

Sometimes it is so annoying to have someone who knows you this well. Dani thinks. *OK, and strangely comforting, too.* Wasn't that what was always missing with Brian? She worked hard to keep up with his changing idea of who he wanted her to be: high-powered career woman, stay-at-home mom, ex-wife . . . Dani stares out the window of the car, watching the scenery.

Suddenly she sees a pink-and-black awning stretching out toward the curb. Her fashion radar goes on high alert. "Stop the car, please, Max."

Max expertly swings over to the curb.

"What are we doing?" Kate asks.

"I just read about this place," Dani answers. "It's a famous French boutique that's opened its first American store."

Dani hops out of the car and strides down the sidewalk, Kate right behind her. She pulls open the glass doors that are etched with a design resembling the Eiffel Tower above discreet black letters that read L'AMERICAIN LAIDY.

"Funny spelling," Dani comments over her shoulder as Kate hangs back.

Inside, the store is a vision of black enamel and watered pink silk. Dani runs her hands along a rack of leather jackets and skirts.

"*Bonjour.* May I be of assistance?"

An impossibly thin young woman appears at Dani's side. She's wearing tight trousers, killer stiletto boots and a low-cut shirt showing cleavage that Dani cannot believe is natural to her skinny frame. Her French accent sounds fake, too.

"I'm thinking about this skirt," Dani says.

The salesgirl's gaze travels from Dani's expensive haircut to her scuffed loafers and back up again. Dani knows she's assessing: Is she a spender?

She coolly appraises Dani's shoes. "Perhaps we can find something in your size."

Dani can tell she's decided they're not worth her time.

Kate wanders over with a pair of pants. "I really like these."

The salesgirl raises a perfectly groomed brow. "I don't think we cut them generously enough for you."

Kate turns beet red as her hands reflexively drop to her hips. Dani feels a surge of anger. *I will not let this little underfed wage slave ruin our day before it even starts.*

Kate begins inching toward the door.

Dani begins to follow her, then turns back to the girl. "Did you ever see *Pretty Woman*? Maybe on video? With Julia Roberts?"

The girl frowns. Dani can't tell whether she's trying to figure out if she's seen the movie or if the question has some other meaning.

"I've seen it."

"Remember the scene where she goes shopping in the ritzy boutique?"

The salesgirl's brows knit together again.

"You just think about it," Dani says, dropping the skirt back on to the rack and steering Kate out the door.

"Maybe we should just try a department store," Kate says.

"We're not trying just any old department store," Dani tells her. "We're going first class today—all the way."

They hop into the car.

"Next stop—Saks," Dani tells Max.

———

Dani and Kate sink into the plush upholstery as the car glides effortlessly through the traffic and soon comes to a stop at Saks Fifth Avenue's front entrance.

"I'll be here whenever you gals are ready," Max says, settling behind the wheel and unfolding a newspaper.

The crowd rushing by on Fifth Avenue flows around Dani and Kate as they stand and take in the huge windows lining the front of the store. Ultrachic mannequins dressed in evening gowns strike poses as if at an endless, glamorous party.

"Welcome to Saks, ladies." A handsome man in an impeccable dark suit with a tiny earphone tucked in his ear smiles in greeting as they step inside. Kate gawks but Dani looks right at home. The main floor is crowded with customers, moving from handbags, to scarves, to sunglasses, taking in the fabulous mix of accessories at each of the dark wood and glass counters. Although the store is busy, the atmosphere is hushed, refined.

A gorgeous dark-haired woman whom Dani recognizes as a film actress currently taking a break to do a Broadway show spritzes perfume on her wrist and sniffs approvingly. Grabbing Kate by the arm, Dani inches closer.

"Sample our newest exclusive perfume?" The girl behind the counter beckons them over to the counter. "It's called Bond New York. It's from the Creed perfume company and is available only here at Saks."

Dani elbows Kate. "Creed makes all the perfumes for the royal family," she whispers.

Kate picks up a bottle and breathes deeply. "What's this called?" she asks.

"New York Fling," the salesgirl says, spritzing the perfume on a thin strip of paper and handing it to Kate. "All of the perfumes are named with New York themes."

"Smell this, Dani," Kate says.

Dani takes a sniff and nods approvingly. "You should get it."

"Oh, I don't know." Kate fingers the bottle tentatively. "How much is it?"

"You buy it by the ounce," the salesgirl explains, "and then you can buy one of these totally adorable bottles to put it in. Perfume and the bottle will probably cost you somewhere around two hundred dollars depending on what you choose."

Kate sprays a little perfume on her wrist. "Let me think about it," she says, backing away from the counter.

Dani strides down the aisles, past the makeup counters, heading toward the elevators at the back of the store. She has no doubt where she is headed: the inner sanctum—the hidden jewel of the whole store. She is about halfway to shopping heaven when she realizes Kate is no longer beside her. Turning around, she sees her, planted in the middle of the floor, looking distressed.

"What's wrong? Am I moving too fast for you?" Dani backtracks and takes Kate by the arm. "Do you want to browse down here first? Go back and get that perfume, maybe? I mean, I thought we'd just get right to it and come back to accessories later if we had to, but if you want to take a look at some of these absurdly cute little handbags, then of course we can . . ."

Kate starts to fidget and then blurts out tensely. "OK, let me just say, we are just looking. We can have fun just looking. The hotel, the car—they're bad enough. This is not my money remember? I mean, not all of it. No one gives away a million dollars and even if they did, even if he's done this before, think of all the people who need it. I can give it to some charity, send it to Rwanda, at the very least start saving for college for the boys . . ."

"Hey, Katherine. What's wrong with it being a gift? A gift for *you*. Someone wants you to have it. If Honeywell had wanted the money to go to Rwanda, he would have sent it there. Besides, he probably already has. Look, if it doesn't feel right to you, you can give it back. But aren't we always talking about how we can never catch up, how we never get a break? Someone is giving you a break." Dani gives Kate's arm a gentle shake. "Take it. Kate. Listen to me. You may not see it this way, but you do need it. Trust me. Hell, I need it. We both do. Any mom could use this kind of a break—a little something for herself. So don't think of it as Honeywell's money, think of it as the Mommy Fund."

Dani can't tell if she's getting through to Kate. She half expects her to turn on her chipped boot heel and walk out. But Kate doesn't. Something in her face has changed.

"OK, but we're in this together. Remember, it's *our* money, *our* Mommy Fund," Kate says firmly.

"Er . . . OK." *Who am I to argue?* Dani thinks.

"So I don't know about you, but I need shoes," Kate continues. "I'll bet they'll have some real fancy Birkenstocks in this place."

"I am not sure if the word 'Birkenstock' has ever been uttered in here. As a matter of fact, say that again and I wouldn't be surprised if one of those security guys in the black suit and the earphones throws you out on the street. So, let's try and eliminate the B word from our vocabulary for the next forty-eight hours . . . And while we're at it, how about, 'Payless,' 'T.J. Maxx,' 'too expensive,' 'Andy will kill me,' 'I really shouldn't,' and 'when will I ever wear these?' Now, just follow me. Let's find you those new shoes."

~

On the fourth floor the elevator doors glide open and Dani bolts out. In the shoe department, she is drawn as if by magnetic force to a pair of slender silver sandals. As she turns them over in her hand, she spies a pair of light blue bejeweled ones. They are light as a feather. She begins to deliberate over which pair to select when she realizes that, for once, she doesn't have to choose. There is something so decadent, so unworldly about this that Dani has to catch her breath and savor the moment . . .

"I'll try both of these on in a nine, please."

Kate has latched on to a pair of knee-high alligator boots with fine pointy toes. "Do you have these in an 8½?"

The sales women disappear and reemerge with their requests along with a few ideas of their own. Before she knows it, Dani is surrounded by piles of boxes filled with the most fabulous shoes she's ever laid eyes on, much less squeezed her rather flat, square feet into. She and Kate make their way to the counter and stack their boxes in one pile. Kate slaps down her debit card without blinking an eye. Even Dani is impressed.

"Well, clearly, I now need to pull together an ensemble worthy of my alligator boots," Kate announces. "Where to?"

—

"Designer Collections," Kate reads as they glide down the escalator to the third floor. "You're not messing around here, are you?"

Dani breezes past the racks of gorgeous outfits, past the Blass and Celine, the Dior and the Lacroix without so much as a glance. Then she stops so abruptly that Kate bumps into her. "I'm getting ahead of myself," Dani mutters. Turning to Kate, she announces, "First a tutorial, then you'll be ready."

"Ready? Ready for what?" Kate looks mystified.

"To join the Club, of course."

Without any further explanation, Dani turns and heads back to where they first got off the elevators. Slowly and deliberately, she and Kate make their way around the circular sales floor. They linger over the designer labels, fingering each jacket and pair of suede pants as if they were their own creations. The names begin to roll off their tongues, Marc Jacobs, Dolce & Gabbana, Stella McCartney, Kors, Versace . . .

"I've never seen anything so beautiful," Kate says, pulling a Vera Wang evening gown off the rack.

Dani nods in satisfaction. "I think you're ready."

She gestures for Kate to follow and heads toward a small unmarked doorway, half hidden behind racks of gowns.

"Welcome to the Club," she says, as they step inside.

"Welcome to the Fifth Avenue Club." A tall redheaded woman stands up behind the antique writing desk just inside the doorway. "My name is Margaret, how can I help you today?"

"Total wardrobe makeover, Margaret," Dani says with a grin. "Casual to evening, shoes to bags."

"Of course, dear. You leave everything to me." Margaret smiles warmly as she escorts Dani and Kate to a room lined with mirrors. She gestures to the comfortable armchairs in the corner. Margaret nods and makes notes in a small leather-bound diary as Dani rattles off their sizes and some of her designer preferences. Then she marches off efficiently.

Within minutes, the first salesgirl hauls an armload of merchandise into the room and Dani and Kate get down to business. Kate preens in a Marc Jacobs brown suede jacket that sets off her new blonde highlights beautifully, Dani twirls in front of the mirrors, strutting in an ivory Gucci suit, glancing at her reflection over her shoulder. Dropping the suit on the chair, she slips into in a silver Versace evening gown with a chiffon skirt.

"You are not leaving here without that jacket," she tells Kate, who is still standing in front of the mirrors, apparently awestruck at the pulled-together woman who stares back.

"What about you?" Kate asks. "Are you taking the suit?"

"I love Gucci, but all that white makes me look more like a nurse at a very expensive clinic," Dani says as she checks out her rearview in slim black Kors trousers and a black tank. She holds a brocade Oscar de la Renta jacket up in front of her.

"If I thought I could squeeze my biceps into this baby . . ." She shrugs, and drops the jacket onto an increasingly high pile of clothes. A salesgirl slips into the dressing room.

"Made any decisions?" the girl asks.

"Everything on this one stays," Dani says, gesturing to one of the chairs piled high with outfits. "Everything on that one goes."

While one girl scoops up an armload of discarded clothes, another evaluates the remaining pile. "I'll be right back," she says. "Would you care for anything to drink while you wait?"

"That would be lovely," Dani says. As if by magic, a tray bearing sparkling water and lemon appears.

While Kate and Dani sit and sip, Margaret comes back into the room and arranges the remaining outfits on racks.

"Finished, ladies?" Margaret appears in the doorway.

"Just about." Dani turns to Kate. "OK, now pick your favorite outfit."

Kate pulls out a knee-length camel Valentino pencil skirt, a simple silk T-shirt and the Jacobs jacket.

"Now put them on."

"Again?"

"Trust me. It's a little trick I learned from Bebe."

Dani slips into a gorgeous navy wool Gucci suit. She feels like a movie star.

When the salesgirl comes back, Dani has her cut off the price tags. The girl carefully clips away the little pieces of paper then gathers up their old clothes, carrying them off to be folded and packed with the rest of their new purchases. Dani tosses Kate the box with the crocodile boots and slides her feet into a pair of new Chanel pumps.

Margaret and her staff bustle around packing up shoes and smoothing wrinkles out of outfits. It takes only a few minutes, and then Dani and Kate are left to stand in front of the dressing room mirrors, basking in their reflected chicness.

"So now we just walk out of here in these outfits?" Kate sounds stunned, like she can't believe it's allowed.

"Watch this." Dani strides out to the register and slaps down the cash card. Without even asking, the packages are whisked down to the street and handed off to loyal Max, who's waiting right outside the front door.

They pause by the jewelry counter on the way out.

"It's too bad that gorgeous jacket didn't fit you," Kate says.

"Well, if I were, in fact instead of in fantasy, a size 0, they would have just what I need. Sadly, the size 8 is gone. But, if memory serves, last month's *Vogue* had a gorgeous red Prada jacket that is just what I need to finish the outfit. So now it's all about the thrill of the hunt." Dani grins as the doorman holds the front doors open and they step out onto the sidewalk.

Max is waiting for them right where they left him, with the *New York Times* still propped up against the steering wheel. He gestures to the bags and boxes piled on the seat next to him.

"Looks like you've done well, ladies."

"Oh, we've barely started," Dani assures him.

"Better move this to the trunk then. Where next?"

"Bendel's, but one stop first," she says.

When Max pulls up in front of the pink-and-black awning again, Kate stares at Dani like she's crazy.

"*You* remember the *Pretty Woman* scene, don't you?"

A slow grin spreads across Kate's face as she follows Dani into the store.

The salesgirl appears to have lost another five pounds since the first time they were in the shop, but this time she hurries over to greet them at the door.

"May I help you, ladies?" It's clear she doesn't recognize them.

Kate and Dani have her gather up armloads of clothes and cart them back to the dressing room. They allow her to bring them little bottles of Perrier and crystal glasses garnished with lemon while they chat loudly about their recent purchases.

Then Dani wanders over to the accessories counter. She picks up the perfect pair of black movie-star sunglasses and lays them on the counter.

"I was in here before, do you remember?" she says innocently.

"Of course I remember you," the salesgirl fawns. "You bought the taffeta evening gown that showed off your fabulous collarbones."

"Actually, I was the one who asked you if you'd ever seen that movie, *Pretty Woman*."

"Oh, right, right." The girl is suddenly eager to please. "I did see it. I just *loved* it."

"This boutique is so small," Dani continues wickedly. "With such high-end merchandise. You must work on commission."

The salesgirl nods.

Dani watches, smiling slightly, as realization slowly spreads across the girl's perfect features.

"I don't think I want any of it," Kate announces, emerging from the dressing room. "Let's go drop some real money." Spinning on the heel of her new boots, she strides out the door.

"Sorry," Dani says to the stunned salesgirl.

She follows Kate out to the car where they exchange high fives. "We own this town, baby," she laughs.

Then it's off to Henri Bendel, where the spree continues as they try on hats that would make Audrey Hepburn green with envy. They cruise through the jewelry department. Dani settles on a beautiful silver ring with a large bezel-set aquamarine. Kate sifts through neatly stacked piles of cashmere sweaters in every color under the sun. There are pullovers from pink to puce and cardigans in crimson and caramel. Kate selects a pullover in a beautiful sage green that sets off her eyes. Dani digs out a deep periwinkle blue cardigan that is so soft it practically slips through her fingers. The fact that the sweater matches her new ring seals the deal. She glances at her watch. It's already almost one. As Kate is paying for their latest purchases, Dani discreetly sneaks off to check messages at the hotel. *Where is my damn cell phone when I need it?*

The Bendel staff, after witnessing the fairly impressive little spree in the jewelry and sweater departments, is only too willing to lend her their landline for a local call. She calls the front desk at the Plaza. Checks the room. Nothing.

Well, I suppose Guy's being a guy. Mr. Casual. Can't look too interested, you know.

As they leave the store, she spots a mobile phone store across the street.

"Kate, I have one more stop to make." Kate trots gamely along behind and stands next to her at the counter while Dani peruses the cell phone options.

"Hey, I thought you were going cold turkey," Kate says.

"Well, I think gradual withdrawal is the safer approach. You don't want to be around when the tremors and D.T.'s set in . . . I'll take the little red one."

She puts the plastic on the counter and it's done. Dani can breathe again. Rationally, she knows that Guy does not have any way of getting this number, nor does anyone else who might need to contact her; however, she suddenly feel enormously reassured by the presence of the little red gadget in her pocket.

As they walk back to the car, Kate lets out a squeal. She's pointing at an oversized poster of an attractive-looking, middle-aged woman with blonde hair, standing between a dead ringer for Burt Reynolds circa *Playgirl* 1977 (only properly clothed) and a heavyset woman with dreadlocks. The poster screams:

RECLAIM YOUR DREAMS
Saturday, October 17
at the Javits Center
with Dr. Mia, Dr. Bob, Una and a host of special guests
Meet Dr. Mia in person at the Barnes & Noble
at Union Square on Friday at 4 p.m.

"Dani, that's *today.* Dr. Mia's signing this afternoon. And, oh my God, the rest of them are all here tomorrow . . . Do you believe it?"

"Oh, lucky day . . ." Dani musters.

"Hey, it wouldn't hurt you, you know, to give them a chance . . . You said you liked that book I gave you."

"Yeah, yeah, it was OK in parts, I guess." *If you're into that sort of thing . . . which I'm not,* she silently adds.

Kate's eager face is beaming back at her. Dani softens. "You really want to go to this thing."

"I just can't believe they're in town . . . I mean what are the odds?" Kate is beside herself.

Pretty damn good, Dani thinks. *Far as I can tell they're always out peddling for a buck.*

"OK, OK, let's go to the signing. If I can't bear it, I can always catch up on some magazines or get a brownie at the café. But tell me you haven't lost focus."

"Did you hear that?" Kate asks.

For a split second Dani's afraid Kate is about to reveal that she has tapped into a direct psychic line to Dr. Mia herself. "What, I hear traffic. Hear what?"

"I hear a little red Prada jacket in size 8 calling your name. Don't they have a store somewhere else?"

"You make me so proud. Admit it, you did glance at that *Vogue* I gave you ... the one with that spread on the Prada store in the old Guggenheim Museum downtown."

"Yeah, maybe. What do you say? Let's grab a bite to eat and head ..." Kate bursts into a rousing rendition of Petula Clark's "Downtown." Sure, she only hits about 75 percent of the notes accurately, but still, it's unmistakable ... "*Where all the lights are bright, DOWNTOWN, Waiting for you tonight, DOWNTOWN ...*"

They dart between the traffic like two crazy people. Horns blare but they barely hear them over their laughter.

～

Max steers the car over to the curb on Broadway. "The street's blocked off ahead, so I can't get any closer," he says. "Sorry for the lack of door-to-door service."

Kate and Dani hop out onto the sidewalk in the middle of the block. "It's OK; the store's right on the corner," Dani says, gesturing.

"What's going on? It looks like a construction site around here," Kate says. The street is lined with nondescript beige trailers with thick black cables snaking between them.

"It's a shoot," Dani says. "You know, a movie or a TV show or something. These trailers are the dressing rooms for the stars."

"What stars?" Kate stares at the trailers wide-eyed.

"Let's find out." Dani walks over to the side of the trailer. When no one stops her, Kate tentatively follows.

Dani points at a cardboard sign on the windshield. "RW" is printed in block letters. Motioning to Kate to follow, she walks over to another trailer. The sign reads "KH."

"I have a pretty good idea," she tells Kate, who is still trailing behind her. "But here's how you confirm it."

A plain blue sedan is parked just beyond the trailers. Dani leans over the hood and reads the permit in the window. "Yep," she says, glancing around. "It's a shoot for the new Reese Witherspoon/Kate Hudson movie. I just read about it in Page Six. I wonder where the cameras are."

"Can we find them? Could we watch?" Kate doesn't care if she sounds like a total tourist. "How cool would that be?"

"Can I help you ladies?" A young guy in a tight black T-shirt with a walkie-talkie in one hand and a Polaroid camera draped around his neck comes up behind them.

"I hope so," Dani says confidently. "Where are they shooting right now?"

"In the Marc Jacobs store, around the corner on Mercer," he says immediately. "Come on, I'll take you over right now. You're just in time." He takes off with long strides. Kate and Dani exchange a puzzled look, but scurry to catch up.

"Who says New Yorkers are unfriendly?" Kate puffs, as she trots along in her new boots. "He's awfully nice."

"Here they are."

Kate and Dani come to a halt behind their escort who hands them off to an even younger woman, with long, honey-streaked blonde hair pulled back in a messy ponytail. She is dressed in olive cargo pants and a cropped white T-shirt. She is carrying a clipboard and has an official-looking badge hanging from a chain around her neck.

"You guys look great!" she says. "Very uptown. We won't even need to send you to wardrobe." She stares appraisingly at Kate, who begins to fidget nervously. "Is that a Marc Jacobs jacket?" the girl coos, reaching a hand out to touch the suede. "It's fabulous. I'm going to have to call the agency and thank the booker. She's *finally* sent me exactly what I asked for. The last two she sent over—they looked like they were escapees from a Britney Spears video. I don't know what she was thinking. I mean I *told* her I wanted some *older* ladies."

Dani clears her throat and the girl abruptly stops talking and becomes all business. "Well, let's get you two on the set," she says.

Kate's eyes widen. "What's she talking about?" she whispers to Dani.

"I think we've just become extras," Dani says.

"We can't just walk onto the set," Kate protests.

"Apparently we can." Dani smiles broadly, raising her eyebrows, and follows the woman as she walks toward the Marc Jacobs store. Dani can see bright lights and a knot of people inside the store. A crowd of pedestrians is gathered outside, peering into the windows.

Security guys with walkie-talkies hold the crowd back as Kate and Dani are whisked inside, past the onlookers. Dani can hear the buzz: *Who's that? What show have I seen her on before?*

"OK, let's have you two over here." The woman positions Kate and Dani next to each other on two X's marked on the floor with tape, next to a counter piled with handbags. A woman with a makeup bag comes over and begins dusting powder on Kate's face.

"Don't move from your marks. Just browse through the bags. You can pretend to talk, but no sound, all right?" She flips open a small radio clipped to her belt. "Ready on the set," she says.

Dani looks over, expecting to see Kate ready to hyperventilate. Instead Kate coolly strikes a pose as she picks up a light pink handbag.

The door swings open, and it's Dani's turn to have to feign composure as Reese Witherspoon and Kate Hudson stroll in.

"And . . . action." The group in the store falls silent as Reese and Kate enter the shop. They walk past Kate and Dani, who are pretending to have an animated conversation, and over to the shoes. After after a few lines, the director calls out again. "And . . . cut. Right, we got it. Let's clear this place out," he says.

The blonde girl appears again. "Thanks so much, that was great," she says, herding Kate and Dani back out the door. "Just find the AD and have him sign your vouchers on the way out."

Kate and Dani scamper back in the direction of the trailers as quickly as they can. Once they are out of sight of the crew and the with the clipboard, they stop and stare at each other in disbelief.

Kate loses it first. She grabs Dani by the shoulders and hops up and down with excitement. "I can't believe we just did that. Did you see how tiny Reese is? And Kate? I could have reached out and touched her. I mean, I wanted to ask for autographs, but really, how could I? Oh, no one is going to believe this!"

Dani doesn't even bother to act blasé. "That was so cool. I do believe we have officially arrived!"

Kate stops hopping up and down and grabs Dani by the arm. "Look!" she hisses.

Dani sees the door to one of the trailers swing open, and Reese

Witherspoon steps out onto the street, carrying a water bottle. She pauses to say something to the young guy in the black T-shirt who is walking past.

"Excuse me, excuse me, please!" Before Dani has a chance to ask her what she's doing, Kate has crossed the street and is approaching the star.

"Hi, um, hi," Kate babbles. "We were just in the scene with you back there and, well, I was wondering, could we get our picture taken with you?" Kate turns to the guy in the black T-shirt and points at the camera in his hand.

Dani can actually feel the red creep up into her face. "Cool, Kate," she mutters. "Very cool."

Reese smiles and nods, gesturing for Dani to come stand next to her as Kate stands on the other side and grins like a maniac at the camera.

"Matt is going to *die*," Kate exclaims, gleefully.

"He is, isn't he?" Dani is grinning now as she steps up next to Reese.

"Smile," the young guy says, and the camera flashes. He hands Kate the undeveloped photograph and heads off.

"Thank you so much," Dani says, trying to act like she runs into movie stars every day.

Kate comes over and shakes Reese's hand. "I just want to tell you– I'm just in awe of what you do . . . having two children–I have two kids, too–but you have this whole huge career and, well, wow!" Kate's expression is dead serious. "How do you do it?" she asks, sincerely wanting to know.

The actress smiles gracefully. "It's a lot of work, isn't it?" she says to Kate. "But even when it's hard, well, I just love what I do. Your kids need you to be happy, don't you think?"

"Reese?" The woman with the clipboard is walking toward them, and Dani remembers that they are nothing more than gate-crashers. She takes Kate's arm. "Thanks again for your time," she says to Reese as she pulls Kate along behind her and heads in the opposite direction.

They duck around the corner and lean against a wall. They stare at the Polaroid. A minute passes, then another, as their images come into focus. Neither says a word. And then they burst into laughter. They laugh until Kate is holding her stomach and Dani has tears streaming from her eyes. Kate shakes her head in disbelief. "How do we top *that?*" she manages to gasp out.

Dani wipes the tears from her eyes. "Nothing I like better than a challenge," she declares.

~

The Prada store is beyond anything Dani has ever seen in the magazines. The clothing hangs in midair, suspended on invisible wires from the ceiling. Dresses, separates, suits, coats, all float in space as if dozens of incredibly well-dressed models had vaporized, leaving only their gravity-defying clothes behind. In the center of the cavernous space is a large, swooping wooden floor that slopes at a forty-five-degree angle twenty feet down. Perched at various points along the incline are the most exquisite shoes she has ever seen (with the possible exception of her new Manolos). She is standing in the center of the store, taking it all in, when Kate sidles up beside her.

"Do you think a size 6 would work?" Kate holds up the red jacket.

"Maybe. If it comes with a personal trainer," she says thoughtfully.

"Hmmm . . ." Kate says, scooting away. Dani watches her chatting with a sales person who then glides silently off into the great beyond that is the back of the store.

"They're going to see if they have your size." Kate's voice is hushed as she walks back.

"Why are you whispering?" Dani whispers as loudly as she possibly can. But she understands. The place has an undeniable air of reverence to it, as if you're standing in a Cathedral to the Great Fashion Designer in the Sky. And, in a way, you are. Only he's not a he, and she's more likely to be jetting around Milan than Mount Olympus. Still, it's starting to remind her of sitting in synagogue as a little girl. The quieter everyone became, the more precise the rabbi's singing, the more irresistible the urge became to shout *Praise the baby Jesus, hallelujah* or to do a handstand in the center aisle. Of course, she never did.

Lost in thought, she wanders along the smooth wooden floors un-

til she is standing at the top of the slope. A security guard eyes her suspiciously. And then something comes over her. She lets out a big yelp
and plops down on her behind. The pants of her suit and the back of
the jacket are smooth and take to the highly polished wood much better than she might have imagined. With her feet in the air, she slides
full speed down the incline, her arms wrapped around her legs. She is
flying until she lands with a bit of a thump at the bottom. Miraculously, she's missed the entire row of shoes along the way with the exception of a cute little pair of gray flats at the bottom.

The startled saleswoman suddenly appears, accompanied by the
burly guard.

"Do you have these in a size 9?" Dani manages, glancing up at her.
"And while you're at it, how about a pair of those black trousers, two
of those adorable skinny suits, that print dress over there and that
blouse in the gray and in the white. I'm a size 8 . . ."

The saleswoman stares at her with a look somewhere between fear
and respect, then takes the shoe from her hand and scurries off as
if she just remembered something. As Dani makes her way back to
the upper level, Kate doubles over with laughter and, Dani suspects,
horror.

"Are you OK? I mean have you lost your mind? I mean both," Kate
gasps.

"Yes, both."

In a flash, the size 8 red jacket has appeared, along with all the
other items. Dani leaves with the jacket and the cute gray shoes, and
a new suit that at least Matt will appreciate. Kate scores a great pair of
flat black ankle boots. Handing the bags off to Max, they head back
uptown to Barnes & Noble.

They have to fight their way through a crush of people even before
they get to the third floor where the signing is being held. It's three
thirty and the reading starts in a half hour. Kate buys Dr. Mia's latest
tome, something called *Architect of Your Dreams*. Dani's amazed she
doesn't have it already. Leaving Kate to score seats, Dani heads to the
second floor for a much-needed latte and to check out the pastries—
and OK, yes, she needs to check messages. She's already squeezed in
a few quiet moments over the course of the day with her new cell

phone friend, Little Red and still, nothing. *Maybe he's waiting for dinnertime to call. Of course, Guy assumes that we will be out of the room all day . . . Why bother to try, right?*

"Messages for room 351, please. No messages? Hmmm . . . OK, thanks."

By the time she gets back upstairs, it's nearly four. She searches the crowd for Kate, who has somehow positioned herself in the third row, directly in front of the podium. Dani starts to slink back toward the stairs but Kate spots her and motions to the seat next to her, the one with her coat thrown over it. Dani reluctantly takes her place in the audience. *OK, there's no escape.* She resigns herself to her fate as Dr. Mia steps up to the stage. *The things you do for your friends*, she thinks, glancing over at Kate, whose face is flushed and rapt. But somehow, even with Dr. Mia droning in her ear, there's no place that Dani would rather be.

Chapter Nine

Back in the Oak Bar, Kate absentmindedly stirs the cocktail straw in the vodka and cranberry in front of her. Dr. Mia's words are still floating through her head: *Each and every one of us can build a life in the image of our dreams, but we must first create a blueprint* . . . Dr. Mia was incredible, even more dynamic in person.

Kate has changed into her new green cashmere sweater, and her brown suede Marc Jacobs coat is tossed oh-so-casually over the back of the oversized velvet chair. Dani is wearing her red Prada jacket and the black Michael Kors trousers. She's distractedly nursing a gin and tonic.

"So, you have to admit that Dr. Mia was pretty amazing," Kate says. "I mean, she is so charismatic. I can't wait to dive into her new book."

"Yeah, who do you think does her hair? It's really fantastic."

"I see you really plumbed the depths of the reading."

"No, no, I have to admit, she made some good points. The part about being the architect of your own life instead of inhabiting what's been constructed for you . . . that's true. I mean that's what I tried to do with Brian. It doesn't work. But I'd like to see what kind of castle Guy could show me . . . Kate, why hasn't he called? OK, forget I said that. We're here for fun, right? Who needs a man?" Even as the words spill out of her friend's mouth, Kate can see Dani fingering the cell phone in her jacket pocket. She wonders how many times Dani has checked in for messages today. Dani thinks she's being discreet but Kate is beginning to get concerned.

"I just wish the line wasn't so long. I'd have loved to get the book signed but an hour wait is pretty insane. Hey, mind if I use your phone for a second? I should check in on my boys."

Dani hands over the phone, which feels warm and slightly sweaty. Kate takes it into the ladies' room. She dials, and on the fourth ring someone picks up. She hears the receiver tumble to the floor; there's a brief silence, then a low rumble and for a second, heavy breathing on the other end.

"Hello, Thompson residence, Henry speaking." Her son's voice half-squeaks into the receiver.

"Well, hello there, Mr. Thompson," Kate says, badly disguising her voice. "How much are you paying for your long-distance service?"

"Uh, I'll get my dad . . . hold please."

"Henry, hey, Henry it's me, Mommy!"

There's a short sniffle and a laugh. "Hi, Mom. Where are you? When are you coming home? Dad's making French toast for dinner."

"Are you guys having fun? How was your soccer game?"

"Good. I got a goal . . . hey, Charlie, that's my lunchbox! You can't put your crayons in there . . ." The phone thuds to the floor once again.

"Hello?" Andy's voice comes on the line.

"Hey, honey. Sounds like you have everything under control there."

"Naturally. How about you? You having a good time? You know, mysterious beauty treatments, shopping sprees, hitting the bars, dancing on tabletops–whatever it is you girls do when men aren't around."

Kate cringes and forces a laugh.

"You guessed it! Hey, I heard Dr. Mia speak this afternoon. She's in town for a reading at Barnes & Noble. She was really wonderful. I picked up her new book. We're just hanging out at the hotel now. Maybe we'll grab some dinner. Just wanted to say hi and I miss you guys." Just then there is a loud crash and Charlie starts to cry in the background. "Those are my crayons!"

"Uh, honey, I need to go referee . . . They never stop. I haven't had a moment to myself all day. Maybe we can talk later?"

"OK, bye, sweetie. Kiss the boys for me. Love you . . ."

"Love you, too." *Click.*

Looking up, Kate notices a well-dressed, chic-looking blonde staring at her and it takes her a second to realize she's looking into a mirror. She straightens her sweater, combs her hair with her fingers and heads back to Dani.

As she rounds the corner leading back into the bar, Kate hears a familiar voice. At first she can't place it, then it hits her. Sure enough, seated on a banquette, surrounded by two men in dark suits and a woman wearing a light blue suit, is Dr. Mia herself. Her short blonde hair is cut in a style that is both practical and flattering. Kate stumbles for a second, then makes her way back to Dani. She can feel herself beginning to sweat in her new sweater.

Dani is motioning wildly in the direction of Dr. Mia's group, mouthing something unintelligible. As Kate takes her seat, Dani whispers, "It's her. Right there . . ."

"Shhh . . . I know, I know. Maybe they're staying here. They have that all-day seminar tomorrow at the Javits Center"

"You know you've got to do it," says Dani.

"Do what?" Kate says, slurping her drink.

"You've got to introduce yourself, get her autograph. This is the chance of a lifetime."

"I can't, Dani. It's rude. She's trying to get a little downtime. I couldn't."

"Hey, if you want a little downtime, you don't take guys in power suits to the Oak Bar at the Plaza . . . Come on. She'll be flattered. How many fans have memorized all forty of her books and can quote them by page and paragraph?"

"She has three books, and I just got her new one."

"Just a quick, *Hi, I love your work.* They live for that crap. If she were the kind of guru who wanted peace and quiet, she'd be meditating in some cave in Bhutan, not playing the Javits Center. Come on. You'll kick yourself tomorrow if you don't do it. What does Dr. Mia say? *No dream reveals itself without the potential to make it a reality.*"

She's not sure if it's the vodka, the stylish new outfit, the fact that tonight she is not eating overdone French toast for dinner or her amazement that Dani has actually quoted the good doctor correctly, but whatever the reason, all at once Kate feels herself rising from her seat in her alligator boots and, on autopilot, heading for Dr. Mia's table.

As she approaches the table, she realizes that one of the two men sitting with Dr. Mia is Dr. Bob, the Burt Reynolds look-alike. She has one of his books, *The Lost Art of Listening: Why Men and Women Don't Hear Each Other.* But when she got to the part where Dr. Bob claimed that men are natural-born listeners because, since the Stone Age, as hunters, they've been hardwired to detect even the slightest sounds, she had to put the book down.

There is a brief lull in the conversation as she approaches on Dr. Mia's left. Dr. Bob glances up at her and smiles broadly as Dr. Mia turns her head.

Kate extends her hand. "I apologize for interrupting, but I just wanted to say that I am a big fan of your work. I loved your reading this afternoon. Your new book is wonderful. I think it's truly ground-breaking."

Dr. Mia takes Kate's hand in hers. "How kind of you. Really! You like the new book? Because my agent here," she gestures to the tall, thin man in geometric eyeglasses sitting to her right, "was just saying that he thought I needed to head in a new direction."

"Mia, I said no such thing." The man runs his hand over his cropped hair. "I simply meant that if you expanded your message to the work-place, you might bring in a whole new crowd."

"Well, Mel, I happen to like my crowd." She turns to Kate. "Thank you for your kind words. And your name is?"

"Kate Thompson."

"Very nice to meet you, Kate Thompson. Let me ask you, do you feel that a book on building your dreams in the workplace is a good idea?"

Flashing a look at Mr. Power Agent, Kate hesitates for a moment, then continues anyway. "Well, to be honest, it seems that the princi-ples that you introduce in your books inherently apply to all spheres of our lives. I guess I always saw your approach as more holistic. You talk about not dividing ourselves, about how we should draw our own map of where we want to be and not let external forces define us. So a workplace book seems at best redundant and, at worst, contradictory." *Did I just say that?* she thinks.

Dr. Mia chuckles and breaks into a big smile, "Well said. Don't you think, Mel?"

Mel looks none too pleased but manages a faint smile. Kate shifts her weight to her other foot.

"Well, very nice meeting you . . ." she doesn't want to take up any more of their time or further irritate Mr. Agent Man.

"You too, Kate. Will you be coming tomorrow to the Javits Center?"

"Well, actually I haven't had a chance to pick up tickets yet, but I will certainly try."

Dr. Mia motions to her agent. "Will you please hand me a couple of those passes, Mel?" And then, turning to Kate, "It would be our pleasure to have you as our guest."

Kate somehow stammers out a thank-you and is barely able to restrain herself from breaking into a jig on her way back to the table.

Dani looks like she's about to burst with excitement. "Oh my God, Kate. You've made me so proud. Look at you chatting Dr. Mia up. What did they say? Tell me everything."

"What would you say if I told you that, tomorrow, we will be the personal guests of Dr. Mia at her seminar at the Javits Center?!"

"Uh, shoot me now?"

Kate glares at her.

"OK, I have to admit that's pretty cool," Dani tries again.

Kate fills her in on the conversation, reciting word for word her exchange with Dr. Mia and Mr. Agent Man. Dani beams. "You're going to have Dr. Mia giving Mr. Agent Man the heave-ho and hiring you."

"Yeah, right." But she can't stop smiling. "What do you say we get some dinner? I'm starved."

"Me too," says Dani. "Hey, mind if I just run up to the room quickly before we head out?"

"Sure, no problem."

They move through the crowds of finely dressed couples and tall, thin women, so young they almost look as though they're playing dress-up. Back in the room, Dani inspects the phone, turns it upside down. Kate hears her calling the front desk, asking if they've had any trouble with their voice-mail system.

"Oh, OK, sure. Well, if a gentleman by the name of Guy De Varen calls for Danielle Strauss, would you mind giving out this number? Oh, OK, but if he *does* give his name . . . yes, thank you so much." Dani is now stretched out on the bed and looks more than a bit troubled.

"Kate, why don't you go ahead without me. I just need to lie down for a bit. Pick a restaurant and I'll meet you there in a little bit, OK? I'm suddenly really tired." Dani glances in Kate's direction but won't look her in the eye.

"You want me to go to the restaurant without you?"

Silence.

"You're so tired that you want to stay in the hotel room on Friday night?"

"Yep." Dani rolls over on her side, leaving Kate to stare at her back.

"OK, Dani. I didn't want to say this but I will. If you need to rest, that's fine. But if this is about sitting around the hotel room waiting for some guy Guy to call, I'm not going for it. We have the whole city at our feet. The Four Seasons, Cirque du Soleil, you name it, we can eat there."

"Unless you intend to balance your entrée on the heads of lithe dancers swirling scarves, I think you mean Le Cirque."

"Whatever, you know what I mean. Sweetie, you barely know him. Are you going to let some guy you just met keep you from having fun, from doing what you want to do?"

"I am doing what I want to do," Dani says unconvincingly.

"This is really what you want to do?"

"Yep."

"Let me ask you this. What would Bessie do?" Kate asks, pulling out all the stops.

"Bessie?"

"Bessie Smith, the blues singer you told me about. Strong, independent, doesn't let anyone hold her back, or tell her who to be? Do you honestly think someone like Bessie Smith would be sitting around a hotel room on a Friday night waiting for the phone to ring?"

Dani doesn't say anything for some time, then rolls over and looks up at her.

"Ouch. Shameless. I didn't know you had it in you. OK, OK, I admit it. I'm becoming one of those pathetic women who blow off their girlfriends and their lives for some stupid guy. Well, when you put it that way . . ." She gets up off of the bed, smoothing down her hair. "Hey, throw me my lucky Prada jacket and let's go get something to eat."

~

They decide to just grab a quick dinner at the Plaza Bistro. When they finish, they walk outside to get a cab. The Plaza lights illuminate the red-carpeted stairs and the street beyond as though it were midday. Taxis snake around the hotel driveway as people on foot dodge between them, unconcerned. A cab stops and a bellhop in a gray wool overcoat with gold piping opens the door for another couple. An overweight teenage girl slumps behind them. The woman, who looks to be in her late forties, is draped in a flowing black gown with spaghetti straps; a wrap barely covers her slender white shoulders. The teenager has black bobbed hair streaked with a slender stripe of magenta and is wearing a long black jacket and a protest of scuffed black Army boots. The man, in a perfectly tailored tux, slips the bellhop a bill, and the teenager rolls her eyes and reluctantly slides into the backseat next to them, closes the door and the cab pulls away.

Another taxi appears and Kate hands a bill to the doorman and jumps in next to Dani.

"Where to?" Dani asks.

"I don't know. This is your town. I'm up for anything."

"Uh . . . Let's see, I know—126th and Amsterdam, please," Dani says through the cab's glass-paneled divider.

"Louie's, eh?" asks the driver, looking pleased. He is a clean-cut young man with dark hair and large almond-shaped eyes.

"You know it?" Dani asks.

"Sure, I know it. You know the blues, you know Louie's Rhythm and Blues Café." He glances into the rearview mirror.

"Are you a musician?" Kate asks.

"No, I'm a graduate student–physics–with an unofficial minor in Muddy Waters."

She ponders that for a moment. "You're involved in environmental protection?"

"Excuse me?" the driver asks.

"Polluted river systems . . ."

The cabdriver is suddenly laughing hard, but not as hard as Dani.

"Kate, please tell me you've heard of Muddy Waters, the blues musician," Dani says when she catches her breath.

Kate looks at her blankly but in a second she is laughing, too.

"To Louie's," Dani says loudly, "and not a moment too soon!"

They cruise up the West Side of Manhattan, slowing for traffic lights that seem to anticipate their arrival, changing from yellow to red as they approach. There are fewer cars heading in this direction. Kate looks out the window, taking in the shifting scene. Long stretch limos in white and black wait lazily outside glamorous-looking restaurants, and nightclubs buzz behind red-velvet ropes manned by big-chested bouncers.

Eventually the cab pulls up to the curb, and as soon as the door swings open, Kate can hear the thump of a bass and drums and a muffled guitar. The exterior of the club is unassuming, with large darkened windows and a couple of tattered posters of outdated shows. Dani pays the driver, giving him an extra large tip, and gets out. People are gathered in small clusters outside, smoking cigarettes. At the door, an elderly gentleman sitting on a high stool collects five dollars from each of them.

"Who's playing tonight?" Dani asks.

"Herb Walker and the Crescent City All-Stars."

"Who's that?" Kate whispers.

"I have no idea," Dani says. "Let's find out. Want a beer?"

"Oh, yeah."

Dani buys a couple of chilled Rolling Rocks and they position themselves by the bar. The place is packed. There are small tables near the stage that are full, and the rest of the crowd is lined up behind them. The stage is completely overrun by the five-man band. Herb Walker, the lead singer and guitarist, looks to be in his fifties. He's at least six foot four with dark, weathered skin and a build resembling his mike stand. He's wearing a ten-gallon hat with a speckled feather on one side that shadows his face. He is the epitome of cool. He has a rich baritone that appears to be in deep conversation with his electric guitar. Kate watches, rapt. Herb is working on a slow groove about the sky crying, and the band ambles along behind him. She looks over at Dani who is swaying beside her, the neck of her beer bottle touching her lower lip, mouthing the words to the song. Herb finishes the number to a thunderous round of applause.

"That last one was from the late great Elmore James." He motions to his band, and they rock headlong into the next tune. Dani looks over at Kate. "What do you think?" Her face is flushed.

"It's great. Wow. You can feel the earth move." Dani links her arm through Kate's and they sway together as Herb tells them, "*I'm ready, ready as anybody can be.*" They are hip checking and then Dani steps out and twirls effortlessly under Kate's arm in the small space. "*. . . Takes a whole lot of loving to make me feel good!*" she sings along with Herb. The song ends and Kate buys two more beers. As the set wraps up she notice a couple collecting their coats at a table near the front, and makes a dash for it. Dani catches up with her just as she settles into her seat.

"Well done. I think that move could qualify you as an honorary New Yorker," Dani says. Music begins to play over the sound system as the last band member leaves the stage.

"They'll be back soon. Looks like that's just the first set. This is great, isn't it? We so needed this," Dani says. She grabs Kate's hand and gives it a squeeze. "Thanks, Kate."

"Hey, thank Honeywell, don't thank me. Gerry is bankrolling this fantasy."

"No, that's not what I mean. Thanks for being my friend. I don't think I've ever actually said that to you. I really don't know what I'd do without you."

She squeezes Dani's hand back. "Probably buy a pair of cowboy boots and go trotting off after some smooth-talking, fancy rancher."

"Hey, I'm not that bad, am I? Anyway, you have to admit, Guy's a catch. I mean, if you're looking for that sort of thing—which, incidentally, I am not. If you'll recall, this is a girls' night out."

"Just remember, Dani, *you* are a catch." Kate raises her beer. "To friendship."

"I'll drink to that," Dani says and guzzles the last third of her beer. She hops up, returns with another round, and places two small shot glasses beside the beer.

"What are these?"

"Kamikaze shots."

"What, are we in high school? . . . How about a game of quarters while we're at it?" Kate asks, the shot glass already on her lip. The smooth lime liquid burns her throat. She takes a swig of beer and slams the bottle on the table. Dani follows suit.

"Wow, impressive, Kate. I remember the first time I met you, I pegged you for a lightweight. Boy, was I wrong. Lurking beneath that kind and gentle exterior is a powerhouse."

"Funny, 'cause when I first met you, I thought you were some uptight New York City lawyer who thought anyone who wasn't as cynical as you were was a lightweight." They look at each other and crack up.

They're still laughing when Kate notices a small, stout bearded man wearing a sombrero and a stern expression standing just a few feet away, staring in their direction. As he catches Kate's eye, he gives her a nod and a big wink. Kate looks at Dani who just shrugs.

"Oh, no," Kate mutters as Sombrero Man toddles over. He stops a foot away from their table, glances at Dani, and then looks back to Kate. For a second, Kate feels a rush of sympathy: *Must be some lonely guy just looking for a little friendly conversation*, she's thinking, when he opens his mouth,

"Hey, ladies, I've been watching you." He fixes his gaze on Kate, then his attention drops to her bustline. "And I got to tell you, that is one *sweet rack of nasties*!"

Kate looks at Dani in horror, covering her mouth with her hand, before bursting into uncontrollable laughter. Just then, one of the burly bouncers grabs the man's arm and says, "C'mon, Pops, I told you you've got to be moving along. You can't be bothering the customers."

"I'd sure like to get my *mitts* on *those* fun bags!" Pops shouts as he's hauled away.

"Gee, and I think *I* have trouble hooking up," Dani says.

———

In a few minutes, the All-Stars take the stage again. Herb glides into place and slings his guitar over his shoulder. He launches into the first number, a familiar R&B tune that Kate can't quite place. Sweat is gathering on Herb's forehead under the hat and the bright lights. His hands move fluidly over the strings as he howls out the song. When Kate glances over at Dani, she sees that Dani is quietly singing along. Herb looks down at their table and when he sees Dani's lips moving to every word, he flashes her a big smile. When the number is over, Dani and Kate applaud furiously. The band plays a couple more numbers, varying the tempo from a fast and rocking swing beat to a slow sensual ballad. Dani has her gaze fixed on Herb, who intermittently looks down at her and shoots her a quick grin. While they are playing a song about St. Louis in a nod to their host, Louie of Louie's Rhythm and Blues, Dani leans over and says to Kate excitedly, "This is a Bessie song, Kate," and then she lets out a loud whoop.

Herb looks out at the audience during the bridge and says, "Seems we have some Bessie Smith fans here tonight!" Dani beams. The band closes and Dani jumps to her feet with applause. As the clapping dies down, someone at the back of the bar shouts, "Marvin Gaye!"

"What's that?" Herb says leaning into the mike and looking out over the crowd, shielding his face from the spotlight with his hand.

"Marvin GAYE!" the disembodied voice shouts again.

"Oh, Mr. Gaye! I think we may know one or two of his. Yes, I believe we do, don't we boys?" Herb turns and says something to the band. The band strikes up a few opening chords and Dani lets out a wolf whistle. Herb smiles at her again and then leans back into the mike.

"Ain't no mountain high enough . . ."

Dani is swaying and singing along when Herbie stops midverse and stares down at her. "You know folks, it occurs to me," Herb says now, looking up at the audience as the band softly jams behind him, "Marvin couldn't sing this song without Tammi Terrell. And that's got me wondering . . . I'm asking myself, where's *my* Tammi?" He then looks down at Dani, "What do you say? I *know* you know the words . . . and I could use a little help up here."

With that, he reaches out for Dani's hand. She hesitates for a second but then lets Herb pull her onto the stage. It happens so quickly Kate can't quite believe it, but there's Dani, in her new high heels, squinting into the bright lights as a couple of catcalls come from the crowd.

Herb raises his hand behind him and the band stops. "Now let's try it again and do it *right*." The intro plays and Herb and Dani lean into the mike, their noses inches apart. Herb starts singing but this time a glorious, rich alto floats over his bass as their voices break into perfect harmony, *"Ain't no. . . ."*

Kate can't believe what she's hearing. The voice coming through the speakers is much huskier and more resonant than Dani's speaking voice. It's gorgeous. Dani's eyes are closed and she is gripping the mike.

Herbie laughs as Dani finishes the chorus and motions to her, "Take it." Dani gives Herb a nod, then cocks a hip and points a finger at Kate. Kate smiles as Dani nails the next verse, telling her that she can call her, no matter where she is, no matter how far.

Kate has one hand over her open mouth. Dani is doing her best teen idol strut as she slowly nods her head, promising she'll be there in a hurry.

Dani pauses at the end of the verse, and the audience explodes. Kate's eyes are getting wet. Herb is laughing with one slim hand on his stomach and says, "Hey, I found my Tammi, all right!" The crowd erupts again. "I think we have us a professional here!"

Herb and Dani move through the number as if they'd been on tour together for the past decade, trading lines and exchanging looks. Dani then glances back at Kate, reminding her that if she ever falls short of her desires:

> *"Life holds for you one guarantee,*
> *You will always have me."*

Kate has both hands on her red cheeks. Herb chimes in and they move into the final chorus.

"*Ain't no. . . ,*" sing Herb and Dani, eyes closed.

"*Ow!*" comes a woman's voice from just beyond the stage. Dani looks down and Kate has a fist over her head.

"*I'LL SAY IT AGAIN!*" shouts Kate, slightly off-key but nonetheless clearly working off a post–Marvin/Tammi, Diana Ross and the Supremes interpretation. Next thing she knows, she's being hauled onstage with Herb and Dani. Dani locks an arm around Kate and they are swaying together singing the chorus.

"*Ahhh . . . aaa AAA aa . . .*" A loud moaning sound can be heard through the mike behind Dani and Herb's seamless harmony, a sound not unlike an underwater recording of a whale mating call.

It is Kate. Her eyes are wide as she sings along. "*Ahhh . . . aaa AAA . . . aa . . .*"

She then breaks free from Dani and starts shimmying to the chorus. The band goes into a big finish and the crowd goes nuts. Dani and Kate have their arms around one another again and Herb joins them. The three take a bow. When Kate steps aside and extends a hand in the direction of Herb and Dani, the response is nearly deafening. The crowd is still clapping and screaming as Dani and Kate slip back into their seats. Herb leans over toward Dani from the stage. "What's your name, darling?"

"Dani, Dani Strauss . . ." Dani says, suddenly looking a bit shy. She then turns toward Kate, ". . . and this is Kate Thompson."

"Ms. Dani Strauss, folks, and Ms. Thompson," Herb says, to more applause, as he returns to collect his guitar.

"Hey, thanks for the backup," Dani says, laughing.

"I didn't know you could sing like that." Kate is truly bewildered.

Dani smiles. "I never really sing in front of anyone. I just sort of sing along to records."

"Well, clearly you should. You were awesome."

The band finishes out the set and Herb stops and leans over again to give Dani a big kiss on the cheek before he walks off.

Kate and Dani step outside into the cool night air. A cab appears immediately.

"The Plaza," Kate says, and they're heading back downtown.

—

Dani slides the key card into the door of their hotel room and steps inside with Kate right behind her. The effects of beer and the Kamikaze shot have worn off and have been replaced with utter fatigue.

Dani throws herself onto the bed, then moves to where the phone sits on the nightstand. She picks up the receiver, puts it down in the cradle. She picks it up again, presses the release button repeatedly with her index finger, and places it back in the cradle. She picks up the receiver.

"Rain Man, what are you doing?" Kate asks.

"Just checking messages," Dani says, keeping her back turned.

"Doesn't look like there are any. The light's not on."

"Yep, I know. Wondered if the phone was maybe off the hook or something," Dani says and Kate hears her voice fall. "I'm going to go wash up."

"OK, diva. I will too, if I can ever haul my body off this bed." And that's the last thing Kate remembers until she wakes up at 3 a.m., still fully clothed. She changes into her pajamas, washes up and slips back into bed.

Chapter Ten

"Ain't no mountain high enough
Ooo ooooh ooo . . ."

Kate is sitting by the window in an armchair, flipping through a newspaper and singing at a slightly elevated volume that clearly implies Dani should be awake already.

Dani responds, rolling over and forcing her eyes open. *I've got to get up, if only to stop her from mangling one of my favorite tunes.* She can smell coffee and Kate's pulled the drapes back, letting the sun wash over the gilded furniture and lush carpeting.

"Good morning, diva."

"Mmummph . . . coffee?"

"The reviews are fabulous, darling." Kate flips another page of the paper. "Listen to this: New England mom steals show at Harlem rhythm and blues bar. Talent scouts throughout Manhattan are hunting for the mystery Cinderella who enchanted the ballroom on 126th Street, then vanished into the night."

"What? Give me that!" She snatches the paper out of Kate's hand and frantically scans the type.

From behind the paper she hears Kate snorting with laughter.

"It's not nice to tease a diva before she's had her coffee," she says, lowering the paper and trying to look fierce.

"Well, it should be in there," Kate says adamantly. "You can quit that ol' day job anytime you want. You were amazing, not to mention drop-dead sexy. I think every man in the place wanted you by the time you finished."

"I'll assume that as resident phone fascist you didn't bother giving my number out to any of them?" Dani's tone is not as light as she'd heard it in her head. Kate's smile fades, replaced by a familiar anxious look.

"You're not still upset about the pep talk last night, are you?"

"I'm not, Kate. Honestly. I was trying to be funny. Which I should never try to do before I have my caffeine fix." She pours a cup of coffee. "So what's on tap for today?"

"Self-improvement." Kate's grin is back and she bounces slightly on the chair.

"The seminar." Dani tries not to roll her eyes.

"Yes. You're coming and you're going to like it."

"It's not until after lunch, right?"

"Well it's all day, but Dr. Mia isn't speaking until the afternoon . . ." Dani breathes a sigh of relief.

"Still, there are a lot of other great speakers, and I'm sure we probably *could* spend the whole day there," Kate finishes.

"Mmmm," Dani says. "Too much self-awareness might be a shock to my system. How about we do a little something this a.m. and just ease into the part of the day where I make myself and the world a better place?"

Dani pulls the weekend section out of the paper and spreads it out on the bed. "Now let me see . . . Broadway show? Nope; matinee won't be finished in time for Dr. Mia's talk." She makes a big show of really caring about that one. Kate comes over to stand next to her and peers over her shoulder at the paper.

"Jazz brunch?" Dani continues. "Been there. Done that."

"What about a museum?" Kate asks.

Bingo! I've drawn her in, Dani thinks. Spared the morning of psychic makeovers, she scans the pages with new confidence.

"Maybe something with a little more action," Dani mutters, running her finger down the column of newsprint. Suddenly her heart stops beating.

Viewing of paintings by nineteenth-century American and European landscape artists. Auction to follow Sunday at 3:00 p.m.

She can hear Guy's low sexy drawl in her head: *"And for fun I collect nineteenth-century landscapes of the American West. They're perfect for the ranch in Texas."*

There's a hammering in her ears and she takes a long, slow breath. *What are the chances? It doesn't matter. If there's even the slimmest chance I'll see him again I've got to grab it.*

"Aha! Here we go. Sotheby's. Just the thing," Dani says casually.

"Sotheby's?"

"The auction house, Kate. Really, you're the art history major. They're having a morning viewing of nineteenth-century landscape paintings."

"Well, it was just a minor, but it would be fun to see what I remember. But won't you be bored to tears? Wouldn't you rather go shopping or something?"

Well, normally I would. But since I'm counting on running into the man of my dreams there, the mind-numbing boredom of staring at paintings of cows and hills seems a fair trade-off.

"Don't discount my love for fine auction houses, my friend," she says. "To you it may count as soaking up culture, but for me it's Saturday-morning window-shopping with the Park Avenue crowd. Maybe I'll find a sugar daddy," Dani laughs, as if that's the last thing she wants.

"It might be fun," Kate says. "Frankly, I'm shopped out."

"It *will* be fun," she says. "You'll look at paintings and I'll look at collectors. Besides, if it's just a bunch of boring old suits staring at dusty old paintings, we'll hit the New Age Road Show early."

Kate brightens up at the thought. Taking this as a yes, Dani dashes into the bathroom to get ready.

～

An hour later, they're strolling out the front door of the hotel for a walk over to Park Avenue.

"You're looking stunning today, Ms. Strauss," Patrick, the doorman at the hotel, says, putting a hand over his heart and pretending to lose his breath.

"The Plaza agrees with me," Dani smiles as she hustles Kate down the sidewalk. She knows she's looking good—and with reason. But she's desperate for Kate not to notice the extra effort. If she's grilled too closely, she'll crack and then have to listen to another impassioned, "Bessie Smith you-can't-live-for-a-man speech," or some Dr. Mia psychobabble about living your life for yourself—and frankly, Dani can't decide which would be worse. What Kate doesn't understand is that these opportunities don't come along every day. There are no guys like Guy in Easton. Kate's got Andy; she doesn't know what it's like to be alone.

"You do look beautiful, Dani," Kate says as they stride across Fifth Avenue heading east. Dani catches a glimpse of her reflection in the flat, black windows of the GM building. The woman who looks back at her looks exactly like the kind of woman who would be heading to Sotheby's to buy a few paintings before lunch. Specifically, the kind of woman who would be meeting her multimillionaire, super-mogul husband at Sotheby's to buy a few paintings for the ranch in Texas before lunch. She pauses and takes off her new Gucci sunglasses for a better look.

Her addiction to fashion magazines and the last few days of total immersion in Manhattan's swankiest shops allow Dani to catalog her outfit in a glance: soft black cashmere, slim-fitting trench coat: Ralph Lauren; knee-length pencil skirt in gray flannel: Marc Jacobs; calf-hugging black leather stiletto boots: Jimmy Choo; soft white cashmere sweater: Lucien Pellat-Finet; light pink leather bag: Marc Jacobs. Huge diamond earrings—her own—glitter in the morning sun. Even the hair is perfect: a loose but sophisticated knot, low on the neck.

"I've never seen those earrings before," Kate says respectfully. "We could have sold those and financed this trip years ago."

"I never wear them," Dani says, stating the obvious. Then, deciding Kate deserves more of an explanation, she adds. "Brian gave them to me, right after he made partner. I was staying home with Brianna, depressed about not working, afraid of not being a good mother. Slob-

bing around the house in sweats, wondering when I'd lose the preg-
nancy weight. He just came home with them one night . . . I was
thrilled, then he said something about how maybe now I could have
something to pull myself together around. I don't know. I always felt
like they really weren't a gift for me: that they were for the wife he
really wanted. So I've had them locked away in the safe-deposit box,
thought maybe I'd give them to Brianna some day—or use them to pay
for her wedding, or whatever." She shrugs.

"You should wear them more often," Kate says, linking her arm
through Dani's. "They're worthy of you."

As Dani stares at their upscale images in the smooth glass, Kate
morphs into Guy and suddenly it's him she's locked arms with. She
guiltily remembers the whole reason she chose this outfit: she's her
own vision of the perfect trophy wife.

She shakes her head fiercely, and Kate comes back into focus.

"You know, that outfit just needs one last thing," Kate is saying.

"C'mon, those paintings are calling your name," Dani says, no
longer in the mood to talk fashion, but intent on getting to Sotheby's.

"Dani, wait. I think I'm getting the hang of this fashion thing. Aren't
you a even a little bit excited?" Kate hangs onto her arm. "C'mon, humor me."

They turn down Fifty-seventh Street and Kate darts into the Chanel
boutique.

"I thought you were shopped out." Dani says, following her through
the doors.

"Almost," Kate says, as the leggy salesgirls descend, never suspect-
ing that they're just two soccer moms playing dress-up.

"I'd like to see that, please." Kate is pointing to a cashmere scarf in
a brilliant pink with long, luscious fringe. "That's it. No need to wrap
it," she says, completing the transaction with a decisiveness that sur-
prises Dani. Kate turns and drapes the scarf around Dani's neck, fuss-
ing with the knot so the fringe spills down the inside of her jacket.

"Perfect. You were gorgeous, but subdued. Now everyone will notice you. It's like Dr. Mia says, "*Don't be afraid to shine.*"

It's not a color I would have ever chosen for myself, Dani thinks, admiring the way the pink is reflected on her cheeks. Suddenly, she's filled

with a burst of happiness that has nothing to do with her gorgeous new scarf and everything to do with the friend who just bought it for her. For a minute she thinks of changing the whole game plan. She thinks of strolling with her best friend down Fifth Avenue on a gorgeous fall day and wholeheartedly embracing an afternoon of self-betterment.

But she knows, deep in her heart, that Guy is just a few blocks away, looking at those paintings and so, instead, she gives Kate a huge hug, and then taking her unwitting friend's hand, presses on to her date with destiny.

—

"Good morning, ladies." The gray-uniformed doorman pulls the door open with a flourish and they enter the hushed vestibule of Sotheby's auction house. The foyer opens to a two-story atrium. Sun streams through large spotless windows. To the right, a small crowd has formed in front of the elevator. Kate flashes Dani a look as they crush into a car.

"I see what you mean about your plans, to, er ... browse," Kate says, inclining her head slightly toward a tall, dark-haired man in tan corduroy slacks and a black turtleneck.

Dani tries to look enthusiastic, but when the doors to the elevator slide open she bolts like a racehorse from the starting gate. In the center of the room, she skids to a stop, Kate right behind her. The paintings are hung on the beige walls of the long, narrow room. Groups of people stand in front of them, glancing from the art to the printed catalogs in their hands. She scans the room, but all she sees are the backs of heads. What if she's forgotten what he looks like?

"Oh, Dani, this was such a great idea," Kate says. "Look, there's an Albert Bierstadt. He lived up by us for a while, you know. Then he went out West, did a lot of scenes of the new frontier. I'm sort of surprised to see his work included here. For a while he was rather out of vogue. Critics thought his work was too over-the-top, too emotional. He's done some beautiful paintings of the White Mountains in New Hampshire."

Dani nods, only half listening to Kate's mini art-history lecture.

Kate moves reverently from one painting to the next while Dani circles the room like a shark around a lifeboat.

"Over there!"

Dani's heart skips a beat. He's here. Kate's spotted him.

"Ohmigod, Dani. Look."

She touches her hair and, trying to look cool, spins slowly around.

"Isn't it gorgeous?" Kate's voice is hushed, like she's in church. She's pointing–not at Guy–but at a little oil painting of some brick buildings and trees. "It's a Richard Harraden painting of Trinity College. We went to that very spot when Andy was a fellow at Cambridge. Oh, I want it."

Dani forces herself to stop scanning the room.

"Guess what," she says. "You can afford it!" It comes out snappish.

"What's wrong with you, Dani? You've been jumpy since we walked in the door. If you're not having a good time, we can go." Kate looks disappointed.

"No, it's fine," she says. "It's just that I . . ." She catches a glimpse of broad shoulders and salt-and-pepper hair. She can't breathe. It's him. It's Guy and he's just across the room. OK, he hasn't seen her yet. She needs to make a plan.

"It's just that I have to use the ladies' room," she tells Kate. "You keep looking; I'll be right back."

Leaving Kate to imagine the tiny oil painting hanging in her hallway, she squares her shoulders and heads across the room.

Taking an inside track between the paintings and the crowd, she slips closer to Guy. She can feel appraising and, yes, admiring looks from some of the weekend art collectors as she passes, but she's so intent on her plan for a casual "What a surprise to bump into you here" meeting that she doesn't pause for even a moment to savor the attention.

Like a lioness on the hunt, she stealthily approaches her prey. *Three, two, one . . .* she stops at the painting to Guy's left and tries mind control: *Look this way. This way.*

She wills him to turn toward her. Instead he turns and murmurs something to the very attractive redhead to his right who laughs and puts her hand on his.

Dani freezes. *He's here with her! Abort mission. Save dignity. Retreat. Retreat!*

Flustered, she gazes blankly at the painting in front of her, her brain and heart racing.

"Dani? Dee?" A touch on her back makes her jump out of her skin. She doesn't have to pretend to be shocked. "Guy? What a surprise!"

He envelops her in a hug that is more than just friendly. "This makes my day." The redhead stands slightly behind him.

"Dani, meet Erica. Erica's my art dealer. Dani is a dear friend."

Erica sticks her hand out. "Pleasure." She has a British accent. Dani can tell from her cool appraisal that Erica's instantly pegged her for a forgery.

"Well, Erica, I guess you can just go ahead and bid for those pieces we discussed," Guy says dismissively. He doesn't take his eyes from Dani's as he talks.

"I don't think there's anything else here I need to see." He leans in to whisper in Dani's ear. "Other than the beauty that is right in front of me."

His arm has slipped casually around her waist and together they turn to face Erica. She smiles, but her gaze is hard as it meets Dani's. "Very good, Guy. I'll take care of everything."

"That's what I pay you for." He doesn't even glance back at her as he smoothly guides Dani through the crowd and into a quiet corner of the room. "I didn't know you were interested in this type of art," he says.

"Oh, yes. I'm particularly fond of Bierstadt's scenes of the American West." She frantically tries to remember what Kate had just said. "I'm so glad he's regained stature among the critics again. His work went unappreciated for so long. With all respects to the critics, I happen to love the emotion in his work."

"A woman of excellent taste," Guy says. "And since you have managed to distract me from viewing the rest of the collection, I think you need to make it up to me."

"Actually, I'd think you'd thank me for saving you some money."

"Why don't we see if we can spend the price of a painting on something that will give us just as much pleasure?" Guy says, putting both hands on her hips and pulling her close. Dani's ready to reenact the bar scene from Friday right there in the middle of Sotheby's, when she sees Kate heading straight toward her and Guy. She can't read Kate's expression, but maybe it's because—for some reason—she simply can't look her in the eye.

"There you are, Dani. Hello, Guy."

"Can you believe it, Kate? Guy collects Bierstadt paintings."

"Mmm, what a coincidence." Kate checks her watch. "Ready for lunch, Dani?"

"Dani's having lunch with me," Guy says, smoothly. "I hope you don't mind if I steal her away for a little bit."

Kate's face reddens as she stares at Dani. This time Dani has to meet Kate's eyes, if only to let her see the plea in hers.

"You'll be OK, won't you, Kate? I promise I'll catch up with you in time for our afternoon 'appointment.'"

She's counting on Kate to be graceful and she isn't disappointed. "I'll be fine. Just fine. You two run along and have a nice lunch. Guy, it was nice to see you again." Kate digs into her purse and hands Dani one of the passes to the seminar. "I'll see you at three o'clock, then," she says pointedly.

As Guy whisks Dani toward the door, she glances back over her shoulder to see Kate standing alone, already looking lost, as the well-dressed crowd swirls around her. Dani has a flash of Kate spending the afternoon wandering around the city by herself. *She'll be fine,* Dani reassures herself. *More time at the self-help seminar without my cynical attitude to ruin her fun.*

In the elevator, Guy pulls her in for a deep kiss. His hands are already roaming up under the white cashmere. He pulls back and looks at her, then raises an eyebrow. He reaches over and pushes the emergency stop button and the elevator shudders to a standstill. *This is like a scene from a movie. He can't help himself, he wants me so much,* Dani thinks, her stomach doing flips.

"What about the people trying to get into the auction?" she says as he unwinds her new pink scarf from around her neck.

"They'll take the stairs." He laughs the laugh of a man who does whatever he wants, whenever he wants. Crushing the scarf into a little ball, he stuffs it between the handrail and the wall of the elevator. Dani leans back breathless, totally caught up in the moment. Guy pulls his light blue silk scarf from under his navy peacoat. She waits for him to drop it next to hers. But instead he slowly slides it across her skin. She can smell his aftershave on the scarf as he wraps it loosely around her neck and plays with the fringed ends. She has a moment of irrational panic. *What have I done? I don't know this man. What if he's some kind of kinky serial killer who strangles women in elevators?*

Guy pushes her shoulders back against the wall and leans away, keeping her at arm's length and staring intently. *Will Kate hear me if I scream?*

"You should never wear pink," he says. And he reaches out and starts the elevator again.

By the time they reach the ground floor her knees have stopped shaking. *Good looks, money and fashion sense . . . hardly the Boston Strangler,* Dani reassures herself.

She's following Guy out to the curb when she remembers that the scarf Kate just gave her is stuffed between the rail and the wall of the elevator.

"Just a minute," she calls to him as she dashes back past the doorman. Dani sticks her hand between the elevator doors, which bounce back open. Snatching the wrinkled pink ball, she stuffs it into her bag. In a flash, she's back out the door.

"I thought you'd changed your mind," Guy says as she slides into the backseat of the cab.

"Never," Dani says, settling into the curve of his arm.

"You've got to stop dashing off like that," he says, stroking her hair.

Dani tips her head back and looks into his eyes. She has a flash of guilt as she remembers Kate pressing the ticket into her hand ". . . *See you at three o'clock sharp . . .*"

"I'm not going anywhere, I promise," she tells him.

～

Kate doesn't know whether to scream or cry or chase after Dani and try to save her from herself. *Does she really believe that smooth-talking*

Richard Gere look-alike is her ticket to paradise? So, this whole Sotheby's detour was just a ploy to lure me onto Guy's turf. It's amazing how quickly Dani loses her grip when a man's involved. In the end, she doesn't do anything. As the crowd swirls around her, murmuring their appreciation of this painting and that, she has a sudden, irrational fear that she'll be thrown out for impersonating a wealthy woman. So before the dark-suited guard by the door comes over to ask her to please leave without making a scene, Kate shoulders her way through the throngs and rides an empty elevator down to the street.

When she steps out onto the sidewalk, she takes a quick glance up and down the street. She's hoping she'll see Dani, running back to her, full of apologies and all *"Ohmigod Kate, it's just like with Brian all over again. I really need to break this pattern of self-destructive behavior with men. Let's head downtown and find some answers.* But the only person heading toward her is a young Hispanic woman wearing a maid's uniform and a stoic expression as she is dragged behind a herd of yapping Maltese.

Kate fishes around in her new purse, the butter-soft Coach bag she had been coveting just days ago, and pulls out the packet to the Reclaim Your Dreams event. The glossy promotional brochure shows photos of the speakers and what looks like a setup of booths for shopping.

She checks her watch: 12:00. "Well, maybe if I spend the whole day there I'll be spiritually evolved enough for me *and* Dani," she says under her breath. Kate backtracks to the Sotheby's doorman. He holds his position, all-business, like a British Bobby without the headgear. His hair is graying and thin and his face drawn. *Probably nearing retirement*, Kate thinks.

"Cab, Miss?"

"Actually, no. Can you tell me the best way to walk to the Javits Center?"

"It's quite a walk," he says. "Why don't I call you a cab?"

"No, really. I'll be fine," Kate insists. "I'd just like a little exercise." *How far could it be?*

"You'll want to avoid the area around the Port Authority Bus Terminal," he says, looking at her pityingly. "So head east until Fifth Avenue, then downtown and then across on Thirty-fourth Street."

"Thank you."

"It really is a hike," he says. "It should be pretty easy to grab a cab on Fifth Avenue."

Kate is trying not to dwell on the fact that Dani has broken the first inviolate rule of girlfriendom: *Don't dump your girlfriend for what you think is a better offer from a man.* She decides she just has to make the best of it. What does Dr. Mia say? *No one can alter our peace of mind unless we let them. We alone are responsible.*

She strides confidently down the street, deciding to do some soul-searching in preparation for Dr. Mia. Even though Dani isn't with her, she's starting to feel pretty good. Here she is, alone, navigating the big city, on her way to an afternoon of good advice and spiritual guidance.

Kate makes her way east to Fifth Avenue and begins heading downtown. The city is one big grid. *How hard can this be?* Kate thinks smugly. The doorman was right about one thing, though, it's quite a long walk. The blocks seem to stretch out in front of her, getting longer as she walks. All around her, people, true New Yorkers, Kate guesses, walk with purpose as though doubt or hesitation is not in their repertoire, passing tourists who cluster sideways awkwardly wielding video cameras. By the time she reaches Forty-second Street, Kate is hungry and tired. She stops to buy a hot dog from a vendor and marvels at the wide expanse of the granite staircase leading up to the New York Public Library. One stone lion rests on either side, staring impassively out onto Fifth Avenue.

She walks up the wide steps and follows the signs to the main reading room. The huge space is silent. A few people work at the long tables laid out in rows in the center of the room. Librarians with serious expressions quietly move back and forth from a main desk, carrying armloads of books. Kate sits down for a minute, slips her boots off her aching feet and drinks in the atmosphere. It feels so good to sit down. She likes being surrounded by countless rows of books filled with facts she doesn't know and stories she's never heard. It makes her feel almost like a student again. Kate thinks back to when Andy had his fellowship at Cambridge. She was taking classes and had visions of getting her PhD in clinical psychology, thinking of taking a job at the London Psychiatric Institute where she was working as a research assistant. She and Andy would take long, moonlit strolls along the Thames, a damp chill in the night air. They'd talk about their future as the golden light fell across the moving water. They'd have three—no, four—kids. It was a future that seemed endless, impossibly big. She was going to do something that helped others, something that made a difference. Such big plans.

Shaking herself out of her daydream, Kate slides her feet back into her boots and slowly makes her way out of the library. She crosses Sixth Avenue, then Broadway, awed by the rows of theaters announcing shows she's only heard about on TV and restaurants of every imaginable ethnicity and style, lining both sides of the street. Trying not to gawk like the tourist that she is, Kate picks up the pace and continues across Seventh Avenue. At Eighth Avenue the street grows seedy, Dumpsters overflow and buildings are marred by graffiti and neglect, and Kate's designer outfit and Coach bag are fine substitutes for a sign that reads OUT OF TOWNER: MUG ME NOW.

The shops and theater and crowds drop away and Kate starts feeling a bit uneasy. She knows she should be going downtown, but can't remember which streets the grandfatherly Sotheby's doorman told her to avoid. Forty-second Street comes to an abrupt end at a four-lane highway filled with speeding cars and blaring taxi horns. Beyond the highway is the river. Clearly she's reached the end of the line. Her new boots have rubbed substantial blisters on both heels and frankly, since she crossed Seventh Avenue, her hopes for inner peace have been replaced by a small sweaty-palmed voice that keeps saying, "*Don't look anyone in the eye.*"

Kate limps across the highway. In less than two hours the city has defeated her. She sticks her arm up to hail a cab and holds her breath as one shoots across three lanes of moving traffic, screeching to a halt just inches short of her aching feet.

"Where to?" The driver is a small balding guy wearing glasses with heavy black frames.

"Javits Center, please."

Kate's thrown back against the seat as he burns rubber out into the oncoming traffic. With shaking fingers she reaches for the seat belt and clicks it securely into place.

"You here for that touch-feely show?" The driver rapidly drums his fingers on the steering wheel.

"The Reclaim Your Dreams event, yes."

"That's not where the answers are, you know." He zigzags in and out of traffic, then jams the brakes on at a red light. "I know where the answers are."

"You do?"

"He told me you were the one who needed to know."

"He?" Kate glances at the passenger seat in the front. It's empty.

The driver, growing fidgety, glances over, too.

"He says he'll tell me what you need to know."

Nervously, she cranes her neck, trying to get a glimpse of the street signs as the cab careens around a corner. *Where the heck is the Javits Center?*

The driver wipes sweat from his forehead and glances to his right again.

"What do you mean I can't tell her that?" The tires screech around another turn. The driver catches Kate's eye in the rearview mirror. "He's afraid you won't believe me if I tell you. He wants to tell you himself."

OK, now just pretend that you're playing the game where Charlie has the talking dinosaur friend. Kate tries to arrange her features in an expression of polite interest.

"I'd be interested to hear his point of view," she says, unbuckling her seat belt so she can fling herself out of the cab if necessary. The driver's got one hand on the wheel, the other gesturing wildly.

"Don't you talk to her like that," he barks. Taking his eyes off the road to glance over his shoulder, he says, "Sorry, but he's getting all wound up. I hope you're not offended. He does this sometimes."

"Of course, I understand completely. Maybe you should just pull over so you two can take a minute to work it out." Kate says in her best "now stop this nonsense or the playdate's over" voice.

"Maybe we should," he says, nodding meaningfully at the empty air beside him.

The cab lurches over to the curb. "Javits Center," he says inclining his head toward the opposite corner. "Hang on and I'll make a U-turn, drop you right off at the door. Just as soon as I settle a little something." He jams the cab into park and pushes his sleeves up past his elbows.

"Oh, no, I think you should just work things out with your, er, friend here." Kate pushes a ten-dollar bill up through the divider and jumps from the cab, leaving the driver in the midst of a heated argument with his invisible copilot.

—

The huge, sprawling glass-and-concrete complex in front of her covers several city blocks. Kate tries four different doors: all locked. With a growing sense of despair, she checks her watch. Two-thirty. Dr. Mia is starting her speech in half an hour, and she can't even get into the darn building.

"Excuse me, ma'am?"

Kate turns around and faces a young girl. The girl is painfully thin with long, dirty blonde hair that hangs in front of her face. She smiles shyly at Kate.

"Do you know where the seminar is meeting? I just took the bus in from New Jersey and I got lost coming over from the Port Authority and I'm afraid I'm late." She clutches a woven Guatemalan bag close to her chest and looks at Kate imploringly.

She can't be more than fourteen years old, Kate thinks, trying to decide whether she should be impressed that someone so young is already embarking on a course of self-awareness, or appalled that the girl is in this slightly dodgy part of town on her own.

"I'm looking for it myself," Kate says to her. "But I can tell you for sure, it's not through any of the doors on this side or around the back of the building."

Kate starts walking around another corner, eyeing a set of double metal doors that look promising. The girl trots along behind her, then catches up alongside.

"Who are you here to see?" the girl asks.

"Dr. Mia. How about you?"

"Yeah, Dr. Mia for me too," she says. "I watch her on *Oprah* all the time."

"Aren't you at school when *Oprah* is on?"

"Uh, yeah. But, like, we have TiVo, so I can see it anytime, you know?"

They reach the doors together, and Kate gives them a tug but, like all the others, they're locked tight. Aware of the impressionable youngster beside her, she keeps her frustration in check and keeps walking. As they round the last corner, Kate sees a wide plaza with colorful banners announcing the Reclaim Your Dreams event. *Duh. The front door. Why didn't I think of this before?*

"This looks promising," she says, cracking a grin. "We're going to be late, but at least we can sneak in together."

The girl is digging through her bag as they approach the check-in desk.

"Tickets?" A guard in well-pressed khakis and a navy blazer holds out his hand and Kate pulls the envelope out of her purse.

"Oh my god! My ticket!" Her young companion bursts into tears. "I've lost my ticket. I remember looking at it on the bus."

"Sorry, kid. No ticket, no entrance."

The girl looks around wildly. "But the tickets are, like, one hundred dollars. I saved for months to buy one."

"Sorry, kid." The guard seems unmoved. *Probably doesn't have kids of his own,* Kate thinks. He hands Kate back her ticket and motions for her to step through the turnstile. She glances back at the girl who has slumped against the wall, the picture of dejection. She imagines her walking back to the bus station and taking a long bus ride back to New Jersey. The girl catches Kate's eye and, biting on a nail, takes a chance.

"Um, hey, you seem really nice and everything. Do you think you could loan me the money for a ticket? I'll have my mom send you a check if you give me your address."

Kate takes in the pinched, eager face. And suddenly she is suffused with a feeling of purpose. Here's her chance. She can make a difference in this girl's life. She can reward her for beginning this search for herself. And if they're a little late for the seminar, then so what?

"Sure, honey," she says. "Let's go over to the ticket window."

"Oh, I don't want to make you any later for Dr. Mia," the girl says. "I can run over and get it."

Kate glances at the big clock across the lobby: 2:50. *I really do want to get to the seminar,* she admits to herself, reaching into her purse and pulling out her wallet. She peels off five twenties and hands them to her new friend.

The girl stuffs the bills into the pocket of her jeans and heads off at a trot.

"Hey, kid! The ticket office is over there." The guard gestures in the opposite direction.

"Suckah!" the kids spits back, giving them the finger and breaking into a full run as she dashes out the doors. Kate watches through the glass as she disappears between taxis lining the curb.

"She oughta get an Oscar for that performance," he mutters, shaking his head.

Kate's mouth drops open. "You knew? You knew and you let her scam me?"

The guard raises a bushy eyebrow. "You would have listened to me if I tried to say something?"

Kate stands there openmouthed, but doesn't have an answer.

"The lady you're looking for is giving her talk in the Grantly Theater," the guard says gently. "You don't want to be late."

Kate doesn't know what she's feeling as she slips into the darkened auditorium. There is a podium lit by a spotlight in the center of the stage. She breathes a sigh of relief. Dr. Mia hasn't started speaking yet. As she makes her way down the aisle toward a front-row seat, a man steps out from behind the stage curtains. It's the agent who was with Dr. Mia the other night in the hotel bar.

"Thank you all for coming to Dr. Mia's presentation of "Building from the Foundation." Today, you have the good fortune to meet a woman whose books have become international bestsellers. Her insight and wisdom have been applauded by everyone from Oprah Winfrey to world leaders in business and politics. Ladies and gentlemen, it is my honor to introduce to you, Dr. Mia!"

He steps aside with a flourish and Dr. Mia walks out onto the stage to a swell of applause. She strides across the stage in her sensible heels, her red, tailored suit a bright beacon for the audience to fix on. She looks like a corporate executive and carries herself as if well aware of her own power. Dr. Mia studies the podium, the microphone on the stand, and then frowns slightly and steps away.

"Mel?" Dr. Mia says in the direction of the wings. Kate watches as agent man comes back on the stage and Dr. Mia speaks softly to him. He turns and moves off stage as Dr. Mia returns to the microphone.

"We just have a few technical glitches to clear up," she says in her beautiful, calm voice. "Please bear with us and take this time to free yourself from thoughts of what is behind you today. Do not think of what is ahead of you. You are here because you have important work to do and you must come to it with purpose and focus."

Kate closes her eyes and tries to quiet the inner turmoil. She tries to erase the image of a scrawny teenager giving her the finger as she makes off with her money. She tries to forget that her last attempt at a meditative walk ended with her trapped in a cab with a homicidal maniac. She tries to block out the vision of her best friend walking away with a man who is all wrong for her. She tries to forget that she can't seem to do anything right at all.

When Kate opens her eyes, she sees that the podium has been removed, replaced by a tastefully upholstered wing chair, and that soft lighting has come on in place of the harsher spotlight. Dr. Mia settles herself comfortably in the chair, a glass of water and a pitcher on a table beside her, a small headset replacing the larger microphone from the podium.

"And now, if you could just turn up the houselights," she says to someone in the back of the auditorium. The lights come on and Dr. Mia smiles.

"Good. It's nice to see all of you. Now I have what I need to talk to you. But the real question is: Do you have what you need to hear me?"

Kate leans forward, sitting on the edge of her chair. *What? What do I need?*

As if she can read Kate's mind, Dr. Mia continues.

"You must build your life as an architect builds a structure. Whether an architect builds a business or builds a home, he or she must first build the solid foundation that sustains either. I'd like you all to take a moment and examine your foundations. Whether you want to work on the strength of your business life or your home life, you must be sure that the heart of the structure is strong. Some of you must start at the beginning: find a level ground and dig deep to establish a base. That base is your sense of self. The source of your deepest desires and inner peace. Some of you may have that base, but it may be cracked or need repair. To strengthen and repair the base, you must accept yourself fully, accept your desires and accept your dreams."

Kate glances around and sees people in the audience nodding.

"Now before we begin the first exercise, I want you all to go down into your foundation. I want you to be able to tell me if the systems that support the structure above–the one that everyone sees–are strong. Have you built a strong foundation for your life? Have you maintained the hidden support of your being?"

Dr. Mia steps down off the stage and moves through the audience with a microphone. She pauses and looks down.

"Kate," she smiles warmly. "I'm so glad you could come."

I can't believe she remembered my name. Kate can feel her ears start to burn as the full attention of the audience turns to her.

"So tell us, Kate, what do you see?"

Fighting back an urge to hide under her seat, Kate instead closes her eyes and really, truly, tries to picture her foundation.

"Well, it's definitely dark and probably kind of cobwebby," she begins. The audience laughs and she opens her eyes. Dr. Mia is nodding encouragingly.

". . . and I keep bumping my head on all the water pipes. Everybody tells me how solid the walls are, but I can see them sagging and I'm afraid that one of these days they're just going to collapse."

"Look around a bit more and tell us what else you're seeing. What do those cobwebs mean?" Dr. Mia prods gently.

Kate closes her eyes again and lets the images flood her mind. "I think it's totally empty down here. I want to believe that maybe if I had a flashlight I could illuminate something of value in the corners, but . . ."

She opens her eyes to see Dr. Mia still smiling at her. "Eloquently put, dear."

"But it's a disaster." Kate chokes back the urge to burst into tears.

"Has it always been in such disrepair?" Dr. Mia asks. "Probably not. Did you build poorly, or have you just been lax about maintenance? Perhaps the core, your foundation, has been ignored. Sometimes, from the outside, everything looks fine, but we must remember to take care of the parts others don't see. When we neglect the foundation, we jeopardize the structure of our lives."

"It hasn't always been this way. Not like this."

Around her, people are nodding in agreement—or sympathy—Kate can't really tell which.

Dr. Mia looks around the auditorium. "Everyone, take a moment to see if you can be as honest with yourselves as Kate has been. As for you, Kate, why don't you grab a flashlight and take a look into those corners."

"I would, but I'm sure Charlie's hidden it, or Henry's used it for a science experiment, and even if they've left it alone, I know my husband forgot to buy batteries, But it's not their fault I've gotten into a situation where I can't see clearly. I have to find a way to shine my own light. After all, this foundation was built from my own blueprint."

"Then let's go back to your blueprints," Dr. Mia says gently. She walks back to the stage and takes a seat.

"Sometimes you can only strengthen the design of your life by going back to the drawing board. Sometimes there's a flaw in the major plan, and sometimes you can see where you didn't follow your own good advice," Dr. Mia says. "Let's try an exercise to see if we can uncover where we each have to start our own process of restoration or repair."

And for the first time all day, Kate has the feeling that she's in the right place at just the right time. She reaches into her bag for a notebook and pen, ready to write down everything she needs to know, the plan that will fix the crumbling structure of her life.

Chapter Eleven

Guy and Dani are sitting in the corner of a large banquette in the main dining room of Le Cirque, sipping champagne out of tall flutes. Even though it's Saturday, the place is filled with men and women in serious suits and illicit, improbable couples playing footsie under the table. Dani scans the menu but it's hard to focus on the words in front of her, and the champagne hasn't even started to kick in. At the moment, the menu is a mere prop keeping her from gazing like a schoolgirl into Guy's green eyes.

No, I'm the urban sophisticate–don't forget art expert–who just happened to bump into him at Sotheby's, she reminds herself, hardly believing her good fortune. *So he made a few creepy, controlling comments about the scarf, but hey, no one's perfect.*

In fact, instead of studying the day's specials, Dani is mentally decorating the living room in their palatial weekend getaway when the waitress interrupts her reverie.

"Do you know what you'd like?" The waitress is a tall, curvy brunette. Her hair is slicked back in a tight ponytail and her dark eye makeup is perfectly applied. She looks as though she just stepped out of a Robert Palmer video circa 1987. Dani dislikes her immediately.

"Why, yes," Guy flashes the waitress a big, toothy smile. "Do you have the lobster salad today? I didn't see it on the menu. Don't tell me the chef's not making it anymore."

"That item is usually on our summer menu, but I am sure he'll be able to accommodate you." Video Girl shoots him a smile that suggests that she just might be able to accommodate him herself. She then shifts her weight so that her hip grazes the edge of the banquette. Dani's dislike blossoms into deep hatred. *I bet she wouldn't know a Bierstadt if it hit her on her head.* (The fact that she herself wouldn't have known one either a few short hours ago is beside the point.)

"Anything to start?" Video Girl grins at Guy.

"Well, let's let the lady order first."

Guy turns to Dani, who swoons inside, but gazes up at Video Girl with a cool confidence that says, *That's me, the lady here, don't forget it.* Then she orders the first item she sees on the menu.

"Yes, I'll have the caviar blintzes. And a Caesar salad as well."

"An elegant choice," Guy says approvingly. "Make that a double order of the blintzes, with the lobster. And I think we'll need another bottle of the Dom Perignon when you get the chance."

Video Girl slithers off and Dani's good mood is immediately restored. She feels Guy rub his knee against hers, ever so slowly.

"Did I mention that you look remarkably gorgeous today?" he asks.

"Why, thank you . . . maybe once or twice."

"Blue really is your color." He fondles the scarf–his scarf–still draped over her shoulder. He leans in and kisses her on the mouth. She can smell his cologne. It smells expensive. On an empty stomach, the champagne is already starting to take effect. She feels a sudden wave of nausea but it passes quickly.

"There's a place I'd love to take you, Dani. It's in the Islands, in fact, it's where *Islands in the Stream* is set."

"I love Hemingway. I know that's politically incorrect of me to say, but I always have. That misogynist pig sure knew how to string a sentence together."

Guy nods approvingly. "That was one of the moments when I knew my first marriage was over. My wife heard me mention *Islands in the Stream* and told me that it was her favorite song, too. She thought I was referring to some Dolly Parton duet . . . Can you believe that? She was a bit of a hick, anyway."

Dani cringes at his callousness, but Guy doesn't seem to notice.

"That's one of the things I liked immediately about you. You're sharp. You're intellectual. You get me."

Dani softens a bit. "Thanks, but tell me . . . Why didn't you share the book with your wife? Why didn't you ever take her to the Islands? I mean, if it was important to you?"

Why I am going down this path? Dani instantly wonders. *The handsome man next to me who is presently stroking my knee with his smooth hand has practically suggested that we jet off immediately to a remote island together and I'm doing ex-marriage counseling with him? What is wrong with me?*

Guy stiffens in his chair. "She would never have appreciated those things . . . And I don't really feel like talking about my ex-wife at the moment . . . Let's talk about you, Dee. What's important to you?"

Dani takes a long drink of champagne, which does nothing to clear her head. *Is it too soon for me to tell him that he's important to me?*

She reaches across the table and rests one of her hands on his. At that moment, Video Girl returns and slides a plate of lush caviar, capers, sour cream and fresh blinis under Dani's nose. Her stomach growls.

"At the moment, this is important to me . . . mmm . . . very important."

She slathers a blini with sour cream, a lump of caviar and a few capers and pops the contents into her mouth. She can feel a dab of sour cream on her lower lip. Guy swiftly wipes it off with his index finger and then pops the finger in his mouth.

"Delicious," he says drawing the finger out slowly. His eyes look glassy.

Bizarrely, Dani doesn't know if she's repulsed or turned on. When Guy proceeds to slide his hand up her thigh, she concludes it's the latter. Guy takes another sip of champagne and offers her his glass. She drinks deeply until it's empty.

Dani's barely set the glass down on the table when the next bottle arrives. The rest of lunch is a bit of a blur. Unfortunately, the blinis and salad don't quite slow the flood of champagne into her system. Guy settles the check—leaving a nice fat tip for Video Girl, she can't help noticing. As they retrieve their coats, Guy holds onto Dani's left elbow, using it like a rudder to steer her through the incoming patrons. She's not smashed, but she's pretty damn close and, at the moment, she realizes, she couldn't care less. She falls into a waiting cab, giddy with champagne and anticipation.

"Downtown–to the Hotel Grand," Guy says to the cabdriver without missing a beat.

"Guy De Varen, do you really think I'm that type of *grill*?" She says smiling coyly, an effect completely undone, to her horror, by the slurred speech.

"Maybe that's what's making me so *hot*."

Even in her semi-drunken stupor this line sounds absurd. Unbidden, Bryce's face flashes into her mind, and Dani realizes with a feeling bordering on queasiness that it sounds like something *he* would say. For some reason, this whole scenario suddenly strikes her as incredibly ludicrous and all of a sudden, she is laughing hard, tears beginning to trickle down her cheeks.

All the while, Guy is looking at her with an odd expression, a half-smile frozen on his face. It's as if he doesn't know whether to laugh along or be very concerned . . . *Is he in the company of some dynamic, good-time gal or a complete madwoman?*

At the moment, Dani isn't sure how to answer that question herself.

"You have a great laugh, Dee," Guy says at last and puts his arm around her. Dani can feel the heat of his body pressing up against hers. And that's all it takes for thoughts of Bryce to vanish. The cab is flying down Fifth Avenue. She stares up at Guy, not believing how utterly good-looking he is. He leans down and kisses her hard on the mouth. His tongue brushes up against her teeth for a split second. This man knows what he's doing.

Dani loses herself in the moment and soon the cabdriver is getting quite a show. But when she glances up and removes her booted foot from its temporary place on the glass separating her and Guy from the front seat, the driver barely looks up.

The cab stops in front of the Hotel Grand and the driver asks "Receipt?" and tears off the paper from the dispenser sounding incredibly bored. With his hand firmly on her back, Guy leads Dani up the stairs and into the hotel lobby.

"Good afternoon, Mr. De Varen," says the concierge.

"Good afternoon, Roger. Gorgeous day out."

"Certainly is," says Roger, giving her, Dani swears, the once-over.

As they take the elevator up to the second floor, she sneaks a look at Guy in the elevator mirror. His head is tilted to one side and he is leaning back against the wall. One of his hands rests on her hip and the other is thrust inside the pocket of his navy blue cashmere overcoat. He catches her watching him and smiles warmly. She slips her hand inside his coat and wraps it around his back as they head toward his room.

The door opens onto a modern room of impeccable design. The floors are of a high-gloss, dark wood. All the furnishings, from the square sofa to the rectangular lampshades to the oversized TV and the large area rug, are an immaculate white. A vase of long, slender calla lilies stands imperiously on the oversized coffee table.

But Dani barely takes it all in before Guy grabs her firmly, sweeps her off the ground, takes her into the ultra-white bedroom and deposits her in the middle of the massive bed. Her head is still spinning from the champagne. There is some fumbling of clothes and limbs, and it all feels as though it's happening fast but somehow not too fast. In the next moment, they're both wearing only underwear, and Dani doesn't want to stop. Her mind drifts for a moment and it occurs to her that she hasn't slept with anyone on a first date since her senior year in college when she beat Todd Windham in a frozen Margarita-drinking contest and powered through the ice-cream headache it induced into an intermission of lame sex back in Todd's dorm room. As she recalls, the sun rose to reveal her lacy purple panties draped delicately over the lampshade on his desk. She had no idea how they got there.

But this, this is different, she thinks. We're adults now. Guy is a successful businessman, man of the world and my future husband. Things happen faster when you're older, she reasons. We don't have time to play games, to take it slow. As Guy is kissing her, she realizes that she could be happy being kissed like this for the next fifty years. So happy. His shoulders are broad, and as she lies beneath him she feels utterly safe. Nothing in the world can touch her.

When they finish, the room is utterly still. Sunlight glows at the edges of the pulled white velvet curtains. Dani strokes Guy's hair. His head is resting on her chest. She starts thinking that, in spite of his few gaffes (probably nervousness on his part), they fit together so well. They want the same kind of future; though, if pressed, she realizes she couldn't really say what Guy sees in his future. Nonetheless, he feels so relaxed in her arms, so comfortable. She muses over what it will take to get him to relocate to the East Coast and whether they should live full time in the city with a weekend getaway in the Hamptons–or Connecticut perhaps. She pictures them walking hand in hand with Brianna along the beach, barefoot and laughing. Dani exhales, softly says his name, and kisses Guy on the top of his head. Guy makes a strange snorting noise. He jerks suddenly and pulls away until he is sitting upright on the edge of the bed. Running a hand through his hair, he rubs his eyes. "Wow, I must have dozed off there for a second. Sorry, babe."

Hey, falling asleep is not a crime, she tells herself, fighting off a pang of disappointment. Oldest cliché in the book. An article in O magazine recently said the post-sex hormone crash is so severe in men you may just as well shoot them with a stun gun.

Guy leans over and caresses her hair, then gets up and picks his watch up off the bureau. "Damn, it's 2:45 already. I'm due uptown for a meeting in fifteen minutes."

It's Dani's turn to be stunned. Even Todd Windham had the good manners to take her to breakfast, albeit at Denny's, but still. "A meeting, on Saturday?" she manages.

"Yes, didn't I mention that? I'm so sorry. One of my associates from the Chicago office is in town and wants to go over his projections for next year." Guy is hopping on one foot, pulling one leg into his pants and trying to button his shirt at the same time.

"I'll call you later at the hotel. God, I hate to run out like this," he says unconvincingly. He is fully dressed now and sitting beside her on the bed. Dani pulls the covers up to her chin. "Forgive me, Dee. That was beautiful, really." He kisses her on the lips, more a dry peck than anything else, and he's gone.

Dani throws down the covers as the door closes behind him. *Who's running away now?* She fights the rising humiliation as she sprawls, naked as the day she was born, on the thousand-thread-count sheets. Then her mind kicks into overdrive. *Why am I making such a big deal of this? Grow up, Dani. Relax. He'll call later. He didn't know you would be at Sotheby's. In fact, he didn't really even have time to take you back to his hotel. He had important business plans. He only did it because he couldn't help himself. Something bigger took over. Yes, something bigger than both of you. Madame Fate stepping in.*

Her head is beginning to throb. She picks up the phone and dials room service.

"Yes, this is room 216. Yes, that's right, this is Mrs. De Varen." *I'll try it out. What's the harm?*

"Yes, coffee please. No, black is fine. Thanks so much."

She hangs up the phone and then it hits her. *Ohmigod, Kate is going to kill me.* She glances at her watch and it's five minutes to three. She's supposed to be at the Javits Center in five minutes. Suddenly she feels quite sober. She dresses quickly, wipes the smeared mascara from underneath her eyes, reapplies concealer and some lipstick and is gathering up her scarf and purse when there is a knock on the door.

She opens it and a young gentleman in a spiffy white uniform hands her a silver tray. Dani tips him five bucks. She pours the coffee into the cup, then grabs a couple ice cubes from the refrigerator freezer and plops them into the steaming liquid. She waits a few seconds and chugs the whole thing down. Then she dashes for the elevator, which arrives immediately and deposits her back into the lobby. She's racing through the lobby heading for the main door when she hears a voice.

"Mrs. De Varen. Mrs. De Varen." It takes her a moment to realize that she is the one being called. She turns and sees Roger clutching a bundle of clothes on hangers sealed in clear plastic. He is looking at her expectantly. "Mrs. De Varen, your dry cleaning is here. I know that you needed it for this evening."

Dani opens her mouth but nothing comes out.

"Room 216, correct? I spoke with you last night? Nice to see you in person. Mr. De Varen dropped your things off this morning. Just wanted to be sure you knew it came in."

"Thank you, Roger." Dani manages to keep her voice level. Roger Dodger, indeed.

Her throat tightens. She is walking down the stairs toward the front door when her vision starts to blur. She sees an empty cab pulling in front of the hotel, stuffs a twenty in the doorman's hand and slides onto the cold leather of the backseat.

"The Javits Center, please." Before she knows it, she is blubbering pathetically in the backseat of the cab. She wants desperately to hate Guy, to expose him for the cad that he is, but she can't muster it. He just seems kind of shallow and predictable. And, worst of all, so does she. Dani pulls out tissues to wipe her eyes, her insides heavy with the weight of her shame, her sadness. *May Brianna never know this feeling*, she thinks. *If I have to lock her in her room until she's forty, I will make sure that she never knows this feeling.*

The cab turns a corner and stops at a light in front of a small park. A group of four children are chasing one another around a swing set, a small dachshund running close at their heels. One of the kids breaks away from the group and leaps over a small wire fence encircling a flower bed. The other kids follow, pursued closely behind by the dachshund, who gamely attempts the jump, only to be repelled like a comic-book character by the loose fence. The dog bounces on its side and does a quick log roll. Unperturbed, the creature then is back on its stubby legs and trotting around the fence to catch up. The kids stop, see this and break into laughter. In spite of herself, Dani cracks a smile.

The coffee is starting to ease her headache but Dani still feels miserable. When the taxi pulls up in front of the Javits Center, she pays the fare and hurries inside.

It's three fifty when she finds the room where Dr. Mia is speaking. The door creaks as she opens it, and a few heads turn around to catch a glimpse of the interloper. One of them is Kate's. Dani slinks along the back wall, giving Kate a quick wave and a feeble smile. "Sorry," she mouths. Kate looks half annoyed, half amused. *She will be mortified when she hears what I've been doing*, Dani thinks. Though Kate has never been one of the I-told-you-so kind of gals. That's just one of the many things Dani loves about her.

～

Kate tries to turn her attention back to the lecture, but she can only think of Dani, slinking through the door. Even from a distance, Kate can see that Dani looks like hell. Her eyes are puffy and she's pale and drawn. The pink cashmere scarf Kate had bought her is peeking like a captive out of the top of her bag. Kate can only imagine what she's been up to.

She wonders how Dani, her strong, independent, sharp-tongued friend, could fall for someone like Guy. She knows what Dani's looking for, what she thinks she wants. She's heard it from her a thousand times. Looks, cash, power . . . *But she had all that with Brian. She wasn't happy then and she doesn't look happy now. If only she would just lose the Cinderella fantasy and all the wrong assumptions that come with it, she might have a chance of meeting a decent guy.*

As she tries to sort through her feelings about Dani's taste in men, Kate realizes that Dr. Mia is wrapping up the seminar. "So, we must remember to take care of our own foundations. By focusing on others to the exclusion of ourselves, we weaken our base and our lives will eventually break down. We are the architects of our dreams. We can live those dreams but we must build from a strong foundation and learn to maintain it. Then, and only then, can we truly benefit others."

Kate nods in agreement. *Dani is the architect of her own life. And, unfortunately, she can take a wrecking ball to the thing if she so desires. Still, it's hard to watch.*

Dr. Mia walks to the edge of the stage to thunderous applause. Kate looks around at the crowd. Some are smiling, others are dabbing their eyes. (Though one or two appear to have dozed off.) They are old and young, black and white and everything in between, slim and overweight, male and female, fashionably dressed and frumpy. They are all here looking for something. Dr. Mia extends her arms outward to the crowd and claps her hands together. She, too, is smiling. She descends the stairs at the far end of the stage and wades into a swarm of fans who have already gathered, many with books in hand.

Kate looks back to where Dani had been standing and sees that she is making her way toward her. Dani looks as though she's been crying, but when she catches Kate's eye, she grins apologetically.

"OK, missy, what do you have to say for yourself?" Kate asks. She reaches toward Dani and gives her a big hug. As she lets go, Dani pulls her back and holds on tight. When Dani lets go, Kate sees that her eyes have begun to tear again.

"Kate, how do you stand me? I am such an idiot."

"It's OK, sweetie. Let's get out of here, get a cup of coffee and you can tell me everything." She takes the new pink scarf out of Dani's bag on the floor, smooths it around Dani's shoulders and gives her a kiss on the cheek. She takes her arm and they make their way out into the hallway. A number of seminars are scheduled to start shortly, so the halls are filled with people milling about. They're headed toward the nearest exit when Kate feels a sharp pull on her arm. Dani has stopped, fixated, in front of a poster outside one of the lecture rooms.

LOOKING FOR THE PRINCE BUT LOVING THE FROG:

A WAKE-UP CALL FOR SISTERS

WITH UNA

"We're going in," Dani says impulsively, and marches inside before Kate can respond. The crowd is just starting to settle into their seats and Dani spies a couple of free chairs toward the front. Kate follows somewhat reluctantly behind her. Frankly, at the moment, she'd much rather leave and find out exactly what's been going on with Dani, but clearly this pit stop is nonnegotiable. She can't really believe it. Dani's hardly cracked open the Dr. Mia book she gave her two years ago and now she's the one dragging Kate back into the self-help-athon.

Just then, an enormous, six-foot-tall, redheaded woman with faint freckles on her swelled pink cheeks and large, luscious lips highlighted, improbably, with orange lipstick, whizzes through the door. She is wearing a huge orange, brown and magenta caftan and her hair is studded with colorful beads that run through the thick dreadlocks flopping down her back. She actually sets off a faint breeze that smells of patchouli as she enters.

Kate is immediately transported back to high school and the enormous crush she had on a shaggy-haired derelict named Boffo who was the lead guitarist for some third-rate Southern rock band. At the time, she firmly believed he was brilliant and destined for greatness. As she recalls, there was a serious semi-clad make-out session in the dressing room after one of Boffo's gigs and one too many Black Russians. And when he dedicated "The Devil Went Down to Georgia" to her–live, from the stage–in front of her best girlfriends and the other thirty audience members at Bub's Roadhouse, Kate felt like the Confederacy's answer to Linda McCartney. Patchouli was Boffo's signature scent.

The full-breasted, Rasta Pippi Longstocking now shuffling toward the front of the room can only be one person. This is not someone about to blend into the crowd. Sure enough, Una assumes her rightful place at the podium to a round of spontaneous and enthusiastic clapping from the audience. Una scans the crowd, deadly serious, then raises one hand solemnly over her head.

"Sisters!" Dead silence.

"Do you hear me, Sisters?!" Halfhearted affirmations along with some more clapping from the group.

"We have some serious business to discuss here today. Am I correct?"

More silence.

"How many of you here today have let a man lead you from your true path? How many of you here today have given up your dignity, your womanhood, your *self-respect*, because some smooth-talking, sweet-smelling Lothario led you down the path to servitude? Each and every one of you is unique. Is special. How many of us throw that away for some fantasy man that doesn't exist? Am I speaking the truth for any of you out there?"

Dani moves forward in her seat and Kate hears her mutter a small "Yeah" under her breath.

"I am asking you, Sisters! Let me hear you!" In that moment, there is a whir of pink to her right and Dani suddenly shoots up with both arms over her head.

"Hallelujah! We hear you, Sister!" Dani shouts. Kate can't believe it.

Una smiles for the first time. "Now, that's what I like to hear. We have a Sister here who can hear–can acknowledge–the truth. The truth is in her. It's in all of you."

Dani takes her seat.

"Let's hear it for the Righteous Sister."

Enthusiastic applause with some *Amen*s thrown in. Kate tries to catch Dani's eye but Dani is transfixed.

"Ladies," Una lowers her voice, "how many times have you made a *man* the answer to your rainbow? How many times have you put all of your eggs in one basket only to realize that you're spinning in a vicious cycle? How many times have you climbed that endless ladder to your dreams only to realize that you missed the boat?"

Una is mixing metaphors so fast Kate's starting to feel dizzy.

"Bless you, Sister! Right on!" Dani shouts over the crowd, jumping to her feet again. This time a number of audience members join her.

"Do we have a testimonial?" asks Una, looking directly at Dani. "Do we have a witness?"

"I'll testify," Dani chimes.

That's right, Sister. Listen up, everyone. Let's hear what our sisters have to say," Una bellows.

Una motions Dani forward. Dani looks up at the crowd. Some of the color has returned to her face.

"Listen, girls. I'm here to tell you that everything she's saying is true. I make the same mistake over and over, and each time I convince myself it's going to be different. Even this weekend, I met this incredibly handsome man. Before I could see what a total player he was, I had us married and living in the suburbs in Connecticut. It was right in front of me and I couldn't see it. He looked like a prince but he was the same old frog. He's two-timing if not three-timing me . . . He's probably married for all I know. I feel like such an idiot. But I won't do it again. I won't give up my power."

"Amen, Sister. What's your name?" Una thunders.

"Dani. Dani Strauss."

"Well, Dani, thank you. Thank you for your words and your honesty. You have true power. Seize it. It's yours. Take it back. Anyone else? . . . Yes, you!"

A mousy-looking brunette with short, puffy hair and large, thick glasses scurries toward the front of the room. Her eyes dart back and forth across the audience before she begins. At first her voice is barely audible. She reminds Kate of Dana Carvey's Church Lady, only not as cute.

"When I first met Greg, I was convinced that he was my prince."

Una gently touches her shoulder and whispers something in her ear. The Church Lady raises her voice, now speaking into the mike. There is a brief crackling noise.

"I told myself that it was OK that he didn't want sex 24/7 like I did . . . that it was all right that he didn't want to gratify me orally."

"He didn't *satisfy* you," Una roars. "How did that make you *feel?*"

"I thought his pleasure was more important, I thought that if I made him happy I could be satisfied." Church Lady is on a roll. "I lied to myself and to him."

"What *lies* did you tell, Sister?"

"I told him he was a great lover. I told him his penis wasn't small."

"*Uh-huh,*" someone cries out from the audience.

Church Lady closes her eyes and clutches the microphone.

"I told myself you have to sacrifice for your man."

"And what did you *learn* from these lies?" Una steps behind the little woman, resting her hands on Church Lady's shoulders.

Church Lady's face is red and her voice is rising. "I learned . . ."

"*Yes?*" Una encourages her.

"I learned . . ."

"Speak the *truth,* Sister." Una sways back and forth, rocking the smaller woman off her feet.

"I learned that pencil-dick had a few dishes on the side!"

Una throws her hands up in the air.

"I won't ever give up what's important to me again." Church Lady pauses, smiles sweetly and says, "Amen, Righteous Sisters."

She gingerly makes her way back to her seat. As she passes their row, Kate sees Dani reach out, grab Church Lady's hand and squeeze it. Dani glances over and, for the first time since Una began, seems to notice that Kate is sitting next to her. Dani leans in and whispers.

"Guy may have been a dick . . . but at least he was a *big* dick, if you know what I mean." Then she giggles.

Kate raises her hand to her mouth and tries not to laugh out loud. "Danielle Elizabeth Strauss. Clearly, we need to get that cup of coffee."

Una goes on to talk about how and why women give their power up to men. Her voice rises and falls, increases in intensity and volume, then dropping to a mere whisper for effect. Her large hands gesture wildly to punctuate a point. She talks about the ten steps women need to take to reembrace their own power. There are a lot of *Amen*s and *Hallelujah*s emanating from the crowd, more than a few coming from Dani.

Una then calls for women to stop being so hard on themselves. To not chastise themselves for their mistakes. To let the mistakes make them stronger.

"Don't let the man win *the race*. It's *your race* you're running. You may go into tunnels and out of tunnels. You may go up and down mountains. A truck may go by and splash you with a puddle, it may even *hit you*. It might put you in the hospital with a few minor injuries but *it won't kill you*. And even if it *did* . . ." Una goes on, and, Kate has to believe, shatters the *Guinness* world record for the longest sustained metaphor.

"Go at your own pace. Get in touch with your power. And let it work for you. Don't bite the candle off at both ends," Una cautions in a somber yet sympathetic tone and then closes the seminar to a roar and standing ovation from the audience. Stacks of books for sale miraculously appear on a card table at the back of the stage.

"We'll go, I promise, but I just want to buy a book," Dani says pleadingly.

"OK, honey, that's fine. Hey, you waited with me at the bookstore to see Dr. Mia. And what do we have to do, anyway? We've got nothing but time," Kate says. And it occurs to her that for the first time in seven years, it's true.

They wait in line and finally it's Dani's turn. Una motions her over with a huge smile on her broad face. "Hey, Sister. I love your enthusiasm. You really shook some of the sleepers up. Thank you."

Dani blushes slightly. "Well, I just felt that what you said was so important. So real. Thank *you*."

Una scrawls her name across the front page of Dani's book with a bright purple marker. "I'd love to talk to you some more, but I've got to run—there's a cocktail party to wrap up the conference. Would you and your friend be interested in joining us?"

Before Kate can say anything, Dani tells Una that they'd love to and is jotting down the address and directions.

Then Kate and the newly converted Dani head out to get that cup of coffee.

Hallelujah. Amen.

⁓

"Una is amazing, isn't she?" Dani's got Kate by the arm and she's pulling her through the crush of newly inspired, self-actualized souls clogging the hallway, each awaiting a glimpse of their own particular life-changing guru.

"She's something, all right. You know, Dani, I never thought I'd see the day."

"What day is that?" Dani asks, expertly maneuvering Kate around a short, plump woman with thinning red hair who's stopped to adjust her espadrille.

"The day you'd sign on to the self-help circuit."

"Oh, please. Trust me, I won't be talking about cleansing my aura anytime soon. Unless, of course, it would help me shape-shift into Heidi Klum. We'll just check it out—have a drink or two. Besides, it will be cool to hang out with her. She's such a force. I mean, I really get what she's saying about the whole man/woman thing. Who knows what those people say *after hours*."

"About that man/woman thing...How was your lunch?" Kate asks.

Dani's stomach drops and for a minute she loses the buzz of empowerment. Or maybe it's just the last of the champagne leaving her system.

"Oh, fine." She decides to go for dismissive in the hopes of side-tracking Kate. "And how was Dr. Mia's talk?"

No dice.

"Oh, no, Ms. Danielle Strauss, I want all the gory details." Kate is relentless.

"We went to Le Cirque. Katie Couric was at the table next to me," Dani offers.

"I want to hear about Guy—you know, the person who was at the table *with* you."

"Jeez, Kate, what's with the interrogation? It was a lunch. We ate food."

Kate stares at her, her brows drawn in concern. Dani can't bear her sympathy.

Somehow cutting Guy down in front of a roomful of bitter women was much more satisfying than having to admit to her best friend that she had really, really screwed up—again. It's righteous indignation that Dani's after and that's not exactly a specialty of Kate's.

"Why are you looking at me like that? You heard me in there. I got up and told the whole room how I screwed up. How I always screw up. How my prince was a frog. Why do you want me to relive the whole shameful episode?"

Kate's whole face softens.

"Oh, Dani, I'm so sorry. I never meant . . . I mean, I thought you'd want to talk, maybe . . ."

"I'm done talking. I'm all about action now. You heard Una: 'Don't waste your breath on a man. Save your breath for the race.' I've left Guy eating my dust and I'm not looking back. So how about you tell me about your day instead?"

Kate laughs ruefully. "You really don't want to know."

"I really do," Dani says, relieved. "How about you tell me the whole story over coffee before we go to the party."

"When and where is this shindig, anyway?" Kate asks.

Dani digs the passes out of her coat pocket. "Six o'clock at the Peninsula Hotel. That's just a few blocks from our place. What say we head uptown for a little room service before we risk any more insights?"

Back in the room, Dani can't get into the shower fast enough. Standing in the steam, she idly traces patterns on the marble wall. *Maybe I'm overreacting. What if it really was just a business meeting? What if there's a perfectly logical explanation for the dry cleaning? What if Guy calls me tonight?* Wrapped in a towel, she picks her clothes up off the floor. They still smell of his aftershave and a wave of fury and embarrassment washes over her. She balls up the gorgeous skirt and the soft sweater and stuffs them to the bottom of the hotel's laundry bin.

"I don't deserve to be treated like this." She wipes the steam off the mirror and stares hard at her reflection. "What would Una say?"

"She'd tell you to take back your power, Sister," she says to the steamy mirror. "Run your own life. Please yourself first and others will please you."

It's working. She's feeling better. "Affirm yourself," she shouts.

"Are you OK in there?" Kate calls from the room.

Dani grabs a hairbrush for a microphone, flings open the bathroom door and slides out.

"I'm better than OK. I have found my affirmation! I ask you, girl: What would Bessie do?"

Dani launches into a version of her favorite Bessie tune, and it comes straight from the heart:

> *"Once upon a time, I stood for all he did*
> *Those days are gone, believe me kid*
> *I've be mistreated and I don't like it, there's no use to say I do . . ."*

Dani finishes with a flourish of her hairbrush, one hand clutching at her towel, which has become unwrapped during the performance.

Kate is on her feet applauding: "Ladies and gentlemen" she beams, "Dani is in the house!"

~

"Sister!"

Kate and Dani walk into the rooftop bar at the Peninsula, and Dani is immediately crushed in a patchouli-scented bear hug.

Una is resplendent in a purple, green and gold caftan. It's so similar to her last outfit that Dani wonders if she has changed or, in fact, discovered the "mood" caftan. A rainbow-colored scarf pulls her flaming red dreadlocks up into a spout on the top of her head. Her wrists are laden with bracelets and prayer beads. The whole look is finished off with a pair of bright purple "fashion" Birkenstocks.

Dani considers that Una is truly free of the shackles of dressing to impress men—or apparently anyone else for that matter.

"Sister, you are here tonight to celebrate your liberation!" Una booms.

Throughout the room heads turn; people stare. Dani gets the feeling that Una couldn't be more pleased.

"You remember Kate?" she says, wriggling free of the embrace.

"Of course I do. You must be so proud of your friend." Una opens her arms and reaches for Kate.

"I think I'll go get something to drink," Kate says, stepping out of arm's reach. "Can I get something for you?"

"I'll have another of these delicious concoctions," Una says, holding out her nearly empty glass.

"What an interesting color." Kate peers at the radioactive green beverage. "What's it called?"

"It's my signature drink. Invented it myself at last year's conference." Una gestures grandly. "I call it the Melon Ball Buster because after *two*, that's exactly what you'll *do!*"

"Care to try one, Dani?" Kate grins wickedly.

"Red wine, please," she says and Kate scampers off to the bar with what Dani swears is a look of relief on her face.

"Now, Dani," Una puts her arm around her shoulder. "Let me introduce you to some of my colleagues."

In short order Una introduces her to a pet psychic, a woman who reads auras, and a man who has a radio show that puts callers in touch with spirits who have "departed the audio frequencies of this earth."

Kate materializes at her elbow with a glass of wine and Dani takes it from her gratefully.

"What took you so long?"

"I was talking to Dr. Mia at the bar. She asked me what I did and instead of telling her I was just a mom, I totally babbled on about my time in London and my research at the Psychiatric Institute–turns out Dr. Mia knows the director of the project I worked on." Kate frowns.

"What's the matter?"

"She's so nice and I probably bored her to tears with the dull details of my failed quest to do something important."

"Honey, you do tons of important things. Every day." Dani reaches out and gives Kate a one-armed hug.

"Keep the pep talk coming," Kate says urgently. "I'd really like to talk to Dr. Mia some more, but I'm afraid that between today's seminar and my babbling at her at the bar, she realizes what a total loser I am!"

"Kate Thompson, you are not a loser," Dani says firmly.

"Certainly not," Dr. Bob materializes behind them. He's casually dressed in pale-colored trousers and an eye-popping Hawaiian shirt that clashes painfully with Una's outfit. "I stopped by Mia's seminar today and I must say, Kate, your self-assessment was eye-opening. Simply inspiring. Mia thought so, too."

Kate is beaming.

Dani turns to Una, expecting her to say something affirming about *her* breakthrough, but Una is focusing a venomous glare on Dr. Bob, and Dani senses it's not related to the fact that his outfit is competing with hers for attention.

"Kate seems to have an innate understanding of the kind of work we're doing," Dr. Bob says to Una, raising his eyebrows. "Something it usually takes people *years* to come by."

Una sputters into a coughing attack that only abates after four or five swigs of her Technicolor cocktail.

"Much as I'd love to chat–*Bob*," Una says, pointedly leaving off the *Dr.*, "and there's much we could talk about, I'm sure you'd agree–I'm eager to introduce Dani to some of the wonderful *forward-thinking* professionals here today."

"That's certainly one way to describe *your* colleagues," Dr. Bob retorts.

Kate and Dani exchange bemused glances.

"Oh, there's Bruno," Una glances around wildly. "He's absolutely the most gifted spiritual financial planner . . ." She grabs Dani's arm and begins to haul her away

"Coming?" Dani asks Kate weakly.

"I think I'll stay here and chat with Dr. Bob for a few more minutes." Kate gives a little wave as Una drags Dani off toward a skinny little guy wearing a green sports coat and a tie covered with dollar signs.

Twenty long minutes later, after Dani's promised to incorporate more green (the color of wealth) into her workplace, and to consider investing in companies that honor the spiritual inclinations of their clients—apparently you can tell from looking at their brochures—Una proposes another glass of liquid empowerment and Dani's more than ready.

Five steps from the bar, Church Lady, from the afternoon's seminar, pops up in front of them.

"Una," she squeaks. "I've been looking everywhere for you."

"I'm so glad you made it, darling," Una trumpets, burying the mousy creature in a great expanse of emerald-draped bosom.

When she resurfaces, Church Lady introduces herself as Crystelle, Una's "number one fan."

"You really inspired me to speak out at today's meeting," she tells Dani.

"Yes, Dani reached the first stage of her empowerment today," Una says proudly.

"That's me," Dani says. "An independent, empowered woman."

"Well, you can't just rush off with this sort of thing," Crystelle says, knowingly. "You'll need some follow-up maintenance to make sure you don't backslide. Where do you live? Maybe we can find some gatherings for you to go to."

"Crystelle comes to every one of my talks," Una says.

"I'm so committed to her whole life plan," Crystelle nods.

"Uh, I'm not sure I remember the life plan part of today," Dani says.

"It's a whole way of life for today's woman," Una explains. "If you follow it, you can remove yourself from the destructive cycle men impose upon us. You will never fall victim to a smooth-talking man—and they are everywhere—even in this very room."

Una shoots Crystelle a meaningful look.

"I can't believe he has the nerve to even show up—after what happened last year," Crystelle says righteously.

"Who?" Dani looks around the room.

"Dr. Bob." Una's voice is dripping with sarcasm. "With his half-baked ideas of opening up communication between men and women."

"He's best known for full-body communication, if you know what I mean." Crystelle's eyes are bugging right out of her head.

Una nods sadly. "I hear so many stories from Sisters who have fallen prey to his smooth deceptions. Under the guise of communicating, he has taken advantage of so many weak souls."

"In fact, Una believes that communication between men and women isn't just difficult; it's useless," Crystelle says with fervor. "When you have fully evolved by following her plan, you'll never need to have a conversation with a man again."

Dani glances at Una and Crystelle's smug faces. She tries to imagine a scenario where she never has to speak to Bryce or Brian again, and for a moment it sounds good. And then it just sounds simply ridiculous. Dani nearly laughs out loud as she admits to herself that she's just had her first actual self-help realization: *All men aren't bad*, she thinks. *I just make bad choices about men.*

Una and Crystelle are staring at her. "I have a six-day seminar cruise coming up," Una is saying. "More than 150 women just like us. 'Free at Sea,' I'm calling it."

Inexplicably, Dani's amusement turns to a sense of irritation. *Did I really waste a whole afternoon listening to this nonsense?*

With a growing sense of urgency, she looks back to where she had left Kate and Dr. Bob talking. Kate is nowhere in sight. *She would never fall for that charlatan's spiel.* Dani scans the room again. Finally she spots Kate and Dr. Bob sitting next to each other at a quiet table across the room. Dr. Bob is leaning in, as if imparting urgent wisdom. He reaches across the table and touches Kate's hand. Dani sees Kate nod and stand up. They cross the room and step out through a doorway and out of sight.

"Thanks for everything, Una," Dani says. "But I've really go to go now."

"OK, but *don't forget*," Una says now practically shouting, "You need a man like you need a *fish* who can ride a *bicycle!*"

Dani rounds the corner and to her horror, sees that Dr. Bob is standing closer to Kate than a professional should.

". . . It's so rare that someone like you—someone who truly understands what I am trying to say—comes along," he murmurs, moving one hand up to rest on the wall too close to Kate's shoulder.

"I don't *feel* like I'm particularly good at understanding communication between the sexes," Kate says. "My own husband is a mystery to me half the time."

Dr. Bob moves his other hand to rest on the wall near Kate's elbow. Dani knows this body language only too well. Hell, if they were in an elevator, well . . .

"Maybe it's your husband who's the problem . . ." Dr. Bob says suggestively.

"And maybe it's your lack of professional ethics," Dani says, striding up and slapping his hand down off the wall.

He loses his balance and falls into Kate.

"Perhaps your friend has had a few too many of Una's cocktails," he says to Kate.

Kate gasps and turns scarlet.

"Dani!"

"Oh, c'mon, Kate, can't you see what's going on here."

Kate grabs her firmly by the elbow. "Excuse us, Dr. Bob. I apologize for my friend," she says, and steers Dani down the hallway. They pause near the elevators.

"Believe it or not, I know exactly what's going on," Kate says. "But how about you give me a chance to handle it in my own way?"

Dani stares at the floor ashamed.

"I'm sorry," she finally manages to say. "All of a sudden they all seemed like a bunch of charlatans."

"It's OK, really. He is a bit of a close talker . . ." Kate says, trying to make it better, like she always does.

"Let's just get out of here," Dani says miserably, punching the DOWN button on the elevator. "Until I snapped out of it, I think I was truly in danger of dressing in wearable art."

Kate laughs and takes her arm as they wait for the doors to open.

~

"All right, as our CPA friends would say, 'Let's party,'" Dani proclaims as they hit the street in front of the hotel. It sounds forced.

"I'm not sure I feel much like partying," Kate says. "This day has been kind of intense."

Dani replays the whole day, flinching at some of the memories.

"I know what you mean," she says. "It's as if I'm living in some bad soap opera."

Kate stops walking and Dani turns to face her.

"Has this all been some huge mistake?" Kate's expression is somber. "I mean, all we've done is indulge ourselves and where has it gotten us?"

"Well dressed and full of cocktails?" Dani says, trying to lighten the tone.

Kate doesn't even crack a smile.

"You're mad at me, aren't you?" Dani says.

"No, I'm not mad. But honestly, Dani, you're like Dr. Jekyll and Ms. Hyde where men are concerned. They're either the answer to your every problem or you don't need them at all. It's hard to watch."

Dani knows Kate's right. Still, it stings.

They trudge along in silence for a few minutes.

"Remember that time last year when we went out—me and you—for drinks at that Italian restaurant?" Kate asks suddenly.

"We stayed out way too late." Dani smiles, thinking about how she had walked Kate up to the door, half expecting Andy to be standing on the porch, arms crossed, ready to accuse them of violating curfew.

"We just talked and talked—and for days afterward I felt like everything was somehow OK," Kate says.

"We don't do that enough, do we?"

"We don't," Kate says. "Something always comes up: no babysitters, or late nights at the office, or guilt over not spending enough time doing quality things with the family . . ."

"Are you thinking what I'm thinking?" Dani's smiling now and her steps are lighter and quicker.

"There are no such excuses on vacation," Kate begins.

"And it seems like there's a lot we could talk about," Dani finishes.

Kate is smiling now, too. She trots a few steps and then matches her stride to Dani's.

"I always thought I'd like to try one of those bohemian coffeehouses in Greenwich Village," Kate says. "You know, drink cappuccinos in front of a fireplace and everything."

They arrive in front of the Plaza. Dani glances down at her gorgeous high-heeled boots. Truth is, they're killing her toes.

"How about a quick change before we head downtown?"

An hour later they are comfortably folded into big overstuffed chairs in front of a low-burning fire. Two cappuccinos and a plate of cookies sit on the small table between them.

"Ahhh," Kate lets out a sigh. "This is what I needed."

Dani picks up her mug, slides her feet out of her new Puma yoga shoes and sits cross-legged in the chair.

"You look like you should be in a *Vogue* article on working out and looking fabulous," Kate says. "I hope you wear that stuff at home when you go running."

Dani glances down at the navy velour Juicy sweatpants and hoodie that somehow fit better and look cooler than any workout clothes she's ever owned.

"Bebe's a big fan of sweatsuits," she says thoughtfully. "Me—I always thought they were a little Atlantic City, if you know what I'm saying. But I think I'm a convert. Either that or I'm turning into my mother."

Kate laughs. "If it were nylon and bright orange, I'd have to agree. But I think you look pretty stylish."

Kate stretches her legs out and props them on the edge of the fireplace. She's wearing her old sneakers and a pair of jeans she'd brought from home. But with her artfully tousled and highlighted hair and the ivory cashmere turtleneck she's wearing, the whole effect is shabby chic instead of plain shabby.

"Well, it's better to look good than to feel good, as the saying goes." Dani tries to pass it off as a joke, but her attempt at humor falls flat. "How did today start out so great and go bad so fast?"

Kate fixes her with a steady look.

"How about you tell me?"

Dani thinks about deflecting Kate with a flip answer, but instead finds herself spilling all the details of the day. From her masterminding of a "chance" meeting with Guy, right up to the humiliation at the hands of the concierge at the hotel.

"I really screwed up," she says miserably when she finishes. "I'm so sorry."

"Oh, honey," Kate says and reaches over to give Dani a hug.

Tears are brimming in Dani's eyes and she sniffs loudly.

"He's not worth it, you know," Kate says, settling back into her chair.

"I know," she says miserably, swiping at her eyes with the sleeve of her sweatsuit.

"You've got so much to offer someone, Dani," Kate continues. "You don't have to keep offering up different versions of yourself trying to please these jerks."

"That's easy for you to say," Dani says. "You've got Andy. I'm telling you, Kate, I get so tired of doing it all this by myself."

"Doing what?" Kate asks.

"You know, all of it. Going to work, paying the bills, doing the housework, being a good parent . . ."

"OK, so let's break it down." Kate is suddenly all business. "If you found the perfect guy, would you stop working, like Brian wanted you to?"

"I think it's well established what I'm like if I'm not working," Dani says. "I wouldn't feel like me if I didn't work. But I sure as hell wouldn't choose to work for Bryce."

"Well, you don't have to work for Bryce, whether or not you have a wealthy husband," Kate says. "So, next: Would you hire a full-time nanny, or maybe one for each of your many houses, to look after Brianna, while you spent your weekends jetting around with someone like Guy?"

"Never. I don't want someone else–or a whole team of someone elses–raising my kid." Dani doesn't even have to think about this one.

"So a man like Guy–just what parts of your life would he fix?"

Dani sits quietly for a long time. Kate just watches her.

"More shopping sprees like this one?" Dani finally offers halfheartedly.

"*We* made this happen for ourselves," Kate says. "*We* took advantage of what was in front of us and wrote our own destiny."

"But Guy was right in front of me. Wasn't I taking advantage of that?"

"But accepting this money as something that was meant to happen to us hasn't changed who we really are. Wardrobe and hair don't count," Kate quickly adds. "Was Guy really going to accept you for who you are–a working single mom with a seven-year-old daughter?"

"He never knew who I was." It slips out so quickly Dani knows she's spoken the truth.

"I do believe you're destined to find love right in front of you," Kate says. "But until you do, you can always count on me." Kate swings her legs off of the fireplace and rises to her feet. "I'll be right back," she says heading in the direction of the hand-painted door marked LES FEMMES.

It's true, Dani thinks, watching Kate go. *I could count on her from day one.* If Dani hadn't met Kate at the playgroup, she would have gone mad. She and Brian had just moved into the neighborhood and Brianna was desperate to meet other kids, so Dani had signed them up for an afternoon playgroup at the local community center. Brianna loved it immediately, dashing away from Dani to join a group of wilding toddlers who were leaping from a climber onto a pile of colorful tumbling mats.

Dani had stood awkwardly near the arts-and-crafts area, realizing she just wasn't going to blend in. The other moms sat cross-legged on the floor; for the most part, they looked like they'd just rolled out of bed. Ponytails and barrettes tamed hair that, even generously, couldn't be called styled. Indian print dresses, cutoff shorts and sweatpants seemed to be the preferred group uniform. At the mother's group Dani had gone to in New York, playgroup had meant choosing an outfit that was fashionable, yet casual—just to prove that your sense of style hadn't been thrown out with the placenta. Dani had agonized over how to dress for her first meeting with this group, finally settling on black capris, sandals with little kitten heels and a sleeveless turquoise shell. She'd pulled out some chunky silver bangles and dangling turquoise earrings. She'd wrestled her curls into sleek waves with the blow-dryer. She'd felt so proud of herself for making the effort when she'd left the house. Clearly, it was wasted.

Finally a tall, thin woman, with graying hair styled in a crew cut and sporting cutoff army fatigues and a baggy olive T-shirt, had motioned Dani over to the mother's "sharing circle." Dani had joined the circle, sitting cross-legged and arranging her face into an expression she hoped conveyed interest.

"I was just saying," an earnest young woman with blonde hair pulled back in pigtails began to speak again, "that it is such a shame that women don't take the time to enjoy the miracle of motherhood. Rushing back to work, paying virtual strangers to raise your children, is no way to promote the values of family and home."

Dani's face flushed. "Don't you think that's sort of a retro attitude?" she asked, trying to keep her voice neutral.

"Mothering is about devoting yourself to caring for your family," the woman said condescendingly, staring pointedly—Dani thought—at her painstakingly pedicured toes.

"Maybe some families are better off if the mother's happy working," Dani shot back.

The group stared at her as if she had sprouted two heads.

"I know what you mean," a woman who had been standing by the snack table piped up. "Sometimes I feel like I'd be a better mother to Henry if I could just get some time to myself."

Dani smiled at her savior gratefully as she backed out of the circle and went over to where the woman stood.

"Dani Strauss," she said, sticking out her hand.

"Kate Thompson," the woman replied. "I love your top; that color's wonderful on you."

Dani grinned. "I guess I'm a little overdressed, huh?"

She had felt immediately at home with Kate, whose natural warmth and sly sense of humor made Dani feel like they'd known each other forever.

Their getting-to-know-you conversation was cut short by a wail from the direction of the climbing tower. A small blond boy with his hand pressed against his forehead was stumbling toward them.

"She hit me with a toy," he wailed, burying his face in Kate's khakis.

"Who did, Henry?"

"She did." To Dani's horror, he had pointed directly at Brianna, who was standing at the top of the climber's slide, brandishing a plastic horse.

Before Dani knew it, Brianna was down from the climber and running over to where she, Kate and Henry stood.

"Here, boy. I want you to have a present," Brianna said, nearly bopping Henry on the ear with the horse.

"Brianna, careful! . . . No hitting," Dani had snapped. The horse clattered to the floor. "I am so sorry," Dani had said, turning toward Kate.

But Kate had knelt down to Brianna's level and gently picked up the toy. Holding Henry safely out of the fray, she had begun a long conversation with Brianna about horses. Before Dani knew what was happening, Brianna and Henry were happily sitting on the floor babbling about horses and animals and favorite videos.

Dani had been awed. The woman was a natural.

"Classic case of the Electra complex." The woman with pigtails had appeared next to Kate and Dani. "The fascination with using the horse to inflict damage to the male. Are you having problems with her father?" She had stared at Dani.

Dani had opened her mouth to tell the woman to mind her own business, when she caught sight of Kate smirking and rolling her eyes. Dani had felt her own mood lighten. "Actually," she said, "I don't believe in anything as classically patriarchal as fathers. No actual men were involved in her conception."

The woman's mouth had dropped open. She had looked fascinated.

Fighting to keep a straight face, Dani had taken Kate's arm. "Want to get some lunch?"

On the way home from playgroup, Brianna had announced, "I love Henry and I love his mama."

Dani couldn't have agreed more.

Dani had never gone back to that playgroup, but she and Kate had become best friends. It was Dani whom Kate had called to come stay with Henry when her water broke and she went into labor with Charlie. And it was Kate whom Dani called first when she decided to leave Brian.

~

Kate returns, selects a cookie from the plate and, taking a bite, collapses back into her seat in front of the fireplace. She smiles, her cheeks flushed from the heat.

"I know I can count on you, Kate," Dani says thoughtfully. "I could count on you from the second we met. I was just thinking about that wretched playgroup."

"'*Classic case of the Electra complex*,'" Kate says in a mock serious voice and then laughs.

"Right. *'Having problems with her father?'* I should have gagged that pigtailed pip-squeak with a hemp rope," Dani says, smiling, and leans forward to take a sip of cappuccino.

"But seriously, Kate, sometimes I worry that there won't be any 'you' there for me to count on," Dani says.

"What do you mean by that?"

Dani thinks for a moment. "It's just that so many people count on you for so much–the kids, Andy, the people at READ, me–I'm afraid we'll suck you dry. That there'll be nothing left of you for *you*. You're so busy taking care of everyone else that you never take care of yourself. I guess I wish you'd be a bit more like your mom."

"My mom?" Kate looks totally surprised. "My mom never did anything for herself. She never left that house, or us kids, or her gardens. She's never even been to a spa. That's partly why I wanted to take this whole trip. So I wouldn't look back and say I never got away from it all."

"Seems to me your mom feels as though she's always had everything she's needed. You're the one who couldn't find anything to be grateful for. You're the one who's always looking for the answers in self-help books."

"But I like helping people," Kate says slowly. "I like it when people need me. I just wish I felt like what I did really mattered. Really made a difference to someone."

"But you never take the credit; you never acknowledge what you've done. Look at the whole Honeywell debacle. You let him take all the credit for your idea. Andy and the kids—they know you'll always be there for them—they take you for granted, and you try to convince yourself that that's what being a good wife and mother is all about."

"Maybe you're right," Kate says slowly. "Maybe I need to think more about what I need. About what makes me feel worthwhile. I wish I could be like Dr. Mia—she helps so many people every day. You saw that seminar. You saw how inspired everyone was—how she made a real difference in their lives."

"Well, for what it's worth, Katherine Thompson," Dani says, "you make a real difference in my life."

Kate smiles, then stands up and gives her a big hug. "And that matters to me. Really, it does, Dani."

"So you can start from there and we'll figure out the rest as we go along. And that concludes today's session," Dani jokes.

She flags the waiter over and gives him a twenty. Taking her best friend by the arm, Dani walks out into the hum of Manhattan at 2 a.m. Despite the muted hustle of the city, she feels quiet and calm. She feels like maybe, just maybe, it's all going to be fine.

Chapter Twelve

Kate rolls over, yawning and stretching luxuriously. She feels more truly rested than she has in years. She savors the quiet of the room, the silkiness of the sheets.

"Morning," Dani sings out from her bed.

"What time is it?"

"Ten o'clock," Dani giggles. "Can you believe it?"

Kate sits bolt upright in bed, feeling like she's wasting time. "Oh my god! I haven't slept until ten since before I was pregnant with Henry."

"Relax," Dani says. "We've got no plans. Nowhere to go. No men to chase. Why don't you call down and order up a copy of the *Times* and some coffee. We can have breakfast in bed and read the paper."

"Pure decadence," Kate says, reaching for the phone.

The red message light is blinking furiously.

"Dani, was there a message when we got in last night?" A little flicker of worry flares up in her stomach. What if something's wrong with one of the kids?

"Honestly, Kate, I didn't notice."

"What if something's happened to Charlie?" she worries aloud.

"Listen to you," Dani says sharply. "It's probably nothing. Probably just the desk calling to say our dry cleaning's ready or something equally mundane. In fact, I say, let's just ignore it until we've had breakfast, read the paper and had our showers. Then we can face checking messages."

"OK," Kate agrees, uneasily.

But she can't stop worrying. She had wanted to call home yesterday, but first she had gotten caught up in the seminar and then in Dani's saga. Now she's feeling completely guilty that she's neglected her family. She thinks back to her whole lecture to Dani last night and decides to practice what she's preached. Kate is going to put her own needs first. And what she needs to do is listen to the messages. She picks up the phone and dials.

Message received, Saturday, 9 p.m. To hear your message, press 1.

She hits the button.

Kate, darling, it's your mother. Your package arrived this afternoon. That's how I got your number. Imagine, a special delivery from the Plaza in New York. I'm so surprised–and grateful, of course–but honey, I just don't need a weekend at a spa. In fact, sweetie, I really don't want to go anywhere. I have everything I need right here–always have. Just the fact that you were thinking of me makes me happy. I can't wait to hear about your adventures. You and Dani enjoy the rest of your little vacation.

Kate smiles as she follows the automated prompts, hitting 7 to erase the call.

"Who was it?" Dani asks.

"My mom."

Kate thinks she sees a flicker of disappointment cross Dani's face. "See, it could have waited."

Before Kate can hang up, Dani takes the phone from her hand and pushes the button for a dial tone. Dialing room service, she places their breakfast order.

"Ten minutes until breakfast," Dani says. "Go make yourself presentable."

Kate disappears into the bathroom and takes a quick shower.

When she comes out, Dani's already set the small table near the window and is contentedly reading the "Style" section of the Sunday *New York Times*.

"First time I've been able to read the weddings section without substituting my name in some of the profiles," she jokes. "You should open a practice, Kate."

"Those who can't do, teach, right?"

"OK, I can see last night wasn't as uplifting for you as it was for me." Dani folds the paper and leans forward in the chair. "What's up?"

"I don't know," Kate says, honestly confused. "I feel like yesterday's seminar was just the start of something I need to do, but I've only got one more day and then it's back to Easton and the same old Kate."

"We figured out last night that it doesn't have to be that way," Dani says. "You've made a start. You can keep going."

"There's no Dr. Mia back in Easton," Kate says glumly. "I'll just be back to trying to read her latest book in between laundry and Charlie's nap. Feeling guilty for not being able to fill out my gratitude journal."

"You don't need some Dr. Mia holding your hand," Dani says annoyed. "Jeez, Kate, I thought we addressed this issue of your not giving yourself enough credit."

"Maybe I'm just feeling sad about our adventure coming to an end," Kate says, trying to change the subject.

"We've still got twenty-four hours." Dani brightens up. "And more money than we can hope to spend. I'll grab a shower and we can figure out how to go out with a bang!"

Dani bounces off to the bathroom and Kate absentmindedly spreads jam on a croissant. Sighing, she flips through the paper. But she can't shake a vague feeling of unease.

She notices the message light on the phone is still blinking.

"Dani, did the phone ring while I was in the shower?" she shouts.

"Nope," Dani shouts back.

Frowning, Kate crosses the room and picks up the phone.

Message received at 11:45 p.m. To hear your message press 1.

She hits the button.

This is a message for Kate Thompson. Kate, hi, it's Mel Fieldstein, we met at the Oak Bar the other night. Please call me as soon as you get this message. A rather unusual situation has come up. There's an opening in one of the organizations I represent, and we feel that you're an ideal candidate. We'd like to talk to you about a possible position with us. There are some time constraints, so we need to gauge your interest as soon as possible. Call my cell anytime: 917-555-5678. Looking forward to hearing from you.

The automated voice comes back on the line.

To erase this message press 7. To hear this message again, press 1.

"Dani. *Dani*," Kate screams.

Dani dashes from the bathroom, her wet hair dripping. "What is it? What's wrong?"

"Listen." Kate punches the button for speakerphone and hangs up the receiver.

"Is it Andy? The kids?" Dani stares at Kate like she's lost her mind.

"Just listen."

Kate presses 1 and the message repeats.

Dani's mouth drops open as Kate forces hers closed with an effort.

"What the . . . ? Who the hell is *Mel Fieldstein?*"

"He's that agent, the guy we met at the Oak Bar. He was with Dr. Mia and Dr. Bob."

"Dr. Bob! I knew it. The little weasel!" Dani's eyes have narrowed. "And to think that I didn't rip his head off last night when I had the chance!"

"What's Dr. Bob got to do with it?" Kate's head is already spinning and Dani's rampage is failing to provide any clarity.

"Don't be naive, Kate. Clearly Dr. Bob's sent his agent to do his dirty work. He couldn't score with you last night, so he's trying to lure you back into his clutches. Una was right–he is totally unethical."

"Mel didn't say the position was with Dr. Bob's practice," Kate protests weakly. She feels a sinking sensation in the pit of her stomach.

"Of course not, that would make this obvious ploy *completely* transparent." Dani is so worked up she's pacing the room.

Kate's beginning to believe Dani's right. Why would a professional organization, one that has helped millions of people, want *her* to work with them?

Dani is still raving.

". . . so you pick up that phone and tell Mel whatshisname that you're no sucker. No, wait, tell Mel you want to talk directly to Dr. Bob and then you can give that wolf in self-help clothing a piece of your mind."

"Maybe I should just ignore the call."

"You'll do no such thing, Kate." Dani is already dialing. She hands Kate the phone.

"Mel Fieldstein."

"Mel, uh, hi. It's uh, Kate. Thompson. Kate Thompson." she stammers.

"Kate. I was just getting ready to try your hotel again. So you got the message."

"Yes, I did and I, uh, I just wanted to say . . ." she glances desperately at Dani for guidance.

"What. Would. Bessie. Do." Dani whispers.

Maybe Dani can channel Bessie at will, but the best Kate can summon up is a polite refusal. "I wanted to say that it was very nice of you to call, but I'm sure I don't have the qualifications for the position. You'll just have to tell Dr. Bob that I . . ."

"Bob? What's Bob got to do with this?" Mel says sharply. "Has he approached you about a similar situation?"

"Well, no, he didn't exactly . . ." Kate's voice trails off.

"God, Mia hates it when he tries to poach talent . . ." Mel is still ranting.

"Dr. Mia?"

"Look, Kate, time is of the essence here. Let me lay it all out: Mia loved your take on her whole philosophy. She's looking for a director for her new center in London. She wants you. In fact, she's set on it."

"Dr. Mia? London? Me?" Kate repeats blankly.

"Dr. Mia? London? You?" Dani echoes from across the room.

Kate listens in stunned silence as Mel goes on about interviews, salary requirements and booking airline tickets so she can meet with the existing staff in London. Gradually, she becomes aware of a silence on the phone line.

"So does this all sound doable?" Mel's tone is impatient and she realizes he's been waiting for an answer for some time now.

"Well, I mean, thank you for thinking I could do this," Kate begins. "But I really can't . . ."

Dani grabs the receiver out of her hand.

"Mel? Dani Strauss here. I'm Kate's lawyer. I think Kate would like to discuss this directly with Mia. You'll agree that it's a decision with enormous import for both her and her family. Can we set up a meeting in the next few hours?"

"Dani," Kate hisses, "what the hell are you doing?"

Dani waves her hand at her. "Great, Mel. Kate will be there. You too. Bye."

"Are you out of your mind?" Kate blurts out. "I can't take a job in London. I couldn't take a job at one of Dr. Mia's centers if it was in Easton. I'm not qualified. I'm not together. I'm not . . ."

"You're not giving yourself credit." Dani's voice is firm. "Now it's my turn to be counselor." She pushes Kate down into the chair and begins to pace. Kate's seen this before. Dani's in courtroom mode.

"Kate, the things you said last night made more sense to me than years of expensive therapy with Park Avenue shrinks. You have a way of getting to the heart of a problem and a gift for seeing the best in people. You have taken a small charitable organization in a backwater town and made it into a national award-winning example. You've sustained a loving marriage; you have a home where people always feel welcome. You have the least dysfunctional family relationships of anyone I've ever met . . ."

Dani stops pacing and pauses for breath.

"But I don't have any credentials, and I never even finished my doctorate. Why would anyone listen to me?" Kate wails.

"You have a good heart. I believe in you. Dr. Mia clearly believes in you."

"I couldn't run an institute," Kate begins again.

"Snap out of it!" Dani has lost all patience. "Everyone thinks you can do this but you. Last night you made me see that my problem is that I am always looking to other people for validation. Well, you pretend you don't want any validation at all. And all that does is make you feel insecure and insignificant."

"That's pretty insightful," Kate says. "Maybe you should put yourself up for the job."

Dani grins. "That's me, all New Agey and in touch with myself. Seriously, I don't care if you take the job or not. But if you don't get dressed and march yourself downstairs and listen to what this woman has to say, you will spend the rest of your life wondering what you missed."

Kate doesn't want to admit it, but her friend is right. All her life she's been telling herself that just taking care of everyone is enough.

But it's not enough anymore, she thinks. *How can you tell if you're doing a good job at something when no one ever tells you? If you can't even tell yourself.*

Kate watches Dani pull outfits from the closet and lay them on the bed, saying something about the right look for an interview, but Kate's not listening. Even as she looks around the luxurious room, and she stares at the mounds of designer clothing, Kate's picturing herself standing at a lectern talking to an audience who will go home feeling better than they did when they came in. She hears Dr. Mia's voice: *No dream is out of reach. You dreamed it because it has a place in your life. It is up to you what you do with it.*

Kate stands up, squares her shoulders and crosses the room to where Dani is still laying out clothes. "So what do you suppose directors of European self-help institutes are wearing these days, anyway?" she asks.

~

The plan was to meet in the Palm Court on the first floor of the Plaza for tea. Kate arrives five minutes early, but when she walks in she sees that Dr. Mia is already there. She is sitting at a table with a steaming pot of tea, a delicate china cup and saucer, and a stack of papers in front of her. She is thumbing through the paperwork and removes her reading glasses as Kate approaches.

"Kate," she says rising from her chair and extending her hand. "So kind of you to meet me on such short notice. Have a seat. What can we get you?"

A waiter appears and Kate orders a mint tea. Dr. Mia sits and considers her with an expression that is intent but gentle.

"I'm opening a center in London and we need to hire a program director. I don't know if Mel mentioned it, but we have another candidate we're seriously considering for the spot. We had some reservations and when we met you, well, it seemed almost meant to be."

"How could you think that? You heard me at the seminar. My foundation needs work," Kate says bluntly.

"We all feel that way inside," Dr. Mia says. "But it's not what others see. I think you just need the opportunity and you will fully realize your potential."

"Well, as you say, we create our own reality and must accept full responsibility for what we find in our lives."

"Yes, I do believe that's true. Let me tell you a bit about the spot." As Dr. Mia fills her in on the position and the goals of the London program, Kate gets more and more excited. Dr. Mia tells her that from their first meeting, she had a sense that Kate was just what they'd been looking for.

There's a long pause until Dr. Mia prompts her. "What do you think, Kate?"

Kate's not sure what to say. "I think it sounds wonderful. I think, as you say, circumstances present themselves because they hold a lesson that we need to learn. That we need to follow the map of our lives, that . . ."

She feels a warm hand on hers as Dr. Mia interrupts. "Kate. I am flattered that you've read my books so closely. I hope that my words are somehow helpful. But as an old teacher of mine once said—and she was much wiser than I'll ever be—truth is only meaningful when you are able to put it in your own words, when you make it your own."

Kate feels the blood rushing to her cheeks. For a second, she feels ashamed, but when she looks in Dr. Mia's eyes, she sees only kindness and is reassured. Dr. Mia takes Kate's hand in hers.

"You are an impressive young woman with a great deal to offer. Why don't you think about the position and let us know what you've decided. I know you'll make the right choice."

〜

". . . So I would have to go over to London for the final interviews," Kate is saying.

Dani leans forward and rests her elbows on the table.

"So what do you think?" she asks, touching her fingertips together and resting her chin on them.

"I think it's crazy."

"Crazy good? Or crazy you could never do anything like that?"

Kate sighs. "I don't know. I mean, Dr. Mia really made me feel like I could do this. That it was possible. And maybe Andy would be able to get a sabbatical, or teach at one of the London universities. And it could be really great for Henry and Charlie to see another part of the world . . ."

"Do I hear a 'but' . . . ?"

"*But* it still all seems like someone other than me is going through this. Like I'm just watching some woman, wearing glamorous clothes, getting a chance at a glamorous job."

"You could do it. You know that, don't you?" Dani has lost some of her earlier cheerleader pep. She's been subdued ever since Kate sat her down to tell her the details of the meeting. Maybe Dani's worried she might actually go to London.

"Could I?" Kate muses.

"So you're on a pretty tight deadline, huh?"

"Dr. Mia said they need to know by six o'clock tonight," she tells Dani. "They've got another candidate who is expecting to hear from them by this Thursday. They've already offered her a position pending references. So I'd need to leave for London with them tomorrow night, meet with the institute staff on Tuesday and make a final decision by Wednesday."

"Well, maybe Andy would let you extend your little vacation by a few days," Dani says.

"I think I need to call him," Kate hears herself say.

"Oh my God, Kate," Dani says. "You're actually considering this."

She nods slowly. "I think I may be. Like you said, if I don't at least take the chance, then I'll always wonder what I missed."

"Do you want me to leave while you call Andy?" Dani asks.

"No, please stay," Kate says, grabbing Dani's hand tightly. "I could use the support."

〜

Andy answers the phone on the first ring. Kate can hear the sounds of the TV in the background. Closer to the phone she can hear Charlie whimpering. Her radar goes up.

"Is everything OK?" she asks.

"Hi, honey, everything's fine," Andy says.

"It's not fine," she hears Charlie sob.

"Charlie's a bit under the weather, says his throat hurts. We're just sitting here on the couch watching TV and eating Popsicles." Andy says.

"Did you take his temperature? How long has he been feeling sick?" Kate gets the frantic feeling she always has when one of the boys is sick, only now it's multiplied exponentially because she's three hours away. She needs to hold her baby.

"I felt his forehead," Andy is saying. "Maybe he's a bit warm . . ."

"Please, hon, it could be strep. Maybe you should call Dr. Hilton."

"Kate, it's Sunday. He's fine. Probably just a cold. Do you want to talk to him?"

"I wanna talk to Mommy." Kate can hear Charlie working his way up to a full wail and then his voice on the line: "I'm sick. I want you to come hoooome."

"I know, baby. Daddy's taking good care of you, though."

"I want you." Charlie sniffs loudly. "Henry does too."

"Yeah, Mom, come home," she hears Henry yell in the background.

"Put Daddy back on the phone, baby."

"OK."

The phone drops to the floor with a thud and Kate hears the sound of sock-clad feet pattering toward the kitchen. As she listens to the TV in the background, her mind is racing.

I need to be there. Charlie needs me.

She has a flash of herself standing onstage, before an audience. Hopeful faces gaze up at her, waiting for direction. *They will all think they need me,* she realizes.

"I'm back." Andy picks up the phone. "Just got another Popsicle. I think I've bought another twenty minutes of peace."

She can hear how tired his voice sounds. *He needs me, too.*

"I miss you," he's saying. "Are you having fun?"

And suddenly everything is clear to her. She knows exactly where she's needed and it's not in London. But it's more than that. It's about where she *wants* to be.

"I think we'll head home a bit early," she says.

"Aw, Kate, it's your last night. Don't come home just because Charlie's a little under the weather. We'll be fine until tomorrow night."

"That's not why I'm coming home. I'm just ready." Really ready, she realizes. "I've missed my guys." Kate says. And she's never meant it more.

"We've missed you." Andy sounds relieved.

"Tell Charlie I'll be home to kiss him good night, tonight. And give him some Motrin, please."

"All right. See you soon. Love you."

"Love you, too." Kate hangs up the phone.

"Everything OK?" Dani asks.

"Never better," she says, smiling.

Without hesitation, Kate crosses the room to her purse, finds the phone number she's looking for, picks up the phone and dials again.

"Dr. Mia? Hi, it's Kate Thompson. I've given careful thought to everything we discussed and I'm sorry to have to tell you that I must decline your offer of a position at the institute."

"I'm very sorry to hear that, Kate. You would have been an asset to the organization, as I hope you realize." Dr. Mia's voice is warm; Kate swears it sounds like she's being congratulated for something.

"Dr. Mia, I couldn't have made this decision without all of your guidance," she says gratefully.

"I'm glad I could help."

"You help so many people," Kate says. "I think I'm just meant to help a few at a time."

Dr. Mia laughs. "It sounds as if you've found your calling."

"I think it took your offer to show it to me. Thank you for everything," Kate says, her voice breaking with emotion.

"Take care of yourself, dear. And stay in touch. I could always use someone with your talents."

"Thank you. I will. Good-bye." Kate hangs up the phone and for the first time since she started making the calls, glances at Dani.

A huge smile that manages to show both relief and pride is spreading across her friend's face.

"So you've decided to limit your practice to Easton, Dr. Kate?" Dani says.

"I believe it's where I can do the most good," she replies with a grin. "And you know, I'm itching to get back to my followers. I hope you don't mind cutting our vacation short by a night?"

"I'm a little homesick myself, right at this moment," Dani agrees. "Ready to have our carriage turn back into a pumpkin?"

"Not quite yet. There's one more thing I need to find out on this trip."

"What's that?" Dani raises a brow.

"Just how extensive is the Game Boy section of FAO Schwarz?"

~

A few hours later, Patrick the doorman is loading up the substantial trunk of the Cadillac. Brand-new garment bags containing magazine-worthy wardrobes are laid carefully across the backseat. Stacks of shoeboxes take up all the legroom in back.

"It's been a pleasure, Patrick," Dani says giving him a big hug.

"Come back soon," he tells her.

Kate thinks of the receipt for their room, folded into a tiny little square and tucked into a corner of her purse with the rest of the evidence of their fling with a high-living lifestyle. "Not likely," she says under her breath.

Dani slides behind the wheel, waves a cheerful farewell to Patrick and then with a screech of squealing tires, the Caddy is flying across Central Park South, the Plaza fading behind them like a desert mirage.

"Put the pedal to the metal, baby," Kate says. "It's time to go home."

Part III

~

"The joy that isn't shared . . . dies young."

—Anne Sexton

Chapter Thirteen

It's early evening when Dani pulls up to Kate's house.

"Do you want some help getting these packages inside?" Dani asks.

Kate's expression, which has been happy and relaxed the whole drive home, suddenly changes. Small worry lines appear between her eyebrows.

"All this stuff," Kate says, almost to herself.

"Oops, that's right. Andy has no idea that you're rich," Dani jokes. "Maybe now's a good time to tell him—since you got him that expensive telescope and all."

"I think I'll just take the gifts for the boys, if you wouldn't mind keeping the other stuff in the car, at least until tomorrow."

Kate reaches over the seat and pulls and FAO Schwarz bag into her lap. Dani opens the trunk, puts Kate's suitcase down on the sidewalk at her feet and gives her a big hug.

"Thank you for the greatest four days of my life," Dani says.

"Thank *you*," Kate says, squeezing her tightly.

Dani watches as Kate heads up the walk to the house, then turns the Caddy around and heads home.

Dani lets herself into the house and drops her bag on the tile floor in the entryway. Suddenly she feels as if the car in the garage, filled to overflowing with boxes of gorgeous clothes and shoes and accessories, is just part of a dream. That tomorrow morning she'll wake up and open the door to find her battered old Volvo waiting. It's too early to go to bed, so Dani grabs a bottle of beer from the fridge, finds a bag of not-too-stale tortilla chips in the cabinet and flops down on the couch to watch some CNN. The house is quiet and she realizes, to her shock, that she is completely relaxed.

~

As Kate turns her key in the lock, she hears a rumbling from deep inside the house. She opens the door to see Henry and Charlie's faces beaming. They are poised with their hands in front of them and, on the count of three, they throw their hands over their heads and a flurry of small pieces of paper fall around her as she steps into the entryway.

"Welcome home, Mom!" They are giggling.

"Hi, guys! Wow, what a welcoming committee!" She sets down her bags and picks a piece of confetti off of her eyelash. She can see balloons dangling from the chairs in the hallway. The banister is wrapped in light blue crepe paper left over from Charlie's birthday party.

"It looks beautiful. Thank you so much." She reaches over and gives Henry a big hug. She leans over to hug Charlie, who throws his arms around her neck so hard she fears she'll pitch forward.

"Now, that's a hug. You must be feeling better!" She touches his forehead. It still feels a bit warm and he looks pale.

"That's the magic of Motrin. Hi, sweetheart. Let me take your coat." Andy grabs it from her hands, not noticing the Marc Jacobs upgrade. *There'll be time to discuss that later,* Kate thinks with a twinge of guilt.

"Thanks, honey."

"How are you feeling, buddy? I am so sorry you've been sick." Kate tries to smooth Charlie's hair down, but it pops back into its upright position as soon as she takes her hand away.

"I'm OK. Mommy, we made you a surprise!" Charlie's small body begins to wiggle with delight.

"Yeah, Mommy, come in the dining room!" Henry shouts.

"The boys have been working very hard," Andy says wryly. "I want to hear all about your weekend."

Where to start? Kate pictures the whirlwind shopping sprees. She sees herself falling off the bar at Hogs and Heifers and Dr. Bob's smarmy face leaning into hers. She feels a flash of panic. But then she thinks of Dr. Mia, of how she actually wanted her–Kate Thompson–to run the London office. But even that doesn't stick. It all passes through Kate's mind like a favorite old movie. *You have to find your own words.*

It is good to be home. I belong here.

She leans toward Andy and gives him a kiss on the cheek. "I'll tell you all about it."

"What kind of kiss is that for your long-lost husband?" Andy grabs her, and in a large sweeping motion, dips her to one side and gives her a long kiss on the mouth. Kate kisses him back, hard.

"Ewww . . ." says Henry.

"Mommy, let's go!" demands Charlie.

Andy lifts her back to her feet and then takes a closer look. "Your hair looks different."

"Yeah, Dani and I went to this amazing place. Do you like it?" Kate touches the side of her head.

"It looks great. But you always look beautiful." It really sounds as though he means it.

Kate feels a tug on her hand. Charlie is pulling her toward the dining room. "Come *on*, Mommy. Come see the surprise!"

With Charlie leading her, and Henry pushing from behind, she is propelled into the dining room.

"*Surprise!*" They both shout at once.

On the table is a large chocolate cake leaning precariously to the left. There's a landslide of fudge frosting in the same direction and a small gouge in the right side of the cake has been filled in with more frosting. The top is speckled with brightly colored M&M's and declares in neon blue frosting: "Welcome Home, Mommy!" It is the Charlie Brown's Christmas tree of cakes. It's beautiful.

"Oh, wow. I didn't know we had such expert bakers around here. Where did you get this from, Edelweiss? Easton Bakery?"

"No, Mommy, we made it ourselves!" Henry shouts.

"We made it. We made it!" says Charlie.

The boys look very pleased with themselves.

"It tastes good! I tried it," Charlie adds.

"Oh, I can see that." She smiles.

Andy appears with a stack of plates, forks, napkins and a knife.

"Thank you so much, guys. I love it. I have the best boys in the world."

They all sit down and watch as Andy cuts big fat slices of cake for everybody. When they're done, Kate collects the dishes and takes them into the kitchen. The sink is stacked high. There is a large mixing bowl dripping with batter, a smaller bowl caked with frosting, enough silverware to serve a State dinner and assorted cups and dishes. Kate just smiles. It can wait until tomorrow.

As they head upstairs, Charlie snuggled in Kate's arms and Henry excitedly retelling her how Daddy took them to the grocery store in their pajamas one morning, Kate realizes just how little sleep she's had over the past few days. Once the boys are in bed, she curls up in Andy's arms on their bed and, before she can tell him anything about her trip, falls into a deep, contented sleep.

Monday Morning

Dani is standing in a vast, open field high in the mountains like Julie Andrews during the opening credits of The Sound of Music, *only minus the drab attire. The sun is beaming through thin, wispy clouds and the air is sweet. She's wearing a long flowing dress and is barefoot. She sprints into the expanse of grass and flowers in front of her, only the faster she goes, the lighter her steps feel until she is slowly lifted into the air. It seems the most natural state in the world, as if she's done this all her life. Below, she can make out a small herd of mountain goats. A well-built man with good posture and thinning hair is standing near the flock. As she approaches overhead, he looks up, smiles and waves. It's Rudy Giuliani. Dani gives Rudy a wave and he smiles back, not that familiar pinched, teeth-slightly-clenched smile, but a real smile. He turns back to his herd.*

She sails over the next peak and sees two figures in the distance. Suddenly she hears the strains of a saxophone and sees the unmistakable mop of wavy hair on the slight fellow playing the instrument. Louis Armstrong, his round face shining, shakes his finger at Kenny G, but the young man doesn't seem

*to notice. Dani begins to address Kenny: Hey, what are you doing in my
dream?*

Before he answers, Dani opens her eyes to a roomful of light and
her clock radio blaring Kenny G's remake of "What a Wonderful World."
It's 7:01 a.m. She must have forgotten to switch off the alarm. She
reaches over and turns off the radio, feeling surprisingly rested. She
hears the wind rustling through the trees outside the window. Brianna
isn't due back until 6 p.m. *I can do anything I want. I can read the newspaper, or scan the new magazines that arrived just before we left. I can examine my new wardrobe. I could even dip back into the Mommy Fund and
have another spa day. I could catch up on some work.* But there's only one
thing she really wants to do. She hauls herself out of bed with purpose, takes a quick shower, and throws on a T-shirt and some old
jeans. She slurps down some coffee, grabs a piece of toast, and is in the
car by 7:45 a.m.

Moving along the familiar roads, Dani passes Mallone Cleaners,
where Brianna can always count on getting a lollipop with the dry
cleaning, and Starbucks, where she gets her coffee every morning. She
only has to show her face and there's a Grande half-caff with 2 percent waiting for her on the counter. She passes the playground at Brianna's school, where she first learned to "pump" on the swings. It feels
as if she's been gone for ages. Dani's mind drifts back over the past few
days. Images of shops and ritzy hotels run past like a tourist infomer-
cial. What she remembers most is singing full voice to a crowded room;
watching the answering machine light blink, knowing she had no desire to pick it up. She thinks of Kate.

When she pulls into Brian's driveway, it's just a little after 8 a.m.
She has no doubt that, with a toddler, they've been up for at least an
hour. Dani rings the doorbell and Allison answers fully dressed and
perfectly coiffed with Connor hanging on her leg. Dani realizes she's
glad to see her.

"Hi, Dani. How are you? I thought you weren't due back until this
evening. Come in. Sorry, the house is a bit of a disaster. You look
rested. Like you actually had a bit of a vacation," Allison says, eyeing
Dani closely.

"Oh, thanks, yeah. We had a great time. I hope this isn't too early." Dani stands in the foyer. To her amazement, she sees toys strewn all over the living room and, on the coffee table, a banana peel mixed in with a collection of wooden cars. She feels a strange sense of relief. "Kate and I got back last night. I don't want to intrude on your plans if you have any, it's just that Brianna has been asking to go the new skating rink that just opened and I thought today might be a great day to do it."

"Yipppeee!" Brianna emerges and hugs Dani around the waist. "Hi, Mommy, I missed you. You look pretty."

Connor runs over to Brianna and she wiggles her fingers in his chubby belly. "Tickle monsta, tickle monsta!" He squeals and dashes away.

Brianna chases him into the living room where he tumbles onto the couch, screeching with laughter. Dani watches her daughter wrestling with the little boy—her brother—and feels a wave of joy.

"It's pandemonium here, I'm afraid," says Allison. "No, that sounds great. We really didn't have much going on. I bet Bree would love that."

Just then Brian walks in. He is wearing a T-shirt, athletic shorts and running shoes. "Hey, Dani. You're back early."

"Yeah, I thought I'd take Brianna to the new rink that just opened. Give those new skates a try."

"That's fine. No problem. Hey, Allie," Brian says turning to his wife. "Where are the shirts that you were supposed to iron? I was just going through my closet and I don't have a single shirt to wear tomorrow." Hearing the tone in his voice, Dani is transported back in time. She has had this conversation before. For a split second, she even feels the blood rising in her cheeks and only then does she remember that she is not the one dropping the ball on the shirts.

Dani looks to Allison for a response. But Allison doesn't flinch or even seem too bothered. "Oh, they're in the dryer, honey. No need to panic."

The moment is a revelation. This kind of thing once drove Dani crazy, but it is barely a blip on Allison's radar. Dani could never get used to it, but then, it hadn't been what she signed up for. She looks around at the house. Her daughter's other home. For the first time, she is glad it is here.

She is also glad–so glad–for her own car keys, her own house keys, in her hand.

"C'mon, Brianna. Get your stuff together."

Brianna races upstairs and emerges moments later with her hot-pink backpack and her stuffed hippo.

"Bye, Daddy," Brianna says. She throws her arms around his neck. "Love you."

"I'm coming to your game, sport. Saturday, right?" Brian has his face buried in the top of her head. He gives her a big kiss. "You can show me the moves we were working on."

"Daddy showed me how to knock a goal in with your head! It was really cool."

Normally, Dani might have used this opportunity to make a comment about Brian and his hard head, but today she doesn't have the heart for it.

"See you all on Saturday. Enjoy your day off," she says. Brianna grabs her hand and hustles her down the front walk.

"Are we really going to the skating rink?"

"If you want to, my dear. You name it, we're doing it! I have only one request," Dani says.

"What, Mommy?"

"We *must* have hot fudge sundaes for lunch."

Brianna laughs and races ahead to the car.

⁓

Brianna is planted on one of the green wooden benches surrounding the rink, lacing up the new skates that Brian bought her for her birthday when he heard about the rink opening. Dani goes to the skate rental office and returns with a pair for herself. She laces them up and hobbles, somewhat stiffly, toward the ice where Brianna is already gliding around.

Dani tentatively steps out onto the smooth surface. Music blares over the PA system as the other skaters whiz effortlessly around the rink's perimeter. Cold rises from the ice and she breathes in deeply.

You used to be pretty good on the ice, she reminds herself. There had been a small lake near the house where Dani grew up in Great Neck. Her dad had her on skates before she could walk. She feels a brief pang and realizes how much she misses him.

Brianna glides up next to her and they synchronize their steps. Brianna looks over at the skater to their left, who is skating with quick backward strokes. "Ooh, that's cool."

"I can show you how to do that," Dani says, her confidence returning. "It's not so hard. Watch your old mother in action. Bet you never knew you had Dorothy Hamill for a mom!"

"Who?" asks Brianna.

"Well, she's like Sarah Hughes with a wedge cut. Now, watch this," Dani says, settling into position.

She pushes off with the jagged end of her toe and is weaving backward. She's just started to pick up speed when her behind connects with a solid object.

"Whoa!" She hears a man's voice cry out.

She regains her balance and whips around to see a tall, dark-haired man in a blue warm-up jacket working hard to stay on his feet. He plants his skates to one side, does a 180-degree turn and stops. He looks familiar, though Dani can't quite place him.

"I must have missed our cue. Is this where I sweep you into the air and spin you over my head like a pinwheel?" He is laughing and his eyes are gray-blue and his hair is slightly rumpled.

"Good luck! Jeez, I am so sorry!" Dani says.

"Hi, Mr. O'Grady!" Brianna shouts, clearly happy to see him.

O'Grady, O'Grady. The name is familiar. Oh, yes: soccer coach.

"No problem," he says. "I was looking forward to your triple lutz . . . Well, maybe next time."

Brianna skids to a stop next to him.

"Hi, Brianna." And with a serious look he adds, "You're not defecting on me and running away with the Ice Capades before our big game, are you?"

"No. My daddy got me new skates for my birthday."

"Well, good. We're going to need you on Saturday. See you at practice." He gives Brianna and Dani a big smile and begins to skate away.

"Bye, and sorry again about the, uh . . . body slam," Dani calls out.

"No problem." He's laughing and it's unclear to Dani whether or not she's in on the joke.

She makes her way to the side of the rink and holds onto it for a minute. Brianna stays in the center and takes a few tentative glides backward. After about a half hour, Dani is coasting again, like she's back in Great Neck with her father. It's exhilarating. The muscles in her thighs start to burn, but somehow it feels good.

An elderly couple skates by in tandem, arms crossed and locked in front of their bodies. They are the very picture of grace. The Fred and Ginger of Easton Rinks. The man whispers something into the woman's ear and she grins, her eyes twinkling.

Dani glides over to the next opening and steps out. Her ankles feel unsteady and a little sore. She sits on the first bench and loosens the laces of her skates. It feels wonderful.

She watches as Brianna further masters the backward skate and begins work on a rather impressive spin. Two of her friends from school show up and they chase one another, stopping only to ice-dance to the 'N Sync song blaring from the sound system. By 11:30 a.m. Brianna's friends have left and she is ready to go, too.

"Where to?" Brianna asks.

"I don't know about you, but I'm thinking hot fudge and maybe some of Flo's homemade mint-chip ice cream."

They go to Flo's Soda Shop down the street and order the largest hot fudge sundaes on the menu. They sit at a small table by the window.

Dani digs deep into a river of hot fudge, slowly removes her spoon and inserts the entire contents in her mouth.

She looks at Brianna, whose face is already streaked with hot fudge. Her daughter stops eating for a second and looks back, concerned.

"Mommy, am I in trouble? . . . Did something bad happen?"

"Sweetie, of course not. Why would you say that?"

"I don't know. You come home early, you take me special places, you let me eat ice cream." There is a long pause. "It's just that usually you have to get to work or it's a special occasion or something." Brianna looks at her, waiting. Dani thinks of the endless hours of overtime, working on vacation days, Bryce's dinnertime calls.

"Brianna." Her throat feels tight. She takes in the curve of her daughter's face, the small dimple in her chin, so much like the photographs of Bebe when she was a young girl. Dani leans in close and puts a hand on Brianna's cheek. "Listen. Every day with you is a special occasion. I am sorry if I don't always let you know that."

Brianna' s face softens. Dani can feel Brianna's foot begin to swing under the table.

"So, does this mean that we can do this again tomorrow?" Brianna asks with an expectant look.

"Nice try, missy. Now eat your sundae."

For the next few minutes, they concentrate on eating, occasionally trading spoonfuls of mint chip for chocolate cookie dough. Then Dani notices a faint rustling of fabric to her left.

"Hello, ladies." She looks up to see Brianna's soccer coach in a navy blue nylon tracksuit. He walks to a table about five feet away and sets down his tray.

"Hi again, Mr. O'Grady," Brianna says.

"Michael," he says to Dani.

"Hello again." Dani gives him a faint wave and feels a surge of embarrassment, recalling their last run-in. "We made it out in one piece."

"How did everyone else make out?"

"I think we only took out one or two. Not counting you."

"That's not too bad. They were probably weak skaters anyway. I'm sure they had no business being there."

"Yeah, Darwinism is alive and well at Easton rinks." Dani sneaks a look at him as he sits down. He is definitely attractive in a low-key sort of way. But for the first time she sees more to him than that. He's enviably confident—at ease. She sees it in the way he carries himself. The way his face comes to life when he speaks. "Are you waiting for someone?" she asks.

"No, just grabbing a bite."

"Why don't you join us?"

He scans his tray and looks up. "Just checking for breakables . . . Thanks. I'd love to." He walks over and sets down his tray. There is a thick turkey sandwich and a large drink on it.

"We're having hot fudge sundaes!" Brianna says excitedly.

"What a terrific idea. They look delicious," Michael says. "Tell you what, I'll be right back."

He grabs his sandwich and walks to the front of the shop where there is a golden retriever resting in the foyer. The dog leaps to his feet, wags his tail and begins to devour the sandwich as soon as it is set down in front of him. Michael goes to the counter and returns to the table with an enormous banana split.

"Much better," he says, sitting down and digging his spoon into the whipped cream. "I don't know what I was thinking. That whole wheat and tryptophan combo will kill you." He sits down.

Dani looks over at the dog sniffing around the floor for crumbs.

"That's Trent, Mommy."

"Trent?" Dani inquires. "The only Trent I know of is Mr. Lott. You're not one of those fat-free Segregationists slumming with the carbo-loading Lefties are you?"

"No," Michael says laughing. "It's a long story. Actually, I'd been thinking about getting a dog and then my brother gave him to me last year for Christmas. The name came with him. My brother thought I was getting a little too worked up about the Republican Party in general. He claimed that it was his effort to try and mend the American brotherhood. He thought if I could bond with Trent, there was hope for us all."

"Hmmm . . . I see. That's the sort of twisted logic I must reluctantly admire," Dani says, cocking one eyebrow.

"Well, that's my brother for you," he says warmly. "Truth is, Trent was the name the dog came with from the breeder." Michael plows ahead with his story. *I hope that he can't tell I'm staring at him.* Her cheeks start to feel warm.

". . . I guess the breeder had a son who was obsessed with Nine Inch Nails. He named every puppy in the litter after Trent Rezner. My brother kind of worked with that."

"My bus driver has nails that are so long they curl at the ends," Brianna chimes in. "She paints them blue."

"Old Hazel Hamilton," says Michael, scooping up another spoonful of his sundae. He wipes some fudge from his chin. "Believe it or not, she's been around since I went to school here."

"You grew up here?" Brianna asks.

"Yep, I went away for college, played a little soccer in Italy, then worked in Europe for a couple of years, but I was glad to come back. My family's still here."

"Cool," says Brianna.

They chat a little bit about Easton, what it was like thirty years ago. He tells them that the street that they live on used to be a tobacco farm. It is relaxed, fun. Before Dani knows it, the bowls are empty, save for a few thick globs of melted ice cream and fudge.

Michael collects his tray and gets up to leave.

"Well, very nice having lunch with you both. Brianna, I'll see you at practice. Dani, a pleasure."

"Thanks for joining us," Dani says. "We'll see you on Wednesday."

As she watches Michael walk toward Flo's entrance, Dani feels a rush, but it's different somehow. It's not the buzz of being dazzled or filled with expectation. It's calmer. Simpler. Like she may have just made a friend.

Trent leaps to his feet when he sees Michael coming.

Dani knows how he feels.

$\sim$

In the morning, Charlie's temperature is back to normal.

"Daddy is taking us to see *fish* today!" Charlie says over his pancakes as Andy pours two cups of coffee.

"I got tickets on Friday to that new exhibit at the aquarium. 'Sharks of the Deep.' I don't know if Charlie's up to it. What do you think?" Andy watches as Kate rests her palm on Charlie's forehead.

"I want to see *sharks*," Charlie insists.

"I think it'll be fine. It's not a long drive and you can bring along some Motrin just in case." Kate finishes wiping down the counter, having worked through the layer of dishes in the sink.

"I only got three tickets. I didn't think you'd be back until later. I'll give the ticket office a call and get one more." Andy hands her a cup of coffee.

"That sounds great." Kate grabs a plate of pancakes for herself, then chases the boys upstairs to get dressed. Andy is in the front hallway as she comes back down. The banister is still swathed in crepe paper and the balloons are drooping off the chairs.

"Kate, I tried to get another ticket to the exhibit but it's completely sold out. Holiday weekend and all. Plus I think it just opened Friday. If you want to, why don't you go with the boys? I'm fine staying here," Andy says.

"Oh, that's too bad. No, of course not. You go ahead. I can just catch up on a few things here."

"You're coming, Mommy, right?" says Henry, coming back downstairs.

"No, Daddy couldn't get another ticket. They're sold out. But you guys have fun and I'll see you when you get back."

~

Kate showers, throws on some clothes and sits down on the couch with a fresh cup of coffee. She picks up Dr. Mia's new book, but before she even opens the cover, she sets it down on the coffee table. The sunlight is hitting the maple just outside the glass door. The leaves are aglow in reds, oranges and yellows and the grass is still deep green. She looks at the overflowing toy box. The head of Charlie's favorite dinosaur, Ralph, is peeking over the top. She can see the kid's books stacked on the bookshelf, half upside down, some sideways, a stray sock wedged between them, no doubt the result of their well-intended efforts to "clean up for Mommy." She begins a mental to-do list:

Vacuum
Find and wash laundry
Make manicure/pedicure appointment
Tell Andy about the little matter of a million-dollar check

In spite of the chaos, or maybe because of it, Kate can't imagine being anywhere else. She stretches out on the couch, taking in the silence and the beautiful fall scene outside. After about half an hour, she decides to head into the READ offices. She has a few things she needs to pick up. She was going to wait until tomorrow, but with the free day, may as well get a step ahead. *How's that for a new concept?*

Kate finds a parking place right out front. The air is crisp and the sun casts long shadows over the quiet street. She enters the building, walks up the flight of stairs to the second-floor landing and is taking out her keys to open the office door when she notices lights on inside. She turns the knob and the door opens.

"Hello?" she calls out as she enters.

"Oh, hi, Kate." An attractive auburn-haired woman looks up from a desk where she is sliding a small stack of papers into a manila envelope. It's Lelia Kelly, former local director of READ, Kate's predecessor, and prior beneficiary of Honeywell's astonishing generosity. Lelia is wearing black wool pants, a cream colored turtleneck and a gorgeous sage green silk scarf that looks very expensive.

"I stopped in to drop off some paperwork," Lelia says. "We just got back from Italy last week. What brings you in on a holiday?"

"Oh, I thought it might be a good time to get ahead on a couple of things. We have that annual fund-raiser coming up soon." Kate drops her bag on the chair in front of her and takes off her coat. "How was Italy? You must have had an amazing time. I didn't realize you'd gone. Martha Wilson told me. That's exciting."

"Yeah, Jared got the fellowship sort of last minute, so we had to make a quick decision. We decided to just go for it. I am so glad we did."

"Fellowship?" Kate asks, confused. *What about the Honeywell-financed European escape fantasy?*

"Jared got accepted for a fellowship at the Economic Institute in Rome. He was sure that he wasn't getting it, but it came through sort of last minute. He had to tell the college on pretty short notice that he was leaving, but it worked out fine. He'll start up here again in January."

"Oh," Kate says, taking this is all in and entirely unsure of how to broach the subject. She plunges ahead anyway. She has to know.

"I just thought," Kate says, trying to sound casual, "I thought that with well, you know, with the bonus or gift or whatever that Honeywell gives . . . I mean, isn't that something? I thought you just ran away and were living in some villa in Florence." She tries to say this with a laugh but it sounds more like a cough, or a honk.

Now Lelia looks confused and it's making Kate nervous.

"Do you mean that fall bonus he always gives his directors?" Lelia asks.

"*Yes,*" Kate says too loudly, but she's already feeling better.

"That is so sweet of him, I know. Actually, I treated myself to this scarf with that . . . *and* had enough left over to get Jared a really nice birthday present. I guess Gerry's been doing it for about five years now. He really is a generous man. I don't know what READ would do without him . . ."

Lelia keeps talking but Kate doesn't hear a word she's saying.

OK, OK, she tells herself. *Don't panic. She said really nice birthday present . . . maybe she got Jared an* airplane . . . *or, uh, a Lamborghini* and *an airplane.*

". . . It's funny because that reminds me. I have to get that canoe out of storage. I gave it to him and then we had to take off for Rome right away."

Kate racing mind comes to an abrupt stop and Lelia comes back into focus. "Canoe?" Kate asks.

"I got Jared a canoe for his birthday . . ."

Kate's stomach does a slow roll . . . *Was that a gold-plated canoe . . . Studded with rare pink Australian diamonds?*

"Jared had wanted one for a while," Lelia drones on, "but he said, 'How often are we ever going to use it?' He thought it was a bit frivolous but . . ."

Frivolous? *A canoe is not frivolous. Frivolous is spending thousands and thousands of dollars buying a whole new wardrobe of designer clothes and staying in the VIP suite of the freakin' Plaza Hotel spending more money in one night than I have ever spent for a month's rent!*

Kate is suddenly afraid that she is about to throw up. She absent-mindedly raises one hand to her forehead.

"I told him that you have to treat yourself once in a while. I wanted to do it for him. I think he really appreciated it . . . Kate, are you OK? You don't look well." Lelia stops talking and looks at Kate with a concerned expression.

"I'm OK. Lelia, how much? How much did Honeywell give you?" Kate has lost all regard for subtlety.

"A thousand dollars, like everyone else." Lelia says, looking puzzled. "Kate, are you sure you're OK?"

I am not OK. I am so not OK. "I'm fine," Kate lies. "So nice to see you Lelia. I'll be back in just a minute."

"Nice to see you. I'm sure we'll catch up soon."

Kate is already out the front door and making a beeline for the bathroom down the hallway. With her breakfast still churning in her stomach, Kate throws cold water on her face and mops it off with some paper towels. She stands with two hands on the sink, hunched forward. *Breathe,* she tells herself. *Breathe. I knew it. I never should have listened to Dani. No one just hands over a check for a million dollars. What was I thinking?! I was too stressed out. Not thinking clearly.* She hears footsteps and a door closing. Lelia's gone. Thank God. *Dani . . . Must call Dani.*

Back in the office, Kate lifts the receiver and steadies her hand to dial Dani's number. She gets the machine. *"You have reached the Strauss residence. Sorry we can't take your call right now, but if you'd please leave a message . . ."*

"Dani, it's Kate," she is trying to sound controlled. "Dani, if you're there, please pick up . . . Dani, it's *important* . . . pick *up.* OK, I'll try you later."

She rummages in her purse for Dani's new cell phone number. As she does, slips of paper in various sizes and colors—yellow, white, pink, blue—pop out of the side pouch as though they'd been breeding in the pocket in which they'd been stuffed: receipts. Kate feels the perspiration dripping from her armpits, staining her blouse. *Oh my God. Oh my God.* As she rifles frantically through her bag, the porn director's business card falls to the desk. She sees his awkward handwriting: *"I'll make you a star–Call me."* Kate braces herself against the desk.

Come to think of it, there is some serious cash to be made in porn. Maybe if I did a couple of movies and they did really well, we could pay Honeywell back in biannual installments . . . OK, I have now officially lost my mind. An image of Henry and Charlie as teenagers pops into her head. They are guests on *The Maury Povich Show: Our Mother Was a Jailbird Porn Star.* Kate breathes in; breathes out.

She can't find Dani's number anywhere and now she's not even sure she ever wrote it down. She calls Dani's home number and again gets the machine.

"Dani, it's Kate. I really need to speak with you. I'm at the office. Call me there as soon as you get this. I know you have it but . . . anyway . . . the number's 589-0400 . . ." She doesn't want to hang up but can't think of anything else to say and it is then that she loses it altogether. "OH MY GOD, DANI, WE'RE GOING TO JAIL FOR THE REST OF OUR LIVES!" Kate shouts into the receiver.

The machine cuts her off. *Well, that should do it. Now all I can do is wait–and panic.*

—

Kate has been sitting–frozen–in the READ offices for what feels like an eternity. The blank beige walls and the silence are nearly unbearable. She's afraid that if she goes out on the street, she'll run into someone–though she couldn't say exactly who that might be–maybe Honeywell or, she thinks in a flash of paranoia, an FBI agent newly assigned to her case. It occurs to Kate that she has never really been in trouble in her life, never even gotten a speeding ticket.

The phone rings and she picks the receiver up with such haste that she nearly fumbles it.

"Oh! You're open. I was just going to leave a message. I'd like to get some information on READ workshops in the area," a woman with a slow and deliberate voice says.

Kate hustles the caller off the phone and waits. At two o'clock the phone rings again and she pounces.

"Kate? It's Dani."

"Thank God! Where have you been?! You are never going to believe what happened! We are in such *huge* trouble . . . I knew it. I knew it a was a huge mistake . . ."

"Kate, slow down. Take a deep breath. I can tell you're doing your hyperventilating thing again . . . Now slow down and tell me what's going on."

"*A thousand dollars,* Dani. That's all Lelia got from Honeywell. That's all he ever gives. We just milked his account for tens–who knows–hundreds of thousands of dollars! What are we going to do?!"

"OK, let me think. Let me think. It'll be fine. I am not exactly sure how just yet, but it will be fine. I am a lawyer, remember?"

Kate is not at all sure how this helps them at the moment.

"First, we need a plan," Dani continues. "OK, Kate, get all of your receipts. I am going to pull mine together. Where can we meet?"

"Andy and the boys are gone for the afternoon. You can come to my house."

"Good. That's good. I'll bring Brianna. We can throw in a video for her or something. First, we need to assess the damages."

Kate winces when she hears that word—damages—but is glad to have a plan.

"OK, I'll meet you there in half an hour."

———

"Four hundred fifty-two dollars and seventy-five cents," Kate says, popping another Tums in her mouth and chewing as she turns another small slip of paper over in her hand. She is sitting at her kitchen table huddled over a stack of colored scraps. Dani is sitting across from her, working the calculator, all business. Brianna is watching *Just Like Mike* in the family room.

Kate calls out another number and Dani types it into the calculator.

"Sixty-five hundred dollars, three nights at the Plaza and room service."

"The spa treatments are in there, too, you know," Dani says.

"Oh, well then, that makes it practically reasonable."

Kate picks up the next slip, "Laurence Loget: fourteen hundred dollars."

"Well, the makeovers were free," Dani offers.

"Would you stop trying to find the silver lining here?" Kate asks, tense. "Just keep adding . . . $1,875. Holy Toledo. That Prada jacket was almost $2,000?"

"Yeah, it's cute though, you got to admit," Dani says.

"Cute? We'll see how cute we look in *prison jumpsuits*. Remember your name is on that bank account, *too*."

"Don't worry. Don't worry. We'll figure this out. Back to work. OK, what else?"

Kate rattles off the numbers on the last receipts in front of her. Shoes: $600; suit: $2,500; six cashmere sweaters at $200 each; a pair of boots: $895. The list goes on and on. *I had no idea. I never for a moment thought we were spending this much. Or maybe I just didn't want to know. I guess with both of us just slapping down the cash cards whenever the urge struck . . .*

"OK, what else?" Dani asks, not even looking up.

"That's it. That's the last one." Kate says.

"OK then. One stroke and we'll know where we stand."

Dani taps her finger on the keyboard. In a flash, her face changes. Gone is the cool, poised businesswoman. Dani's eyes widen and she looks pale but she doesn't say a word.

"What? WHAT?!" Kate shouts, running to the other side of the table. She stares at the screen and gasps:

$49,204.97

Kate hasn't seen a number that big since she and Andy bought the house. Her stomach starts to turn again. She tries to inhale but can't seem to get enough air. The room begins to blur and the next thing Kate knows, there is a brown paper bag over her nose and mouth and she is taking short breaths.

"*Breathe, breathe.*" Dani's voice sounds far away. Kate's breathing starts to slow and deepen. She imagines holding down three jobs for thirty years to pay it all back. In a flash, she sees herself in a Kentucky Fried Chicken uniform working the deep fryer for seven dollars an hour and realizes that it would take more like forty years to pay back that kind of money. *We could rob a bank. How hard could that be? Yeah, right.* And then Kate remembers that, basically, that is what she and Dani just did. She pictures herself in a bright orange prison jumper, speaking on a phone through glass to Andy and the boys. She tries to picture Andy's face when he finds out. She can feel Dani's hand on her back as the paper bag opens and shuts, crunching with every breath.

I want to die, she thinks.

Chapter Fourteen

"Kate, can you hear me? I'm going to take the bag away. Just keep breathing slowly." Kate's eyes are beginning to lose their blank look and Dani thinks she's finally getting through to her. She slowly takes the paper bag away and drops it on the table.

"Ohmigod, Dani," Kate starts.

"Quiet!" Dani says firmly. "Breathe."

When Dani's sure she has Kate's attention, she begins to speak. "OK, Kate, you've got to stay calm. Andy and the boys are going to be home soon and you can't be a wreck like this. I'll get to the office extra early tomorrow morning and look up some case law. Maybe I can find precedent for making a horrible mistake."

Kate moans. "You'll be my lawyer when Honeywell sues for the money, right?"

"Honeywell isn't going to sue. We haven't done anything illegal. We're going to get out of this just fine, Kate," Dani says, voicing a confidence that she doesn't quite feel.

"Oh, Dani, what did we do?" Kate's eyes are starting to brim with tears.

"Kate, you've got to pull yourself together. I've got to get Brianna home, but I'll call you from the office first thing tomorrow." Dani stands up, moves to the other side of the table and gives Kate a hug. "We're going to be fine. I promise."

Dani calls out to Brianna. "Honey, is that movie done? We've got to get going. It's a school night. Then turning back to Kate, says lamely, "Try not to think about it."

"Right." Kate puts her head down on the table as Brianna comes into the room.

"Is Kate OK?" Brianna looks at her mother, worried.

"I'm fine, honey." Kate picks her head up and Dani thinks she detects a spark of resolve. "Just a little tired after the big vacation I took with your mom."

"You guys had fun, huh?" Brianna asks.

"So much fun," Dani says, meaning it completely. "It was probably the best vacation I ever had."

"It was, wasn't it?" Kate says thoughtfully.

"I'll call you first thing," Dani says on the way out the door.

TUESDAY MORNING

Dani is awake hours before the alarm goes off. She barely slept all night. Every time she closed her eyes she played out a different scenario of explaining to Honeywell how they had come to spend fifty thousand dollars of his money on hotels, clothes and spa treatments, and none of them sounded even remotely rational. She lies in the dark bedroom, her mind racing. *The truth is, I have no idea what we're going to do.* She can see some light beginning to show between the curtains so she slides her legs over the side of the bed and quietly makes her way to the bathroom.

As she is starting the coffee, she can hear Brianna wake up and start puttering around in her room. She calls up the stairs the promise of a ride in the "fancy red car"–the Cadillac, symbol of all their woes–and Brianna is sitting at the door, dressed and ready by seven o'clock. By seven fifteen, Dani's dropped her off at her friend Amanda's house.

"Thanks for taking Brianna to school," Dani says to Amanda's mom as Brianna pulls up a chair at their kitchen table and helps herself to a Pop-Tart.

"Oh, it's not problem at all. It must be tough for you when you have these early-morning meetings," Amanda's mom says with sympathy Dani knows she doesn't deserve.

"Well, I owe you one. Bye, honey," Dani says as she carefully stacks Brianna's lunchbox and backpack on another kitchen chair.

Dropping a quick kiss on her daughter's forehead, she dashes out the door.

⁓

It feels strange to Dani to be back at work—as if she's been gone for weeks, instead of for a long weekend. Her desk is piled high with folders and briefs, all with Post-its bearing Bryce's poor penmanship. She pushes them to the side and heads down the hall to the legal library. The office hallway is lightly populated with long-suffering personal assistants and young paralegals eager to make their mark with an early-morning arrival.

Dani disappears into one of the stacks and an hour later puts the last book away with a sigh. Nothing. There is nothing she can do.

She goes back to her office and picks up the phone.

"Hello?" Andy answers and she can hear cartoons on the television in the background.

"Hi Andy, it's me," Dani says, making an extra effort to speak slowly. *Just a casual morning call*, she thinks to herself. "Kate around?"

"She's still upstairs," Andy says. "She looked awful last night. Said she thought she was coming down with whatever Charlie had."

Good girl, Kate, way to cover. "Oh, that's a shame," Dani says.

"Oh, hey, wait. Here she is now," Andy says.

She hears the sound of a kiss and then Kate's voice comes on the line.

"Morning, Dani. How are things at the office?" Kate's voice is totally calm.

"Pretty good," she says, lying through her teeth. "There are some options we can discuss, but let's do it in person. Can you have a quick recovery?"

"Why, yes, I'm feeling much better this morning," Kate says. "Thanks for asking."

"So can you get away?"

"Oh, no, I'm afraid I can't have lunch today. I'm planning on going in to the READ offices around eleven. Today's my usual volunteer day. Oh, hang on a minute, Dani."

Dani can hear Kate talking to Andy.

"Really, I'm fine. And Claire is supposed to come over to sit for Charlie. I'll just take it easy. No one else will be in today, so it'll probably be easier than trying to catch up on all the housework here. You go ahead and have your office hours—I'll be fine."

Kate comes back on the line.

"Sorry, Dani, logistics. Anyway . . ."

"All right, then I'll meet you there at twelve o'clock exactly. Will there be a quiet place we can talk?"

"That sounds great. Have a good day at work."

"You're good at this, Kate. You should be a secret agent," Dani says and she is rewarded with a small laugh. "See you at twelve."

She puts the receiver back in the cradle and sits at her desk, her hands covering her eyes, frantically reviewing the options. She doesn't know how long she's been sitting that way when she's jolted out of her thoughts by a stack of papers that lands with a thump in front of her.

"Sleeping at your desk your first morning back?" Bryce stands in front of her, arms crossed over a too-busy tie. He looks pleased to have caught her with her guard down.

Dani looks up, as irritated as ever by his greased-back hair and beady little eyes. And then it hits her. Everything Kate said, what she really learned about herself this weekend: she can take care of herself—she doesn't deserve to be treated this way. *Game over*, she thinks.

"Crisis, Bryce," Dani says shortly. "How the hell could you have let this happen while I was gone?" She picks up a random folder from her desk and waves it in his direction.

He immediately looks guilty. "I'm sure you can handle whatever it is, Dani. You should be totally fresh after your long weekend." His eyes shift back and forth from the folder in her hand to the stacks of paper on her desk.

Dani stands up and shoves the folder into his hands.

"Frankly, Bryce, I'm not sure being fresh will be enough. Thank

God I got back when I did or there's no telling how much this could have cost the firm."

He slowly backs toward the door, his sharp shoulders hunched over the folder in his hands. "Well, as I said, I'm sure you can handle . . ."

"No Bryce. I think *you* should handle this one."

Bryce retreats, clearly hoping to avoid further conversation. The door clicks shut behind him.

Who knew it could be that easy?

Dani checks her watch: 9:30. Another two and a half hours until she has to meet Kate and deliver the bad news. With a sigh, she picks up a file from the corner of her desk. Judging from Bryce's reaction, there probably really is a big mess that he is expecting her to clean up.

She shuffles papers for a while, unable to concentrate on anything. She keeps thinking about how she was the one who urged Kate to cash the check. "Free money" she had said, as if there really were such a thing. *And now I have to go over and tell her that there is nothing she can do but own up to the truth—or take the rest of the cash and move her family out of the country.* Dani sighs.

Abandoning any hope of getting work done, she decides to walk over to the READ offices. The building is nearly a mile from her office but somehow tooling up in the red Caddy feels wrong. Walking at a good clip, she covers ground quickly, staring straight ahead. She thinks she hears someone say hello but doesn't realize until it's too late that she's just passed a client on the sidewalk. Dani climbs the flight of stairs to the READ office. She hates to admit it, but she's got butterflies in her stomach. She's also got a plain brown paper bag in her hand. Kate is not going to take this well at all. She taps on the glass-fronted door.

Kate appears out of nowhere and whips it open.

"Hi," Dani says, with what she hopes is an encouraging tone and expression.

Kate face is momentarily hopeful, then her shoulders slump. "You can't fix it," she says tonelessly.

"It's not going to be so bad," Dani says, not believing a word of it.

"Easy for you to say." Kate walks to her small cubicle at the back of the office. She pauses to pull another chair in next to the desk and then drops heavily into hers.

Dani feels a rush of protectiveness. "Kate, I'll call Honeywell. Really. It was my idea to rush off and blow all the money. I was the one who dragged you into the stores. I spent more on clothes than you did. I'm equally responsible. *More* responsible."

"I thought about this a lot last night," Kate says. "I'll tell him what happened, then I'll tell Andy, then I'll call and see if I can still get that job in London. Maybe Dr. Mia can add a series of lectures called 'You *can* buy self-knowledge, but at what price?'" Kate makes a strangled sound that Dani thinks is supposed to be a laugh.

Kate has the phone in her hand. She flips through the card file on her desk and dials. Dani reaches across the desk and takes hold of her free hand.

"Gerry Honeywell, please."

It is so quiet that Dani thinks she can hear Kate's heart pounding and then she realizes it's her own.

"What? Oh, no. No message. I'll–uh–I'll call him at home. Thank you."

Kate hangs up, her breathing quick and shallow. Dani waves the paper bag at her. Kate shakes her head and then rests her forehead on her knees.

"He's not in the office today." Her voice is muffled.

Dani rubs her back. "So we'll call him at home. C'mon, Kate, let's get it over with."

This time Dani picks up the phone and places it in Kate's hand.

"Hello, it's Kate Thompson. May I speak to Gerry, please?" To her credit, Kate's voice is steady.

"Oh, hello, Sunny. Fine, and you?"

"Yes, yes, I did get myself something special with the check," Kate's eyes are wide, her expression panicked. "My friend Dani and I took a little vacation together. But it got a little out of hand. In fact, that's what I'm hoping to speak with Gerry about. Not how the vacation got out of hand, but the check." There's a long silence during which Kate's eyes grow even wider.

"What? What's going on?" Dani tries to put her ear next to the receiver, to hear what Sunny is saying. Color rushes back into Kate's face in a flood and she goes from white to crimson in a matter of seconds.

"Sunny, please, could I put you on speakerphone and have you say that again? My friend Dani is right here. I think she needs to hear this." Impatient, Dani punches the speakerphone button herself.

"Hi, Sunny, Dani Strauss here," she says crisply. "Do you know something about the mix-up with the check Kate received?"

"Just listen, Dani," Kate murmurs.

"Hello, darling." Dani swears Sunny sounds amused. "I hope you girls enjoyed your vacation."

"Well, we did until we got home and realized that we'd financed the trip with stolen money," Dani says.

"Actually, I was the one who did the stealing–if that's what you want to call it. I prefer to look at it as creative accounting," Sunny says, brightly.

Dani stares at Kate who simply nods.

"Look, ladies. As I just told Kate, Gerry and I have been having problems for some time now, and when Gerry took the credit for Kate's program at the luncheon, I decided to take matters into my own hands. It's really too late for me to start sticking up for myself, so I thought that maybe it would feel good to stick up for someone else."

"So you thought you'd just give away a million bucks?"

"Oh, that's the least of it. Let's just say the Food Bank, the ASPCA and the local woman's shelter will richly benefit from Gerry's generosity."

"Call me crazy, but that's quite a chunk of change missing from his account," Dani says.

"I handle the household as well as Gerry's nonbusiness expenses," Sunny explains. "When he told me to write the bonus check for the director of READ, I just employed a little creative bookkeeping. He often has me sign his name to the checks. I took a little bit from here, a little bit from there . . . Trust me. He'll never notice. And if he does, well, I don't want to be too specific, but let's just say that I doubt he wants anyone looking too closely at his books–especially the offshore accounts."

"It does sound surprisingly on the up-and-up," Dani says slowly. "Except for the *forgery* part. Oh, and the dishonesty to your husband part."

"The hell with him. Look, I'm not his first wife and I doubt I'll be his last," Sunny says sharply. "When I married him I signed a prenup and I meant it. I didn't want money for being his wife. When he started using me as a social secretary and a house manager and an accountant, I decided to make sure I felt valued."

"A sentiment I've been trying to get across to a particular someone for some time now," Dani mutters thoughtfully. Kate shoots her a look.

"Well, even if it's all legal, what you did," Kate says. "We still need to pay you back. It's just not right. I certainly have not done a million dollars worth of work for READ."

"You didn't spend the whole check, did you?" Sonny sounds incredulous.

"We spent about fifty thousand dollars of it," Kate says glumly.

Sunny laughs. "That was the best you could do? Really, you girls could use some lessons in conspicuous consumption."

"Sunny, please, let me send the balance of the money back to you. Then we'll figure out a way to pay back the rest over time. It's just not right." Kate is pleading.

"You can't give it back," Sunny says urgently. "If Gerry does find out what I've done, there's no knowing for sure how he'll react. And there are things I definitely like about being married to a man like Gerry. Things I'm not sure I'm ready to give up. No offense, Kate, but it really seemed like you could use a break. I just wanted to make your life a bit easier, to give you an excuse to do something for yourself--to give you a little freedom."

"Well, you were right, it was just what she needed, what we needed. That 'little freedom,' as you call it, made a big difference," Dani says. "We called it 'The Mommy Fund.'"

"The Mommy Fund," Sunny hoots. "That's brilliant. Simply perfect. Look, let's not talk anymore about giving back the money. Just give me an hour or so to figure out how to handle this. I'll call you back."

Sunny's chipper voice is replaced by a dial tone and Kate pushes the speakerphone button. The office is completely silent. Dani is speechless.

"What do we do now, Dani?" Sunny's explanation has apparently done nothing to calm Kate down.

"Go shopping?" Dani jokes.

"Seriously." Kate is wringing her hands. "We're like accessories to the crime, now. If Gerry finds out what Sunny's done, we can still get in big trouble."

"You're watching too much *Law and Order*," Dani says. "Besides, you heard Sunny. She's going to find a way out of this–for all of us."

Dani doesn't know how long they've been sitting and staring at each other when there is a sharp knock at the office door. Kate turns pale but gets up and opens it. Dani walks toward the front of the office. At first all she sees is the coat: a vision of embroidered sapphire suede and Mongolian lamb.

"Girls! I'm so glad I found you here."

Although Dani is unsure of her name, she knows who the woman is. She's one of Sunny Honeywell's friends and one of a select group of ladies who live on their manicured estates in the countryside surrounding Easton. You never see them running errands; they're not really part of the community. They're too busy heading off on shopping expeditions to New York or museum parties in Boston or hopping in hubby's private plane to have dinner on the Vineyard. When they do venture into town for a rare outing or errand, they stand out. Their Pilates-honed bodies are wrapped in designer jeans and "casual wear" that costs more than Dani's condo. Oh, you may not know their names, but you definitely know who they are.

Dani had always thought she wanted to be one of them. Now she's not so sure.

Kate finds her voice–and her manners–first.

"I'm Kate Thompson. I work here at READ." She extends her hand. "And this is Dani Strauss."

"Georgina Gilmore."

Dani shakes her perfectly manicured hand, trying without success not to gawk at the at-least-three-carat, emerald-cut diamond.

"Sunny said I could find you here. She told me about what you're doing and I just have to tell you—I think it's wonderful. You girls are just a marvel. Now, here's a check for fifteen thousand dollars." She waves a piece of paper in Kate's direction. "I've made it out to your fund. The Mommy Fund . . . Really, darlings, it's so clever. I wish there'd been such a thing when I needed it. Maybe I wouldn't have ended up with such a windbag second husband. Well ta-ta, girls. And good luck."

And before Kate and Dani can so much as draw a breath, she swirls back through the doorway, a flash of brilliant blue disappearing down the dim hallway.

"What just happened?" Kate's voice is barely a whisper.

"I think you've just been handed a get-out-of-jail-free card," Dani says.

They both stare at the check in Kate's shaking hand. The phone rings. Kate jumps a mile and Dani cracks up.

"READ, Kate Thompson speaking. "Yes, yes she was just here. Well thank *you*. Yes, I'm sure that would be fine. Yes, that is the correct address. No, *thank you*. Good-bye."

Kate hangs up the phone and starts to laugh.

"Sunny?" Dani guesses.

"Another donation," Kate gasps. "Ten thousand dollars! For the Mommy Fund."

"This is it, Kate." Dani is suddenly so excited she can't get the words out fast enough. "This is it. It's what you want. The Mommy Fund . . . why didn't I think of it? It's what you can do. It's how you can make a difference."

Kate stares at her blankly.

"Think. Think about what this weekend has done for us. Think about what we've learned about ourselves. Here's your chance, Kate. You wanted to help people. Now you can."

Dani's inspirational speech is interrupted by a ringing telephone.

In the next fifteen minutes, she and Kate take a few more calls from Sunny's "ladies." By the time they're done, they've recovered most of the money they'd spent.

Kate's manic laughter has settled into fits of sporadic giggles, and

Dani doesn't even care that it's already three o'clock and she's probably as good as fired the minute she turns up in the office again.

At last the phones are quiet. A minute passes, and then ten.

"What just happened?" Kate says.

"I think we just became a charitable organization," Dani says. "I mean, there'll be some paperwork, but nothing I can't get going on right away . . ."

Before Kate can protest, the phone rings again. Dani reaches past her and hits SPEAKER.

"The Mommy Fund," she says. "Danielle Strauss speaking."

"Kate, Dani, it's Sunny."

"What have you done?" Kate says. "The phone's been ringing off the hook and Georgina Gilmore just . . ."

"Oh, I've been very busy indeed," Sunny cuts her off. "I'm just having a few girls over to lunch later this week to talk about your wonderful organization. Of course, you two will speak about your fund and your plans for future recipients. I'll call you in a few days with a firm date. And congratulations you two—it's a brilliant idea."

There's a long silence while Kate and Dani each process what this means.

"What are we going to do?" Kate finally asks.

"I don't know about you," Dani says, "but I'm definitely going to wear the Prada jacket!"

Chapter Fifteen

Dani arrives to pick Kate up at two o'clock on the dot as directed. She had been thrilled when Kate asked her to extend the rental on the red Cadillac for one more day.

Showered and having manhandled her new haircut back into some semblance of what Mr. Loget had originally intended, Kate sashays down the walk wearing her new Marc Jacobs coat, her alligator boots, a pink cashmere sweater, chocolate brown Jil Sanders trousers and makeup. She feels good, but somehow it's not about the clothes or the makeup, and it's not because she is someone's mother or someone's wife or is doing someone else's work. All those things matter, but right now she is doing something for herself. Henry has an afternoon school program and Charlie's just left with Claire for the library. She and Dani have two hours.

Dani gets out of the car and strides down the sidewalk like it's a catwalk. She executes a perfect turn in her high heels and takes her friend's arm in hers.

"You look great!" she says, strutting around the far side of the car and getting back into the driver's seat. Dani looks great, too, in black oversized Gucci sunglasses and her Prada jacket.

"Thanks, you don't look too bad yourself." Kate opens the door and hops into passenger side.

"So, I don't get it," Dani says as Kate buckles her seat belt. "What are we going to do? Just drive around and look for some beleaguered soul who needs a break? C'mon Kate. We could end up giving it to some total psycho who uses it to finance a hare-brained Home Shopping Network show."

"The Mommy Fund targets a special brand of need; I think we'll know it when we see it. I don't know about you, but I want the satisfaction of handing the money over ourselves. Just us. Just this once."

"You've got a point," Dani says.

Kate looks out the window, the cool air lifting the hair off her shoulders. In two hours, the red Cadillac convertible is going back, she thinks; in two years the new clothes will fade and go out of style, but what she's learned won't change.

"So, I'm not exactly sure how it'll all work just yet. But honestly, do you think we are the only women in this town who need a break?" she asks.

"So, we're playing God? Like we can decide who needs it most?" Dani persists.

"Maybe it doesn't matter, Dani. I mean, why us? Why did we deserve it? Because some frustrated wife was looking for payback from her rich, prenuptialed husband?"

Dani is quiet.

"And we figured it out," Kate continues. "Well, eventually."

⌒

They cruise the streets of Easton. It's nippy but not too cold. Stopping in Starbucks for coffee, Kate gets a decaf vanilla latte and Dani gets her usual half-caff. They settle into a couple of chairs and Kate stirs her drink.

"Oh, dear, we may have a winner," Dani says.

Kate glances in the direction that Dani is looking and she sees them, too. Three boys, none older than eight: one is hanging off the back of a bedraggled-looking young woman. The smallest has gotten hold of the milk canister and is pouring it into a plastic plant. The third is pulling on the young woman's arm and she looks as though she is about to cry.

"The Rudling boys," Kate says turning back to Dani, nonplussed. "Accompanied by their–very well paid, I might add–sitter. Eighteen dollars an hour, I hear."

Dani looks on in horror. "That isn't nearly enough. So she's not the mommy we're looking for."

"At least she's well compensated, and I suppose quitting is always an option." Kate goes back to surveying the room.

"I've got it," Dani says a few moments later. "We need to apply logic here. We need to look for her in her natural habitat. Follow me."

Kate doesn't know what Dani's talking about, but follows her anyway because she doesn't have any better ideas. She follows her back to the car and Dani peels out of the Starbucks parking lot.

"Woo-hoo!" she yelps.

"Jeez, you have *got* to stop doing that!" Kate says, but she is smiling, too.

Dani pulls up in front of the Grand Union Super Food Mart and finds a parking space right out front.

"Oh, I get it," Kate says. "I like how you think."

Grocery store; late afternoon: Seventh Circle of Hell for overextended mothers battling their nap-deprived, hypoglycemic spawn.

"Let's go," Dani says, opening the car door.

They step inside the store and head down aisle two, crackers and cereal. The overhead neon lights cast a ghastly pall on the faces of the shoppers. The air is cool and smells faintly of produce and Windex. Kate feels a tug on her jacket.

"I think we've found our gal. Who knew it would be so easy?" Dani says. Kate looks in the direction that Dani is pointing. There are countless shopping carts veering off in all directions. There's a middle-aged woman pushing a cart filled with frozen vegetables and a roast. Further down the aisle, there's a young man wheeling a cart filled only with imported beer, and beyond him a young mother with a car seat inside the cart takes a box of baby cereal from the shelf. Then, Kate sees her.

She is wearing an oversized tan sweater coat that hits just below her knees. Her dark hair is pulled back in a loose ponytail and her hands are wedged under the armpits of a three-year-old boy whose legs are kicking furiously over the cart. Tugging on the back of her sweater is a delicate-looking girl who appears to be about five and is standing over a spilled box of Lucky Charms.

"Mommy, help! It spilled. Mommy, can we get these? *Please . . .* can we?" The girl says in a voice too loud to be coming from her small frame. The woman turns her head to address her daughter, which only makes the toddler boy kick all the harder.

"Eamon, please sit down," she says under her breath, "put your legs through the slots, *please*. You heard Mommy." With that, the young child plants his feet on top of the cart and pushes hard, bucking both feet in the air. A sneaker connects squarely with the woman's jaw. She releases her grip from the child and he falls a few inches back into the seat of the cart, his feet propped up on the handle. He begins to bawl at the top of his lungs.

"AH, YOU HURT ME! YOU HURT ME, MOMMY!" he shouts.

"Wow," Kate and Dani whisper in unison.

Kate nods to Dani, who approaches the woman from behind and taps her lightly on the shoulder. The woman whips around with one hand still holding her jaw. As she turns, she steps on the pile of Lucky Charms at her feet with a loud crunch.

She looks up at Kate and Dani and it is written all over her face as she takes in their sharp outfits, their clean, styled hair. To her, they appear calm and under control, and Kate gets the feeling that if the young woman could will it, the black-and-white checked supermarket floor would open up and swallow her, the cart and the children whole. But instead, she just awkwardly shifts her weight from one foot to the other and sweeps a loose strand of hair behind her ear. Her face fills with shame.

"Oh, I'm so sorry for the commotion. He's fine. He really is, he's just at that age when . . ." she begins, before Kate gently interrupts.

"You don't need to explain to us," Kate begins. "Don't worry, I have one about the same age."

"Yes, we noticed that you could perhaps use a little help," Dani says bluntly, extracting a nondescript white envelope from her purse.

"Really, I'm fine. I think I've got it under control," the woman says unconvincingly. "But thanks, anyway."

Behind her, the little boy works himself upright in the cart and, sensing an opportunity, grabs his distracted mother's open pocketbook and hurls its contents onto the floor.

There is a clatter of loose change on tile and then silence as the woman stares at the floor. Kate bends down and picks up a lipstick that has rolled to a stop at her crocodile boot. Dani picks up the bag and starts refilling it.

The woman just stands there, her shoulders slumping. "Sometimes I just—I just . . ." she says, her voice tightening. Dani gives her the bag back.

"We understand, we really do. Which is why we want you to have this." Kate takes the envelope from Dani and hands it to the woman. "Congratulations, you have been chosen as the first official recipient of the Mommy Fund."

"Open it," Dani says. "Go on."

"*Da*ni," Kate says out of the corner of her mouth.

"Well, you said you wanted the satisfaction of *seeing* it," Dani hisses back.

The woman appears utterly confused. She turns the envelope over in her hands.

"I don't understand." She tries to hand the envelope back to Kate.

"We know," Dani says. "It's OK. Until about three days ago, neither did we. Go on, open it."

The woman looks at Dani and then back at Kate, who nods encouragingly. The woman slides her finger under the envelope flap and peeks inside. Her eyes grow wide and her mouth drops open.

"But what's it for? Why are you giving this to me?"

"Because someone did it for us." Kate reaches forward and places her hand on the woman's shoulder. "It's for *you*, and you alone. That's really all you need to know."

The woman sneaks another peek inside the envelope as Dani links her arm in Kate's. They turn on their heels and head back down the aisle. As they're walking away, Kate, unable to help herself, looks back over her shoulder. The woman still hasn't moved and even the kids have quieted down and are now are staring in their direction. Kate smiles.

"Don't worry," she shouts. "You'll figure it out!"

And somehow, walking arm in arm, back to their lives–to Andy and the boys, and Brianna, and legal briefs, and carpools and soccer practice–back to the car, the one due back to the garage in fifteen minutes, somehow, they know she will.

EPILOGUE

The Mommy Fund is a full-time job now—at least as much as Kate and Dani want it to be. Things got a bit hectic after the *People* magazine piece and after they appeared on one of the big morning shows. *Time* magazine even did a boxed profile in their "The Family Today" issue, accompanied by a small photo. The local *Easton Eagle* did a feature, too, in which, unfortunately, the reporter referred to them as a couple of Ed McMahons in heels. His intention was clear, but Kate and Dani weren't at all sure that that was the image they wanted to promote. But they really knew they'd arrived when they became the subject of an honest-to-goodness backlash. It was brief, spearheaded by a left-wing, nearly off-the-grid women's rights zealot who said on national television that the Mommy Fund sends the wrong message to women: that money is the answer to their problems. She even said that the Fund sounded to her like the death rattle of a rapidly degenerating capitalist society. That was pretty exciting, especially the last part.

But the truth is, it's never really been about the money and the ones who need the fund most know that. And Kate and Dani are good at sniffing them out: They know their people. The ones who make time for everyone—and everything—but themselves. The ones who lose sight of who they really are amid the endless demands of heaps of laundry, soggy diapers, sleepless nights, sticky furniture, evil bosses, runny noses, well-meaning in-laws, flying food, nannies, day care, overtime . . . You get the picture.

Donations roll in pretty steadily and Kate and Dani don't even have to ask for them. But that's not the most impressive part. Individuals, church groups, shopkeepers and even a few corporations have begun offering their time and services in the name of the Fund. Inspired, women have made the time—for pedicures, college courses, shopping, naps, girls' nights out—whatever they thought they needed.

Back in Easton, there is plenty of work, but with Dani handling the legal end of things and Kate taking care of the management side, they keep up. Especially with newly divorced Sunny Honeywell working the phones and, with some supervision, balancing the books. In fact, Sunny made the Fund a full-blown reality faster than Kate and Dani could ever have imagined by officially launching it with a spectacular luncheon for all of her well-heeled friends. Brianna wore a red jacket to match her mother's new favorite. Kate worked the room like a pro, energized by their new mission and liberated from guilt over having neglected to mention "a few significant details" to her husband. (After Andy got over the initial shock of Kate's "news," he became one of the Fund's biggest supporters, even offering *unsolicited* to watch the boys while Kate attended the luncheon. Besides, that new telescope was really great.) Dani, inspired by Kate, gave Bryce just two days' notice. When he sputtered that she'd never make much money working for a nonprofit, Dani snapped back that it wasn't about the money. And, uncharacteristically, she really meant it. Then, more typically, she convinced Matt to jump ship with her as she assumed her new titles of legal adviser and treasurer. Kate and Dani found a light, airy office downtown. They are even considering making the Fund an international resource.

So far, there's more than enough to go around—and they are always on the lookout for the next beneficiary. Life is good. They are grateful.

And at the end of the day, they're home.

© Jeanne Birdsall

Madeleine K. Jacob is a pseudonym for Jennifer Gates and Jill Stern, two friends who are working moms with careers in publishing. They live with their families in western Massachusetts and have been known to make impulsive shopping excursions to NYC themselves. They wish someone would give them a million bucks, too.